THOUGH I LIVE NOT WHERE I LOVE

SUSANNA M. NEWSTEAD

HERESY PUBLISHING

First Published in 2021
by HERESY PUBLISHING
Newbury RG14 5JG
www.heresypublishing.co.uk

Cover design by Charlie Farrow

A CIP catalogue record for this book is available from the British Library.

ISBN 978-1-909237-08-7

For Samos wire haired fox terrier Newstead.
My little treasure.

Savernake Forest c.1200

Susanna M. Newstead © 2017

N

S

Part of Forest
of Berkshire.

Part of Chute Forest

NOT TO SCALE

To Devizes

Avebury

East
Kennet

Ogbourne

Aldbourne Chase

Marlborough

The Common

Manton

Preshute

Castle

River
Kennet

Forest Hill

Grafham Hill

Hungry Pool

West Baily

Glass
Blowers

Clench Commons

Oare

Cadley

Big Bellied Oak

Brayton Oak

Tumuli

Tumuli

Wootton

A345 Shaftesbury Road

Pewsey

Upavon Road

B3087

Easton

Lye Hill

Collingbourne

A 346 Salisbury

Bytham's Pool

Burbage

Southgrove

Tumuli

Oakhill
Pool

Durley

Hungerford Road

A33

Wolf Hall

Bedwyn

La
Verne

The King's Way

A4 London

Cock Troop Lane

Henset

Whitehill

Coppice

Mildenhall

Axford

Ramsbury

Whittonditch

Chilton

Froxfield

Charcoal makers

Le Broyle

Chisbury
earthworks

Hippenscombe

Shalbourne

Bedwyn

Buttermere

Dean

Vernham

Inkpen

Hungerford

To Newbury

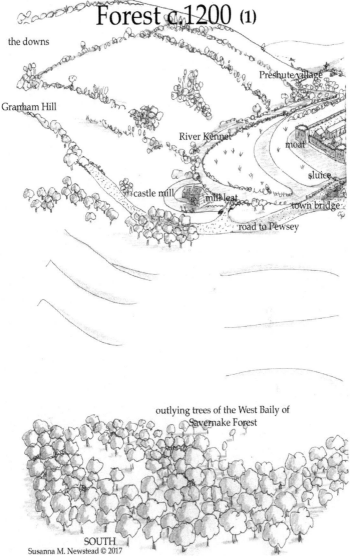

Marlborough and Savernake Forest c.1200 (1)

the downs

Preshute village

Granham Hill

River Kennet

moat

castle mill

mill leat

sluice

town bridge

road to Pewsey

outlying trees of the West Baily of Savernake Forest

SOUTH

Susanna M. Newstead © 2017

Marlborough Town and the forest c.1200 (2)

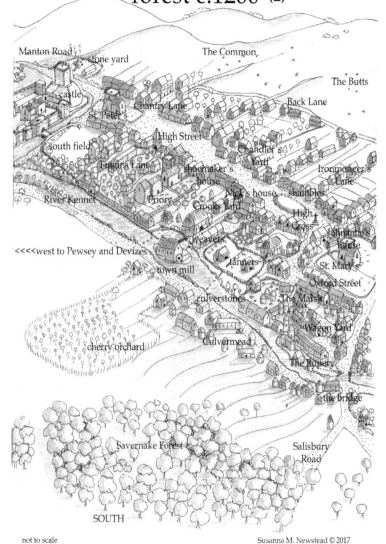

Manton Road · stone yard · The Common · The Butts · castle · Chantry Lane · Back Lane · St. Peter's · High Street · Chandler's Yard · south field · Figgins Lane · shoemaker's house · Ironmonger's Lane · Nick's house · shambles · River Kennet · Priory · Crooks Yard · High Cross · weavers · Johanne's house · <<<<west to Pewsey and Devizes · St. Mary's · town mill · tanners · Oxford Street · culverstones · The Marsh · Culvermead · Wagon Yard · cherry orchard · The Ropery · the bridge · Savernake Forest · Salisbury Road · SOUTH

not to scale

Susanna M. Newstead © 2017

Marlborough and the forest
c. 1200 (3)

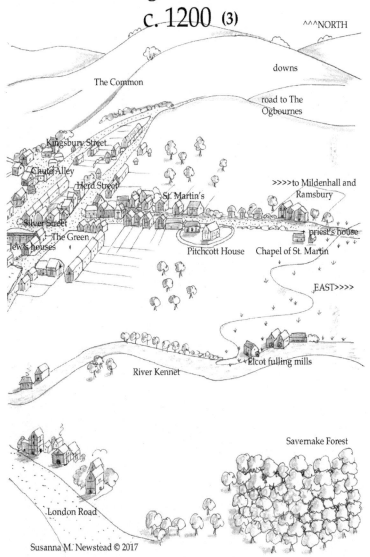

^^^NORTH

downs

The Common

road to The
Ogbournes

Kingsbury Street

Chute Alley

Herd Street

St. Martin's

>>>>to Mildenhall and
Ramsbury

Silver Street

The Green

Jew's houses

priest's house

Pitchcott House   Chapel of St. Martin

EAST>>>>

River Kennet

Elcot fulling mills

Savernake Forest

London Road

Susanna M. Newstead © 2017

THOUGH I LIVE NOT WHERE I LOVE

Come all ye maids who live at a distance
Many's a mile from off your swain,
Come and assist me this very moment,
For to pass away some time.
Singing sweetly and completely,
Songs of pleasure and of love.
For me heart is with him all together,
Though I live not where I love.

When I sleep I dream about you,
When I wake I take no rest,
Every moment thinking of you,
My heart lies within your breast.
And though far distance may be of assistance,
If from my mind your love remove,
For me heart is with him all together,
Though I live not where I love.

All the world shall be of one religion,
All living things shall cease to die,
If ever I should prove false to my jewel,
Or any way his love deny.
Oh the world shall change and be most strange
If from my mind your love remove.
For me heart is with him all together,
Though I live not where I love.

So farewell lad and farewell lassies,
Now I think I've made my choice.
I will away to yonder mountain,
Where I think I hear his voice.
And if he holler, I will follow,
Around the world though it is so wide.
For young Thomas he did promise,
I should be his lawful bride.

So come all ye maids who live at a distance
Many's a mile from off your swain,
Come and assist me this very moment,
For to pass away some time.
Singing sweetly and completely,
Songs of pleasure and of love,
For me heart is with him all together,
Though I live not where I love.

English Folk song.

Chapter One

Tom Potter looked up at me with his large, shining brown eyes.

"Oh well sir. I'm not so sure I can do it. I'll have to think about it."

"You don't think it's possible?"

He scratched his head and the chestnut waves of his shoulder length hair rippled in the watery sun. "Well...I dunno. I'd have to ask Alf."

"Yes, of course, it must be a collaboration. You and Alfred Woodsmith. Hubert too I don't doubt."

"Any metal parts sir, would have to be made by a blacksmith."

"They would. Let's all meet to speak about it. Can you tell the other two, Tom? In the hall at...let's say just after sunset and before supper?"

"Before Vespers, sir?"

"After."

"Aye, sir. You make a rough drawing of what you want and we'll see what we can do."

"Another person who might be useful...Mat Fisher. He knows the river well. We shall need someone who is used to the water, Tom."

"I'll ask him to come too, shall I?"

I looked up at the sky and sighed. My breath turned to smoke in the cold air.

"Aye...you'd better be about it if you're to get to it before dark."

Thomas Potter saluted me and was gone out of the courtyard.

I turned and made my way up the manor steps to the hall screens passageway. To the right lay my little office. I took out the key which I kept in my purse and opened the door.

Sitting at my table I pulled some parchments towards me. A little while before, I had made some drawings and I scrutinised them now making a few changes and annotations with graphite.

We'd had a problem with flooding in Durley village.

1

This was the village of which I was Lord; Aumary Belvoir, Lord of Durley, under constable of Marlborough castle and constable of the northern part of the county of Wiltshire, responsible for the tracking down and arresting of felons, amongst other things. Well, in that year, the year of our Lord, 1207 I was all those things. 1207, the eighth year of the reign of John Plantagenet, God assoil him. He gave me the job, you know. He and I were childhood friends. Now I am an old man and am nothing much. I sit here looking out of the solar window at the courtyard below and you Paul....

Paul, you're not asleep are you? Oh good. I can't go on rambling away if you aren't writing down what I say. You're here to write down my stories aren't you? Just look at these fingers. I can't do it any longer so you must do it for me.

Oh, I've said that before, have I?

Oh well. Doesn't make it any less true. Carry on then my scribe.

In the winter of 1207, I was a young man of thirty-three, with a wife, a daughter, a son and another child on the way. I held sway over the Forest of Savernake of which I was hereditary warden, all one hundred and fifty square miles of it. Trees, glades, meadows, coppices and rivers and the two hundred or so souls living in Durley village and the wider forest.

Yes, rivers. It was my responsibility to look to and manage those hundreds of people and that day in November my mind was exercised with how I was to prevent the flooding of the village in times of severe wet weather.

We'd had two years where the autumns and springs had been wet and some of the houses in Durley had been under water. The river had begun to change its course and homes which for years had been safe, were at risk. Now why, you ask me....

I can hear you thinking it, Paul my scribe, so don't deny it.

Why was I wanting to talk to a potter, a blacksmith and farrier, a carpenter and a fisherman?

Tom Potter was a clever young man who not only made pots and bowls—he could draw so beautifully, anything you asked him to.

He had a workshop in the courtyard but also worked in Cock a Troop Lane close by the nearby town of Marlborough, where there was quite an industry of potters. My drawings were mere scribbles. Tom would turn them into something which folk could understand. Something from which they might be able to work.

I'd explained my ideas to him that late November afternoon, standing by the door of his pottery. Hubert Alder, my farrier, who had the building next door, would be the man to make any of the metal parts. Alfred Woodsmith who also had a workshop in the courtyard might be called upon to fabricate the wooden segments of my idea. Mat Fisher, as I'd explained to Tom, knew our little river well. We'd need a man who understood it, so we knew where best to place our gates.

I had been studying the sluices—the watergates of both the castle moat in Marlborough and that which dammed the River Kennet in the town, to fill the pond of the corn mill.

The Kennet supplied both castle and mill and I wondered if the same type of arrangement might easily be installed in the village. Large vertical gates which might funnel the water to the far bank of the stream, to the meadows where there was no habitation. At the first sign of trouble we might shut the gates and divert the stream, leaving the houses safe and dry.

I shuffled my parchments together and blew on my cold fingers. A warm supper would be very welcome but first, vespers in our little church of St. Mary and a meeting of my village artisans.

My eight year old daughter Hawise came with me to church. Lydia, my wife, stayed in the warmth of the solar with my two year old son Simon. She was eight months with child and thought it best to stay at home and take her ease.

The villagers trooped into the cold church. There was a deal of sniffling and coughing and all those with warm cloaks or blankets pulled them closer around their bodies. It would be a very cold night. Father Crispin began the service and there was a hushed silence, broken only by the hissing of the candles and the shuffling of frozen feet. The sun was westering and throwing shadows across the old stones.

The door banged. Crispin ceased his Latin and leaned sideways and peered through the chancel arch to see who the latecomer was. I turned and caught the eye of the potter Thomas.

"Sorry m'lord," he whispered.

I nodded.

Crispin began again. Thomas found himself a space between Bevis Joiner, one of my carpenters and my man at arms, Hal of Potterne, a grizzled soldier with a grey beard trained into two points and worn long like his Viking ancestors of old. He chuckled at Tom and shuffled up a little. The service resumed.

I yawned. I saw Hawise, to my left hand side, look up at me and giggle under her breath and I smiled. Father Crispin turned; and looking through the chancel arch, caught her eye and he too smiled whilst his Latin continued to drone on.

I looked up at the windows of the church, glazed only a few years ago. It was still very cold in the building but at least it was dry and the wind was no longer whistling through. Try as I might, I couldn't keep my mind on the liturgy. My little drawings kept spinning before my eyes. The river bank swelled up in my mind's eye, as it had been that late autumn of 1207. All the different suggestions for dealing with the problem swam in the rising waters.

I *so* hoped that this would be the answer... but what was this fearful clamour intruding into my reverie?

A screeching and screaming outside the church.

Crispin ceased his loud intonation and almost began to whisper, listening with half an ear to the noise.

Walter Reeve, who always stood at the back of our little church, turned to the door and opened it. Hal went striding down the nave. "I'll deal with it m'lord," he said as he passed me.

Crispin's Latin faltered and stopped.

We could all hear the voice clearly now.

"And you promised.... Oh how you promised. How could you do this to me

Thomas? How could you?"

My housekeeper, Agnes Brenthall, looked over her shoulder. She scanned the people present. Her eye lit on Thomas Potter.

"It's a foul thing to do…you promised me you'd come back and fetch me. It was lies…all lies." The voice broke off and started to cry and scream intermittently.

"Father Crispin… carry on. Hawise: stay here."

"But Dada.."

"Stay here."

I turned on my heel and marched down the nave and through the church door, following Hal and Walter Reeve, the man responsible for the daily running of the manor and the work of all my tied villeins. The sun was setting over the trees towards Ramsbury but there was enough light by which to see. I saw Hal making his way down the slight slope towards the lych-gate where there was a huddled figure. Walter stood a few feet away.

The voice continued to babble and scream.

"Thomas…. Oh Thomas… where are you? You are a cruel and unfeeling man. How could you leave me like this? I hate you. Hate you!"

"Now, now, young lady," I heard Hal say as he came up to her. "What's all this? I in't never 'eard so much yellin' from such a chit as you."

I arrived to stand by my village reeve.

"Do you know her Walt?"

"No, sir. Not one of ours."

"Who is this Thomas she keeps on about?"

"I have no idea, sir."

The screaming and babbling grew louder and a few expletives peppered the sentence.

"Now, now, that i'n't what I like to 'ear. No, not at all," said my man at arms. "I'll thank you to keep yer language nice in front of my lord."

The girl took no notice.

"Argh…." She rose and clutched her middle and I saw her drop a cloth parcel; a roughly bagged up bundle of material, to the floor.

5

"Argh...."

I strode down to the gate.

"Who *are* you?"

The girl was doubled up, her blanket like cloak wound round her body like protective wings.

"He lied to me...he's a lying bastard. What am I to do...?" She stretched up to look at me. The wind buffeted her cloak.

"My lord," said Walter quietly, "the girl's with child."

"Aye, I can see that Walt."

Hal took a step backwards.

"Looks like we shall have a birthing soon." The girl's skirt was wet and my guess was that her waters had broken and that she was about to go into her labours.

She yelled again. "Thomas! Come out, you bastard."

Then she doubled up again.

Hubert Alder, who had not been in church but about some business of his own near the orchard, came running up the lane.

"What's all the noise, sir?"

"Ah... just the man." Hubert was tall and brawny and could easily pick up the girl and carry her into the courtyard.

"Get hold of her, will you, Hubert, and run with her down to the guest room. Get Peter to go for Old Joan. She'll know what to do." Joan also hadn't been in church that evening.

Hubert looked quite shocked but scooped up the screaming and blaspheming girl and ran down the lane, through the gate and into the courtyard.

"I'll go and ask Peter," said Hal and he jogged back up to the church.

I turned to him again just as he reached the church door. "Hal?"

"Aye, sir."

"How many Thomases do we have in the forest and village?"

Hal screwed up his forehead. "I don't rightly know sir... five or six, maybe as many as ten."

I nodded and he disappeared into the building.

So which Thomas was having his parentage probed? Which Thomas was it whose good name was being called into question?

"Walt?"

"Master Hal's right, but here in the village we have only three. We had four but...."

"Tom Potter, Tom Hart and Thomas Hill?" Old Tom had died in 1204.

"Aye sir."

"And Thomas Hill is a grandfather...."

"And a great grandfather," added my reeve.

"Hmm. When Hal comes back, can you get him to take that cloth bag to my office, Walt?"

"Yessir."

"It might tell us something about the girl."

"And you, sir?"

"I am going back to church, Walter," I said.

*****

The service was soon over and we filed out of the church. Hawise ran on ahead. Thomas Potter exited behind me with Bevis Joiner, Phil Wheelwright and the village butcher's only son, Hervey Kellog.

"I'll meet you up in the hall, Thomas," I said and jogged off to join my daughter.

I collected my notes from my office and waited in the hall for Thomas, Alfred and Hubert. They came in shortly after and a few moments later, Mat Fisher scratched at the hall door. The other young men slept in the hall at night and they were used to being here. Mat lived in the village and was very much in awe of such a large place. Usually a confident man, he tiptoed into the hall quietly.

"Come in Mat...come in. Sit yourself here and pour some ale," I said jovially to try to make him feel at ease.

7

Mat was a short, bow legged man in his early forties with hands like huge leather gloves, hard, calloused and chapped. He wrung them together now in nervousness. Many men in the village who laboured with their hands, suffered from broken skin in the winter and Dr. Johannes who lived in Marlborough town, my friend and fellow murder investigator, would make some special ointment to help them through the cold weather. Mat was massaging in some of this unguent now.

I arranged my parchments in front of the men. Tom and Alfred could read after a fashion. Hubert and Mat could not and so we had to explain to them the annotations on my drawing.

"So what we need to do is make a large solid gate which we can drop shut across the river. This will force the water from the river bed and the flood will spill over the uninhabited meadow the other side beyond the old willows," I said finally.

Hubert's brow was creased. "What's to stop the water backing up?"

"It would have to be supervised. We couldn't just leave it, Hube." said Tom. "We'd need to watch it. Watch for debris getting stuck and that but I reckon ...see... look...," and he began to scribble with a piece of charcoal. "If we angled the gate, like m'lord says, the flow would go this way."

"But then the river would be empty. What about the fish?" said Mat.

"There would still be a small amount of water going through but not enough to cause damage, Mat." I answered. "I've watched both the mill sluice and the castle moat gate. It doesn't take much to fill the river again."

"The fish aren't so stupid Mat, as to swim onto grass," said Alf with a chuckle.

"Fish end up in the castle moat and the mill pond," I said, "but they're quite happy there."

"Aye. The pike grow big and fat in there," said Mat. "My cousin Wat says them's some gurt big fish in the moat." Mat's cousin was Wat Fisher, who worked the River Kennet in the town for fish suppers of a Friday and other fast days.

"We are trying to spread the water over the meadow. There may be some casualties but perhaps we can be vigilant and drive them back to the mainstream."

"Might I take your drawings, sir and make some detailed plans?" asked Tom.

"By all means."

"This gate is to be wood, is it, sir?" asked Alfred Woodsmith

"It would but I have a feeling it would need some metal reinforcing and that would be Hubert's job."

"And bars, sir," said Hubert " Some kind of bar so it might drop into the river."

"Just so. Do you think you might be able to make something which would work, Hubert?"

Hubert puckered up his nose. "I'll have a go, m'lord," he said.

"We'll need to measure the river where it's goin'a go," said Mat Fisher.

"It should go where we had the major trouble last year. At the far side of the salleys."

"River's about twenty feet wide there, I reckon," said Alfred.

"And what's more we shall need to raise a mound this side of the river." I added.

All eyes were on the little drawing again. "Here, the river bank needs to be higher. We need to build a dam to the side so that the water backing up cannot spill over."

"Hmm" Hubert fingered his close cropped brown beard. "Where do we get the soil from?"

"The other side you clod," said Tom chuckling. "Lower one side, raise the other. Stands to reason.

His shining face rose up to mine.

"You've thought of everything, sir," he said.

*****

Supper over, I went back to my office to look over some accounts for my thread business located in Collingbourne a few miles towards Salisbury, and the list of cases for the manorial court. A little while later there was a scratching at the door.

"Enter."

Hal slid through the opening and planted himself in front of my table.

"Message from Old Joan, sir."

I put down my pen and scrubbed my eyes.

"Ah yes. Our mystery woman," I said, yawning.

Hal cleared his throat "She says sir that the birthing is a bit of a struggle. The girl is so small and malnourished, see."

"Ah... I see."

"It's goin'a take a while, she says."

"Right. Do we know who she is? Where she comes from?"

"All Joan managed to get from 'er was that 'er name is Cille, she comes from somewhere called 'Ereford, I think and that she was to be married to a Thomas."

"From Hereford. That's a long way from here."

"She walked, she said. Joan says that's why she's in such a poor way."

"Yes, indeed. I'm sure."

I got up and put some more charcoal onto the brazier I had burning in my office. I picked up the bundle which the girl had dropped by the lych-gate.

"Let's see if there's anything here which might tell us something?"

The bundle was tied up with hairy string. When smoothed out, I realised that the bundle was a patched brown blanket cloak which had seen better days. There were other clothes in the pack, all old, soiled, muddy and creased. A comb and some pins were kept in a small wooden box. There was a linen coif of quite good quality, the sort women of a certain class use to catch up their hair in the summer and protect their head from the sun. There were some baby clothes; another tiny bonnet and a shapeless linen baby gown and nothing else. There was no money.

"Did the girl have a purse, Hal?"

"Aye it's with her in the room."

"Why did she leave Hereford?"

"Perhaps she were thrown out. Nowhere to go."

"Likely. Is she talking about *our* Thomas, do you think?"

"Well, I can't see as she can be. 'As Tom ever bin to 'Ereford?"

10

"This Tom is the father of her child is he?"

"So she says."

"Why has she come to Durley?"

Hal shrugged.

"Tom? Hmmm. Tom Potter... a young and very good looking, not to mention clever, young man...," I said.

"Thomas Hart? Well, she in't likely to be lookin' at 'im now is she?" chuckled Hal. "What with his funny eyes." Thomas Hart was forty and had a terrible squint.

"Besides. He never leaves Durley, he's tied to my land."

"And Grandfather Thomas."

"Great Grandfather, Hal."

"Can't see 'im cavortin' about with a young'un, not with 'is gammy leg an 'is stick an' all."

"And we have the same problem. Never leaves Durley."

"No."

"Are we certain that this Tom lives in the village? Might it be one of the forest Toms?"

"Girl said, Tom from Durley."

"Hmmm," I stroked my lips. "Well, then. Tomorrow, we'd better have young Thomas Potter in here and we'd better ask him if he's ever been to Hereford."

Hal shook his head with a strange far away look on his face. "I can't remember 'im ever goin' off anywhere so far. Marlborough. 'Ungerford. Salisbury even...but not this other place."

"No, Hal, it's a mystery."

"Think she's got it wrong, sir?"

I shrugged "I have no idea, Hal. Why walk all this way if she doesn't think she's right?"

"Reckon she's a runaway, sir?"

"She might be. If needs be, I can stretch out a few tendrils and see if anyone is missing a maid servant or a tied villein from Herefordshire."

"Be an Easter couplin' won't it—or thereabouts?"

11

"Pardon Hal?"

This year. Easter. March 28th it was."

"Oh yes. You'd know wouldn't you? It was your birthday."

"So it'd be March 28th when this Tom was in 'Ereford."

"Nine months ago. Yes."

"Do you remember if 'e was 'ere, sir?"

"No, Hal... not..really. I spent a lot of time in Marlborough then, we both did, didn't we?"

"Why would 'e go so far away?"

I shrugged again.

"We must ask him," I said.

*****

Ask him I did early the following morning.

Tom came up the hall steps whistling and brandishing his drawings in his hand.

He bowed.

"Good morrow, my lord. The plans as I promised."

"Thank you Tom. Step into the office a moment will you."

Tom came in grinning and set down the parchment on my table.

I glanced at them. The drawing was neat and perfect. The writing straight and legible, just as I had expected.

"Thank you. I'll look at them later and then pass them on to Hubert and Alf."

"Yes, sir." Tom turned to leave.

"Tom, wait a moment will you."

The young man looked back and turned in the doorway, his hand on the door jamb.

"I want to ask you some questions."

Thomas Potter came back into the room.

12

"Can you close the door?"

I watched him as he quickly grasped the handle and shut the door quietly. Everything this young man did was deliberate and controlled. There was no banging the door, no noise, just the gentle click of the latch.

Thomas was a man of middling height with a profusion of shining, light brown hair falling from his crown to his neck in perfect waves. His eyes were large and dark brown like the skin of a conker, his features perfect. He was a manly shape, broad shouldered, narrow waisted and muscle flanked. His hands were perpetually stained with the material of his trade, the soft rust coloured clay with which he made his pots. He was a genial man, quick to understand and learn and to apply knowledge wherever he found a need for it.

He stood now looking at me, totally at ease and with an open face.

I cleared my throat.

"You came late to church yesterday, Tom. Why was that?"

"I'd been to find Mat as instructed, sir. Only he wasn't to be found easily. I managed to find him eventually but it made me a bit late."

"Ah yes. You will have heard that yesterday when we were all in church, a young woman arrived at the lych-gate."

"Aye sir, I heard her yelling outside like everyone did."

"Did you see her as you entered the church, Tom?"

"No sir. I came in from round the back, Ramsbury Lane."

"You had no speech with her?"

"No sir. Why should I? I don't know her. I didn't see her well. I didn't look down the path."

"I see. Have you ever been to Hereford, Tom?"

"Hereford, sir? Where's that? I don't think it's round here is it?"

"No Tom, it's many miles up country."

Thomas laughed "Well then, no...I've never been further north than Rockley, sir."

Rockley was a small village about two miles north of Marlborough.

"You have never had cause to go to Hereford?"

13

"No sir. Why? Why should I?"

I shrugged. "You aren't a local lad are you?"

The smile left Tom's face. "No sir. If you mean Durley or Marlborough. No. I'm a southerner. I come from Salisbury. I came up here with me da in the Spring of 1199; in the first year of the King's reign."

"Yes, I remember. You were a lad of about seventeen as I recall. Your father rented the pottery from me as do you now."

"Yes, sir." Tom's eyes were now wary.

"The girl at the lych-gate is looking for a lad by the name of Tom. Thomas from Durley."

"I heard that was what she was yelling...."

"You didn't take any notice, despite her calling your name?"

"No sir. Like I say, I don't know her and it's a common name, Thomas...why there are six...."

"In the immediate lands around and about... yes I know."

"I heard sir...." Tom licked his lips. "That the girl is with child."

"You heard correctly. She says the father is a lad called Thomas."

Thomas swallowed abruptly. "Well, it isn't me, sir."

"No. The girl comes from Hereford. And you tell me you have never been there?"

"No sir. Never."

"Right, well then," I smiled, "we are looking for another Thomas."

"Yes, sir."

"Ah well. Close the door on your way out and I'll let the boys have these drawings to look at."

Thomas turned on his heel.

He paused. "I wouldn't leave the girl in the lurch sir," he said. "I wouldn't do that. Even if I did know her."

"No Tom, I don't think you would," I said to his back.

*****

Towards the evening, Agnes Brenthall, my housekeeper and wife to my chief wood warden John, came scratching at the door.

"Sir, I just thought you'd like to know. Joan says the young woman we found by the lych-gate yester eve has just been delivered of a boy child."

"Thank you Agnes." I looked up from my work. "Is all well with them?"

"The child is weak. Joan thinks that he will live but he will need some careful nursing."

"And the mother?"

Agnes shrugged. "It's been a difficult birthing, sir. She is exhausted, quite apart from all the walking she seems to have done, she doesn't seem to have had much to eat lately either."

"Yes, she struck me as all skin and bone when Hubert lifted her up to bring her down to the manor."

"She's a poor piece sir, when all's said and done."

"Do we know any more about her?"

"No more than we did yesterday."

"Her name and where she comes from?"

"Aye sir. She doesn't have the strength for talking."

"Well, we shall have a word with her when she recovers. Do we think that we might need the help of Dr. Johannes?"

"Bless you sir, I don't think so. Old Joan, Janet and Alice Reeve know what they're doing. I think she'll be fine in their hands."

I nodded. "Good."

Agnes cocked her head to one side. "Of course, the thing she kept saying was that Thomas was the father of her child."

"Our Thomas Potter denies it, Agnes."

"He *is* very popular with the girls on account of his good looks...."

"Yes, that's true. However he denies it and I am inclined to believe him. If the girl came from Hereford, our Tom has never been there."

"Of course, he *will* be popular, he's a nice lad. We know there's many a girl in the village gone doe eyed over him, but he doesn't seem to care about it," said Agnes quietly.

"He's twenty five and can choose to ignore the village girls or to engage in a flirtation with them if he wishes, Agnes. I can't stop him. He's a free man."

"Aye, sir. I know. I was just thinking out loud."

I gave Agnes a sidelong smile. "I remember a young lady who was besotted with a young man in Wooton village, who ignored her for ages, Agnes... when I was ooh... ten or so?"

Agnes laughed out loud. "Made him notice me eventually though, didn't I?"

We both laughed.

"So you think that the girl is lying, sir?"

"No not necessarily. It might be one of the forest lads called Thomas."

"She swears he said he was a Durley boy and besides sir, all the Thomases I know out in Savernake are tied to the land. None of them will ever have been to Hereford... wherever that is."

"No. That's probably true. At best I think the girl is mistaken."

"It's a long way to come sir, to be mistaken."

"Yes, it is indeed."

"Sir. Far be it from me to interfere...," began Agnes.

"Doesn't usually stop you, Agnes." I chuckled, leaning back in my chair.

"Oh whisht, Sir Aumary," said Agnes, a smile splitting her face, "it's just well, if we could get the girl to look at Thomas without him knowing, maybe we could convince her that it's not him."

"If we do that Agnes, it will be with the full cooperation of the young man involved. I don't want anything done behind his back."

"No, sir."

"And I'll have no idle speculation or gossip around the village. Leave it till the girl is well and then we shall see what can be done."

"Yessir. And if it is him?"

"If it can be proven and for the life of me I cannot see how, unless he confess, then we shall have a wedding in Durley, shall we not?"

"And if it isn't?"

"Then we shall make further inquiries. The girl may stay until we get to the bottom of this mystery."

"Yes, sir."

"Close the door Agnes. There's a fearful draught coming in. And can you shut the outer door too please?"

"Aye, sir."

And that was the end of that.

Except it wasn't... the end, Paul my scribe. For by the close of that day, the poor girl Cille, who I'd allowed to stay in one of the guest rooms on the southern wall of the manor courtyard—was dead.

And what's more, she was murdered.

Chapter Two

The wind blew around the forest and village that night in a bitter blast that sounded like peas rattling on a drum.

The candles flickered in the draughts and we huddled close in blankets and cloaks for warmth.

I slept well in my deep feather bed and woke to a bright blustery morning and an insistent banging on the solar door.

"Sir, Sir Aumary."

"Yes, Hal. I'll be with you in a moment."

I hopped around on one foot trying to fit my right boot, whilst looking for the other.

"Oh Aumary, you do look funny!" laughed my wife Lydia, who was propped up on pillows in a pile of blankets, a woollen shawl around her shoulders.

"It's there, under the table where you left it."

"Ah...there it is. Coming, Hal." I threw open the door in the action of tucking my shirt into my braies.

"What's so urgent that a man can't put on his boots at his leisure in peace and quiet?" I said chuckling.

Hal's face was dour. "Ah well. If you foller me you'll see what's urgent and why it i'n't so funny."

"Oh dear Hal," said Lydia sitting up a little straighter, her face serious. "What's happened?"

Hal's mouth opened and closed. I could tell he wanted to speak out but felt he couldn't.

I reached for my cotte and threw it over my head and took up my cloak. "Come on then." I leaned over and pecked Lydia on the nose.

"Back soon."

I followed Hal down the solar steps and through the hall. There was a hushed muttering going on there which was silenced as I passed.

A few of my workers, those who laboured in the courtyard in particular, some of the kitchen workers and those who had no place in the village, slept in the hall of a night. Their eyes followed me as I threw my cloak over my shoulders, tucked it around me and exited the room. Behind me the conversation started up again.

"What's all that about Hal?" I asked as we stepped onto the outer stairs.

"You'll see."

I could see Henry, my steward, hovering in the courtyard. I nodded to him. Wyot Gatekeeper was there too, not yet gone to his rest in the gatehouse for he'd been up on watch all night.

I fell in beside Hal halfway across the yard, banging my feet properly into my boots.

"The south range? What's happened there Hal? Something to do with our young mother and guest perhaps?"

"Aye. Something."

Crispin our priest opened the door as we approached. He was white faced and agitated.

"Aumary. I...."

"Crispin, what's the matter?"

Crispin Darrell and I were well acquainted. He was a Durley born boy and we had been friends from childhood. He had once been the aide to the bishop of Salisbury but had retired from the bishop's service and had come here to Durley to be our priest.

He gestured for me to enter the little stone lean-to building which we laughingly called our guest quarters.

It was a small room some ten feet square with limewashed stone walls and a flagstone floor. There was but one small shuttered window, still closed. I dipped my head under the lintel for I'm a tall man, six foot, and screwed up my eyes against the glare of a lamp, set onto the wall bracket directly in front of me.

I shielded my eyes.

"I 'ad that brought in for it were mortal dark and I didn't think the shutters should be opened to the elements and pryin' eyes sir," said Hal.

Old Joan sat on a stool in the corner. She struggled up as she saw me enter and tried to curtsey.

"No, Joan...be seated...no need for that."

She adjusted her gnarled hands on her hazel stick.

"I'm sorry sir," she said, "but when I came in this morning, this is what I found."

She gestured to the bed which was placed up against the wall.

I noticed that Annot Pierson, my steward Henry's wife, was standing by the door. She had a small bundle pressed close to her bosom. The child born here yesterday I supposed.

I nodded at Annot and she bobbed her head at me, "M'lord."

The child gurgled but did not cry and didn't move, swaddled close as it was.

Hal turned back the blanket covering the young woman Cille.

"I found her sir, earlier this morning. I only left her a few hours and went to my rest at home by the wall," said Joan.

Old Joan lived in a small bothy outside the gate of the manor courtyard.

"She were sleepin' well and I thought it were safe to leave her."

"The child?"

"Sleepin' with Jonathan's little one up on the green. This poor chit weren't in any state to feed the lad so Philly said she'd do it. She's got enough milk for two since she had their Gregory sir. Annot brought the littlun' down this mornin'. "

I nodded.

I looked once more at the body of the young woman Cille.

"She's bin wurried, sir."

"Thank you Joan. Henry, might you and Annot take everyone up to the hall and I'll speak to you all later. Crispin I take it you have...?"

"Yes, Aumary, I have cleansed her soul and the child is baptised."

"Thank you. Does he have a name?"

"Aye, Algar," said Hal. "It was what the girl wanted."

"Not Thomas after the father, then?"

No one answered me.

I waited until the room was cleared.

Hal stood in the doorway, his arms folded across his chest.

"So, Hal. What do you know?"

He sighed. "Well. 'Ubert brought her in 'ere as you asked. "E left her in the care of Agnes and Joan. Agnes went 'ome about supper time, sir. Alice Reeve came up from 'er 'ouse to stay with the girl for a while. The child was born in the very late evenin' yesterday and Father Crispin baptised 'im just in case 'e didn't survive. Then Alice took 'im up to their Jonathan's"

"Where Philippa fed him and put him down to sleep with her own children?"

"Yes, sir."

"And then?"

Old Joan stayed a noddin' in the corner and then as she said she went 'ome. She came back in this mornin' and...." He gestured to the bed.

"Was the door locked?"

"This door's only got a bar and it weren't put across, no. We didn't think it would be needed."

I put my head out of the door and yelled across to the gatehouse. "Wyot!"

My diminutive gatekeeper scurried out of his little room and peered at me, "Ah, sir...."

"Last night. You knew the girl was in this room?" Wyot waddled up to me.

"Aye, sir. Who didn't?"

"You heard nothing?"

"No, sir."

"Saw no one?"

"Only them as lives in the yard, sir."

"And what were they doing?"

"Goin' ta bed, sir. Up in the 'all."

"No one went near the room—this room?"

"No, sir. Not as I saw."

I knew that Wyot and his mastiff Thibault would make the occasional foray around the courtyard in the night. He checked the salley port, that small personnel door at the back of the kitchen and unlocked the wicket gate after dark when the main gate was shut, to let in late comers. He had let out Old Joan.

"So you saw only those who had a legitimate business in the manor?"

"Yes, sir."

"No one else was let in?"

"Only young Tom coming in later, through the wicket. Then he ran up to the hall and was up the steps."

"Right. Thank you. Sleep well, Wyot."

He saluted me, "Thank you, sir." I heard him mutter as he walked away shaking his head, "Bad business, bad...."

I turned back to the little room.

I scanned the meagre contents of the space. Nothing there. I checked the floor. I asked Hal to check under the bed.

At last, I stood looking down at the body.

"The girl was weak, Agnes said."

"Aye that she was. She'd laboured all day and night to bring the little lad into the world. An' she weren't a strong chit anyway. She can't 'ave put up much of a fight," said Hal sadly.

"And yet, the bed clothes aren't disordered. Her body has been laid out as if she died in her sleep. On her back, her arms to her sides. The bed clothes are straightened."

"But that in't right 'cos she 'as the 'and print round her neck and her face is all..."

"Yes, precisely, Hal."

"Someone tidied 'er up then. Why?"

"I don't know."

"Father Crispin didn't do it, that I know and 'e's been the only one to touch 'er."

"Hmmm."

I cupped my hand on my chin and rested my elbow on my arm.

23

"Why? Why kill her? Who benefits from her death?"

"No one."

"She had nothing to steal. She knew no one here..."

"Except perhaps this Thomas."

"Well… yes, whoever he is."

"You still don't think it was *our* Tom?"

"Do you?"

"Wyot said that 'e came in the wicket gate late on. Maybe 'e came in 'ere an' thought 'ed get rid of 'is little problem. If problem she was."

I pursed my lips and looked at Hal.

"Ah no...." He scratched his beard. "Don't seem like our Tom, does it?"

"No. But we need to find out where he'd been before he came in through the wicket. And we need to ask around to see if anyone saw someone who shouldn't have been here late last evening."

I looked around once more. "Ah here's her purse. Anything useful, Hal?"

Hal shook his head.

"Nothin'. Poor chit. All that walkin', all that sufferin'. For nothin' ." He crossed himself.

I followed his action.

"We have an orphaned child in the village now, Hal. What are we to do with him?"

"Aye, We shall 'ave to 'ave a good think about that."

"And one other thing we shall have to think about..."

"Oh, aye?"

"Whom shall we send to inform the coroner?"

"And then there's another thing..."

"Yes, Old Hal?"

"Hadn't we better send for the doctor?"

*****

Though I Live Not Where I Love

We asked Dr. Johannes of Salerno who was my especial friend and Lydia's uncle, to come and look at our body, before we informed the coroner of the murder. He and I had a history of looking at bodies together and were more than competent at looking for clues upon a corpse.

He was a big man, tall, over six foot, near to forty five years of age. He had shoulder length brown hair, scrupulously clean and shining, with just a hint of grey at the temples, which was tied back in a queue and he was clean shaven, contrary to current fashion, which dictated that men wore small beards, as I did myself. His eyes were an amber-brown, clear and direct of gaze.

He had learned his doctoring in Salerno in Sicily, (where he was en route from the Crusade with King Richard,) the best school of learning in the world for doctoring, he assured me, and though he had some odd ideas, as far as the rest of the profession believed, he lost fewer patients and cured more people than others could ever hope to send their bills to. Cleanliness and orderliness were paramount to Johannes. He had been born in Oxford of a parchment maker and a seamstress but, upon his return from Italy, finding it hard to pursue doctoring in his home town, had packed his bags and fetched up here in Marlborough. We were all glad he had. He had been a great help to me in my role as constable, responsible for investigating all odd deaths in the locality. This role had been bestowed upon me by the King a while ago and I have to say I could not have done the job half as well, without Johannes' help.

In the afternoon of that day he was looking down at our poor girl, the blanket which covered her drawn back to her feet.

"A woman of about twenty, would you say, Johannes?"

"Thereabouts. Small, poorly nourished. She had just given birth, you say?

"Aye, the child lives and is being cared for by Jonathan's wife, Philippa, who is wet nursing him."

Johannes lifted the girl's stiff hand.

"We know little about her but that she says she came from Hereford. I shall write to the Sheriff of Herefordshire to see if we can ascertain where she made her home and why she left. I'm not hopeful of an answer."

"She left I presume, because she was an unmarried mother and open to censure. Perhaps she couldn't pay the lyrwite?" said Johannes. "She followed the father of her child to the place where he said he came from. I expect she wanted marriage."

"That's our guess, but until we know more, we cannot be sure. She did speak about this man marrying her, yes."

"She is certainly no finely bred girl. See here, her hands are calloused and the nails short and jagged."

I looked over his shoulder. "Might this be as a result of walking so far? It must have taken her quite a while to walk from Hereford to the forest. She won't have had access to the tools with which to keep herself tidy."

Johannes looked at me over his shoulder. "Aumary...you might not believe it but there are some poorer people who *never* have access to such things, walking or not. None of the niceties of life. It's all they can do to keep themselves alive and standing upright."

I put my hand on my heart. "I consider myself well and truly rebuked."

Johannes grunted and let go of the girl's hand. He picked up the other.

"At least she had shoes and didn't walk barefooted."

"Her possessions are meagre and were tied up in that cloak there."

"Hmm."

"So, she worked with her hands?"

"The muscles of her upper arms are quite well developed even if the rest of her is somewhat thin."

"She was used to carrying things—heavy things?"

"Perhaps. And see here, what's this ingrained in her fingers?"

He reached into his doctoring bag, without which he never travelled and brought out a small metal probe.

One nail of her left hand, the little finger, contained a coppery residue.

Johannes fished it out and laid it on a small piece of birch-bark paper.

"Of course this might have been obtained whilst she was travelling but, what does it look like to you, Aumary?"

"Red soil?"

"Aye perhaps. I've heard the soil in Herefordshire is red."

"I think this is clay...," I said peering at it more closely.

I looked up at him. "Potters clay? Tom Potter's hands are this colour. No matter what he does, it cannot be shifted. As long as he works with the clay, it stays with his hands and in his nails."

"Was our girl also a potter or at least worked in that industry? You say he denies knowing her?"

"Aye he does but now it looks like..." I caught my lip in my teeth.

Johannes sighed. "Now let's look at the rest of her."

He pulled down the flimsy shift at the neck and lifted her chin.

"Two sets of thumb prints. The hyoid bone is broken. Strangled from the front, the thumbs pressing into the little protrusion just here at the place we doctors have sometimes called the 'shield'. "

"Because it looks like a small shield?"

"Yes. Suffocation follows."

"Poor girl. She cannot have fought hard. She had nothing left to fight with."

Johannes pulled up the shift again.

"So someone crept in, strangled her, rearranged the bedclothes, tucked her up again and left the same way."

"One door only."

"No one was seen except those with a legitimate reason to be in the manor."

"So we must conclude it's one of your manor folk," said Johannes.

"Thomas?" I shook my head. "I don't like to think of it."

"As to the time of death, well...rigor was fairly well established when you saw her this morning you say?"

"Yes, she was stiff."

"So early in the night perhaps. Before midnight maybe. She is just becoming pliable again now and rigor can wane after about a third of the day. In this cold weather rigor will have been slower."

27

"Hmm. About the time Wyot saw Thomas in the courtyard. I must have another word with my gatekeeper."

I looked Johannes in the eye.

"We must also inform Hugo of Ramsbury, the coroner. Meanwhile can you get the girl to your mortuary?"

"We should leave her here if we aren't to be amerced for moving her."

"I know but..."

"She can lie here until he comes. I'll have the place watched."

Johannes nodded. "And then...will you return her whence she came?"

"I am not going to pay for a lead lined coffin to get her all the way back to Hereford, unless I know there is someone who grieves for her in that town. She can lie in our churchyard. Crispin will bury her."

"God will know where she is. Cille of Hereford."

"Hereford or Durley, it's all the same to God." I said, covering the body with its blanket again.

*****

As the sun was going down later that day, I managed to have further words with my gatekeeper.

"Doctor Johannes has managed to establish that the girl died at about the seventh hour of the night, Wyot."

"Before midnight then?"

"About the time you saw Thomas Potter in the courtyard. Tell me what happened."

Wyot sniffed. "It were a Wednesday see...he's always late of a Wednesday."

"Is he? I hadn't noticed. So what does he do on a Wednesday which always makes him late so that you have to let him in after the gates are closed?"

"It's market day. He loads his hand cart of a Tuesday night and trundles it to the town and then back again. In the winter, it's often got dark before he gets home, so I has to let him in."

"I see. He leaves his hand cart in the hay barn doesn't he?"

"Aye, he does. Loads it and unloads it there. His work shop is next door... well almost."

"So you let him in the hay barn?"

"He comes in the wicket, leaves the cart outside. I open the barn door for him to bring it in and shuts it after him."

"And he did this on Wednesday last?"

Wyot fingered his sagging double chin. "Er no...not on Wednesday."

"But you said...."

"Aye... I said he *does* do that but not last Wednesday. No, then he came in the wicket and ran across the yard to go up the stairs, sir."

"Did he ascend?"

"Aye, he did. He waved at me from half way up."

"And where were you?"

"Me and Thibault were going towards the kitchen."

"Did he leave his cart?"

"Er... no, not right then."

"He came back to do that?"

"Aye, he did."

"So you saw him twice? Once when he came through the wicket and went up to the hall and once when he came again and went to the barn with you?"

"Aye, that's right. I told him I'd already seen him but he just laughed and said I'd bin dreamin'." Wyot scratched his beard. "But then he's always the joker i'n't he, sir?"

"Yes, he does have a reputation for being a bit of a joker... him and Hubert." I furrowed my brow. "So he must have gone out a bit later and retrieved his cart."

"Yessir."

"You didn't see him go out again?"

"No, sir."

"Then why did he go up to the hall?"

"I dunno, sir. You'll have to ask him."

*****

Ask him I did, later that evening. Supper over, I called him into my office and asked him to close the door.

Johannes was sitting huddled over the brazier warming his hands.

"Good evening m'lord; sir," said Tom politely. Johannes dipped his head and smiled.

"Tom. We have a problem... well actually several problems."

"Always pleased to help, Dr. Johannes," said Tom with a smile.

"I expect you have heard that the girl who came to Durley on Wednesday was killed last night."

Thomas looked at his feet. "Yes, sir. I came back from town and went straight to my bed. Hubert told me earlier today that she'd been found strangled."

"It seems she was murdered at about the time you came in with your cart, Tom."

He looked up abruptly.

"I didn't see anyone, sir. Just Wyot who let me in as he always does."

"Wyot tells me he saw you twice that night, Tom."

"Aye, he told me too but I told him that it wasn't possible. I came in as usual through the wicket..."

"Once?"

"Why would I go out again, sir?"

"You tell me Tom."

"I came in through the wicket. Wyot unlocked the barn, I brought my hand cart in and went up to bed."

"And yet he says he saw you going up the steps to the hall at an earlier time."

Tom shook his head emphatically.

"No sir, he's mistaken. I didn't. Not until I had stowed my cart."

30

"Who else saw you, Tom?" asked Johannes.

"Saw me, sir?"

"When you unrolled your mattress in the hall and prepared for sleep."

"Hubert was asleep and snoring. So was Alf. None of the kitchen staff were in at that time. Not yet."

"So no one saw you."

"I don't know, sir."

Johannes brought a candle nearer to him.

"Look at this for me will you, Tom, and tell me what you think it might be."

He unfolded the slight scrap of birch-bark paper in which he had stowed the small scraping of rust coloured clay from the girl's nail and laid it on the table.

Tom came forward and peered at it.

"Looks like clay, sir." He swiftly looked at his own hands.

Johannes took hold of Tom's right hand in his own and said, "Might I scrape some from your nail Tom? I know you will have some lodged there. Just to compare."

Thomas made no demur.

With his little metal probe the doctor ran along the top of Tom's finger.

Once the result was dropped by the first sample, there was nothing to distinguish the two.

We all looked at the paper by the light of the candle.

"It is potter's clay", said Johannes.

"Where does your clay come from, Tom?"

The young man straightened. "There's a deposit by the river almost at Stitchcombe, sir."

"On Cock-a-troop Lane?"

"Yessir, where all the other potters work. I get some from there and I also get some when I can, from a man I meet at the market. It comes from up country, sir...."

"Hereford?"

"No, sir, Warwick. He brings it down to a few of us. It comes from somewhere called Tocilwood, m'lord."

"And is this a rust colour?"

"It is. Marlborough clay is a little more grey."

"I will tell you now Tom, that the murdered girl had this red clay under her fingers. It seems to the doctor and myself that she was working in the pottery industry, somewhere in Herefordshire."

"It's up north isn't it? I don't have anything to do with that part of the country, sir," he answered firmly. "Only Warwickshire...and I have never been there myself, only spoken to men who have."

"Last March, Thomas. Were you missing from the manor for any length of time?"

"March..?" Thomas screwed up his face and the candle shadows danced over his even features with flickering movements.

"This would have been when Master Hal and I were at Marlborough castle for a while. Early March, when the King passed through on his way to Clarendon."

"Why, sir? Can I ask why you want to know?"

"Because if you weren't in Durley you might have been in Hereford getting a child on the girl Cille, Thomas," said Johannes.

"No sir!"

"Answer the lord, Thomas."

Tom swallowed. "Aye sir. I went down to see my mother in Salisbury. I spent some time with her on account of her being very ill."

"Your mother?"

"Aye sir," said Thomas with a blank expression on his face.

"Your mother didn't come up to Marlborough then from Salisbury with your father, when you were younger?"

"No, sir. She stayed in Salisbury with her kin."

He saw the look which passed between Johannes and myself and sighed.

"My mother and father couldn't abide each other, sir. My father decided to make a new life here. My mother stayed with my brother and sister and my grandparents in Salisbury. I came up here with my father."

"When you were seventeen?"

"Yessir. I was apprenticed to him. Apprenticed to my father as a potter, sir."

"So naturally, you would go with him."

"But now and again I go to see my mother."

"Do you have a witness who can guarantee that you were in Salisbury in March, Tom?"

"Will your mother be able to tell us how long you stayed?" asked Johannes.

"No, sir."

"No, Tom?"

"She died last April, sir."

I let out a frustrated breath.

"I must call in the coroner, Tom, for he must come and look at our body and pronounce upon her. I must also tell him that you were seen in the courtyard at about the time the murder was committed and...."

"I didn't kill her, sir!"

"And furthermore that you seem to be the only Tom who...."

"No, sir. There are others...."

"I have asked, Thomas. The Thomases who live in the forest are all tied to my land and have not left it. They all have alibis and all can be spoken for. You are the only one...."

"No sir! I didn't know her. It wasn't me."

"Only one who, at the moment, has no alibi. No one can vouch for you."

"Why would I, sir? Why?"

"To rid yourself of a serious embarrassment, Tom. Though I must say, in my experience... it would be very unlike you to...."

"I did not know her and I did not kill her, m'lord."

"I must do my duty, Thomas. I can do no other. I will however continue to investigate and I'll see what can be done. For example I will write to Salisbury and see if I can find anyone who can confirm that you were there."

"And I'll ask about and see if anyone remembers you sleepin' in the 'all at the right time," said Hal.

"You will let me be arrested and confined for a crime I didn't commit?"

"I will continue to work at the problem, Tom. The coroner must be told but it may be that his jury decides that someone else is responsible for the girl Cille's murder."

"But they might decide it's me and let the sheriff throw me into gaol."

"Thomas, we need to find someone who saw you in the hall at the right time on Wednesday. We also need to find someone who saw you in Salisbury last March. You cannot have been in two places at once."

"No, sir."

"Meanwhile, stay in the manor courtyard. I promise you, we'll see what we can do about finding someone who has seen you."

"And if the coroner finds that I am guilty, m'lord?"

"Then I will work to convince him and the jury that you are not, Thomas."

*****

The coroner Sir Hugo of Ramsbury jogged into the manor courtyard the next day. He was followed by his elderly scribe and secretary a short while later on a mule.

Hugo Ramsbury was a short man of about thirty-five with hair cropped in the Norman fashion. He had put on a little weight since I'd seen him last and his cotte was straining around his middle. He grunted as he stepped down from his horse.

We exchanged pleasantries.

"And I think I am correct in saying Hugo, that congratulations are in order. You have a son I believe."

"Aye that's true. Born in October. John, after my father, you understand."

"And our esteemed monarch."

"Yes... yes... indeed," he sniffed. "So what have you for me, Sir Aumary? The young man you sent said it was only a peasant girl."

"Her name is Cille and she told us she came from Hereford."

"Then what in the name of blazes was she doing here and why am I called to...?"

"She was ...passing through the forest, Sir Hugo, and she suddenly went into labour. We gave her a place in which to bring forth the child."

"So if she died in...."

"No sir, she did not die in childbirth. She was strangled *after* she gave birth."

Sir Hugo narrowed his eyes.

"She wasn't one of *your* villeins then?"

"No. She told us she came from up country, from Hereford, but we know no more than that. We don't know if she is a free woman or a tied villein. She may be a member of the free inhabitants of the town. We suspect she was a potter."

"A potter!"

"Or involved in that trade. Perhaps Doctor Johannes can lead you through what he found."

Johannes stepped forward.

"You here again doctor?"

"Sir Aumary is family, Sir Hugo. I am often to be found at Durley," he smiled.

Hugo of Ramsbury grunted again. He turned to his scribe, "Come on then William. Let's be havin' you," and following Johannes, he marched off towards the room where lay the body.

It was unusual for the coroner to have a scribe for rarely was anything written down at the time apart from the fines. However, the previous coroner had instigated the writing of a list of crimes, the evidence and those swearing for the accused and the practice lingered.

I too lingered a little in the middle of the yard. I looked towards the workshop of Thomas Potter. The door was open and I could see him sitting on a stool, staring at the floor; an ale pot in his hand.

"Look lively Thomas, the coroner has arrived," I shouted.

He looked up but didn't move.

"You may or may not be called. Just be ready."

"Aye, sir."

35

As I reached the little guest room, Johannes was beginning his explanation.

The coroner, hs arms clasped around his body, his head to one side, listened intently. "First finder...?"

"Old Joan. One of my tied women," I said coming in at the door.

"Well, we'd better start to get together my twelve men and then we'll ask a few questions of your first finder."

"I'll have her fetched."

The coroner's clerk went about the village collecting together twelve men over the age of fourteen. They all squashed into the little room on the southern wall of the manor.

Wyot was not called but Hal of Potterne did his duty and acted as spokesman.

Evidence was heard. Many folk told of the girl's arrival at Durley.

Old Joan told of her finding of the body.

It was quite late in proceedings when Sir Hugo asked who was seen in the courtyard at the time of the woman's death.

I was lounging in the doorway listening and stood upright.

"One of my men, a tenant who rents a workshop from me in the courtyard, was seen at about the right time. I must tell you that before she died, the girl named a Thomas as the father of her child and the reason for her long journey to Durley was to find him and make him marry her, I think."

"This lad, the one who was seen, is called Thomas, I take it?"

"He is, though he swears he has never been to Hereford."

Hugo of Ramsbury fingered his chin. "No, no. He might not have been to Hereford. But has he been elsewhere that the girl has been? Did you ask him that?"

"Last March he swears he was in Salisbury. We have yet to confirm this."

"Last March? Ah...I see what you mean. Has this girl ever been to Salisbury?"

"We cannot say Hugo. It's doubtful. I will however be writing to the sheriff of Herefordshire. We need to know more about the girl. If it's possible to know anything."

"They might have met elsewhere you know."

"Yes, I concede that's a possibility. However Thomas has not been missing from the manor for any length of time apart from the time he spent in Salisbury with his mother in March."

Hugo shifted his feet as he thought. "Hmmm. It could be then, that this Thomas of yours got rid of the girl because she had a claim on him?"

"It cannot be proven, sir. It's one person's word against another and one is no longer alive to answer questions," said Johannes.

"Lets' have this Thomas in here. Let's see what he says for himself."

But search high and low, we couldn't find Thomas Potter.

Chapter Three

"Foolish man!" I yelled as I mounted Bayard and dashed under the gate tower of the manor.

"Why did he need to run?"

"'Cos he's guilty sir?" said Hal, thundering after me.

"More likely because he isn't and was afraid he'd be arrested for the crime."

"Well, coroners aren't exactly noted fer their subtlety or impartiality now are they, sir?" said my man at arms. "It's either the first finder or the person first seen near the time of death is guilty and Old Joan can't a wurried the girl, now can she?"

Once it had become obvious that Thomas had bolted, the verdict had been delivered in his absence. He was guilty of the murder of Cille of Hereford. The hue and cry had been called. We were all out looking for him.

"The jury wasn't that 'appy with it, sir."

"I know Hal. I know you did your best. But it doesn't help his cause to run away like that."

"Well, we all know the lad. Only one or two were convinced that he was the culprit but they managed to persuade the rest."

"And you Old Hal?"

"Ah well. I was the only dissenting voice at the end. But Sir 'Ugo will have his way."

"So much for justice."

"Aye."

We turned into the village green. I had arranged for all able-bodied men to muster there. John Brenthall was organising the search groups and I told the men to fan out into the forest. They looked up at me sullenly and loped off on foot, not at all happy with their task. One or two looked back at me with sad eyes. Friends of Thomas. Wilfrid Frithson, Edgar Canty two of my foresters, Bevis Joiner a woodworker, Arthur Pigherder and William Ryder one of my stable hands. They melted into the forest.

John, the best tracker in Savernake leapt up onto his favoured horse Fire.

"I'll see what trail he might have left, sir," and whistling a few men to run with him, he was off across the green in the direction of the village edge.

"John!"

My senior forester looked back, "Aye sir?"

"No violence. He's not to be harmed."

John nodded and disappeared into the trees.

"So where are *we* off to, Sir Aumary?" said Hal turning in the saddle to look back at the manor where more folk were out looking for our errant potter.

"Thomas has contacts by the river at Cock A Troop Lane."

"The potters, sir."

"Aye. Lets ride through the forest and see if he has made his way to friends there."

*****

The lane wound down the side of a steep hill in a 'u' shape where it led off from the road to Hungerford. We trotted down the bank and came out from the trees. There, half way up the hill, the potters had their kilns and workshops which spread down to the river.

I turned into a small stockade and jumped down from Bayard, my roan gelding. Hal stayed mounted on Grafton, his favourite grey.

"My Lord Belvoir." Reginald Croker came out of a small and flimsy building wiping his hands on his apron. " Welcome," he grinned. "What brings you to the crokerers, sir?"

"Hello Reginald. Good day. I'm looking for Tom, Tom Potter. Is he here?"

"I haven't seen him since Saturday, sir." He turned around quickly and located a man wearing a brown capuchon hood.

"Bartholemew, you seen Tom Potter today?"

The man threw back his hood. "No, sir. He'll be here I expect on Saturday next."

"Why do you want him, m'lord?" asked Croker, looking up at Hal seated on Grafton.

" 'E's gone missing from the village," said Hal. 'We need to find 'im."

"Missing you say? He hasn't been waylaid on his way from town?" he asked with a worried expression. "I know he's out in the dark sometimes and I've told him to be careful...."

"No, nothing like that. He returned on Wednesday, Reginald, from Marlborough as usual," I said. "But went missing this afternoon. If you see him can you detain him here and send a runner to Durley. It's important. We need to find him."

"Aye, sir, we can if he'll be stayed. It sounds like he's in trouble, sir?"

"The coroner has declared him a suspected murderer, Reginald."

"NO! Not Tom. It's not possible."

"I grant you it seems impossible to us but the law must take its course. He must be detained pending inquiries. I'll do my very best to clear his name and find the real culprit. He didn't help himself by running away."

A few other folk had now joined the master potter and were shaking their heads in disbelief.

I heard Hal mutter under his breath "He in't got the sense God gave a goose."

"We'll have a look around the locality, sir. See if we can help find him."

I saw one young man backing away down the hill, a shocked expression on his face. He saw me watching him and turned to run.

I nodded to Hal. "Head him off, Hal."

"Right you are, sir."

Hal manoeuvred his big grey horse between the river and the fleeing man. The potter stopped dead and looked around as if searching for another place to run and I jogged up behind him.

"What's your name, man?"

Croker came upon my heels quickly, "Anthony Wright, what do you know

41

about this matter?"

"Nothing, Reginald...nothing..."

Croker planted his feet wide and put his hands on his hips. "This man Wright is thick as pease pottage with Potter, m'lord. Looks like he might know where he is."

"No, I don't, I don't," protested Wright.

"Where do you live, Wright?"

"Towards Stitchcombe, m'lord. Just down there." He pointed with a shaky hand to a small cottage close by the river.

I nodded to Hal who put his feet to Grafton's sides and trotted off down the hill.

"If he hasn't come to you Wright, then, where do you think he might go?"

"I dunno, m'lord, really I don't. I haven't seen him since Saturday."

"That was the last time you saw him?"

"Yes, last Saturday, sir."

"Where?"

"Here."

I looked round at the locality. It was a pretty place. The trees of the forest stopped short of the river bank by about a quarter of a mile. The hillside was stepped with banks and ditches and some crops grew there in the spring and summer. Visible now were the remains of the autumn crop. There were a few houses scattered about. I could see the smoke rising from their fire holes, even if I couldn't detect many of the houses themselves, buried as they were in bushes and clumps of smaller trees. The river Kennet wandered lazily along in its bed, osiers and rushes and in the summer, meadowsweet punctuating its banks. It split up into several tributaries which shone silver in the sunlight. The crokerers, as they were known, had a rambling site along the flattest part of the hill side and the riverbank.

I saw Hal enter the small house. No smoke came from its smoke hole in the thatch.

"Well, if you do see him, perhaps you'll tell him from me that he must either quit the district all together and be declared an outlaw, or he must come back to Durley and take sanctuary or he must answer the questions of the coroner. Those are his choices, Wright."

Wright looked down at his feet.

"Yessir."

I took pity on the man. "If it's any consolation, Wright, we don't believe him guilty but we simply must have him detained pending inquiries. It's the law. We might not like the law but there it is."

"Yessir."

I saw Hal come out of the small house down the hill and shake his head. So Potter was not there.

Wright lifted his head.

"What is he accused of, m'lord?"

I sighed. "It's said that he got a woman with child and then in order for her not to name him the father, he killed her."

Master Croker shook his head and said quickly, " Doesn't sound like the Tom I know."

Wright's eyes had become huge in his face. He closed them.

"Oh no, sir. That cannot be true. It simply can't."

"No, Wright. His friends think it isn't and I count myself one of his friends."

"You, sir?" said Wright in incredulity, his eyes snapping open. "A friend of Tom's?"

"Aye I am. I've known him since he was seventeen, that's nearly eight years, Anthony. A person can learn a lot about a man in eight years and whatever else he might be, Tom is not a cold blooded murderer."

"No sir. He's as gentle as a lamb."

"But that doesn't mean I'll let him go free. It's my job to search out murderers in this part of Wiltshire and with Tom safely tucked away in the castle gaol for a while, I can apply myself to clearing his name and finding the real killer. Is that clear?"

"Yessir."

"If you should happen to meet him, Anthony, tell him to come home."

Hal rode up the hill and slowed as he approached.

"No one," he yelled. "Empty as a nest in December."

"Thanks Hal."

I put my foot into Bayard's stirrup.

Behind me Wright stirred. "My lord Belvoir?"

I looked over my shoulder.

"His ol' da once had a cott over near the charcoal burners. It's been empty these five years since he died but...."

"Thank you Anthony."

I mounted Bayard and turned his head.

"If he is not guilty, I promise he will not hang."

And we rode away.

Hal came up to my knee. "You might not be able to keep that promise you know."

"What? That he'll not hang?"

"If ol' de Devil comes back, it might all be taken out of your 'ands."

"De Devil... I mean, de Neville, might be the constable of the castle Hal, but he isn't the constable of north Wiltshire. I am."

Hal disliked the castle custodian and this was his private nickname for him.

"Ah well. I'm just sayin'. You remember the last time 'e overruled you?"

Hugh de Neville was the chief forester and technically my overlord. He was abroad or travelling the country with the King much of the time. He only rarely made appearances at Marlborough castle. When he did, he was ruthless, hard and merciless.

"Aye I remember."

"So we'd better find the person 'oo did do for Cille of 'Ereford or it's likely that Tom *will* be swingin' on the Marlborough gibbet won't 'e?"

*****

44

Folk were trickling back as we crossed the village green. No one had found Tom. I felt somehow they had not really looked with any seriousness.

"Aren't we goin' out to the charcoal burner's place then?" asked Hal, "since that fella Wright said our Tom might be there?"

"I shall send others to look, Hal," I said. "You can go out with them if you want. But it's very late. It'll be dark soon. Tomorrow will do."

Hal harrumphed. "I'm goin'a 'ave an ale. I'm as dry as a stick."

I handed Bayard to Cedric, one of my grooms. "No luck yet, Cedric?"

"No sir. He's just disappeared."

"Ah well. Tell everyone thank you. The hue and cry is over. We did our duty."

"Yessir. He was on foot wasn't he? He can't have got too far," said Cedric.

I marched on a few steps before I said, "Hal, tomorrow ask Nathan Kennet to get a party out at the Le Broyle end of the forest, towards Ramsbury and Hungerford. He might be going out of the county into Berkshire. Tom knows enough to know that my writ doesn't extend that far."

"Yessir."

I was halfway up the steps when there was a savage screeching and yelling outside the walls.

"What now?" I shouted.

I ran up to the top step where I had a much better view out over the gatehouse wall. There running for his life was Tom Potter, his chestnut locks flying free.

Four or five men were chasing him but when they saw that he was heading for the gate they slowed.

Thomas came skidding in the gate, breathing hard.

"Well!" I shouted and my voice echoed around the walls. "Thomas Potter. First you run out then you run in...."

"Sir..., Tom took in huge gulps of air. He swallowed and wiped the back of his wrist over his mouth.

"My Lord. Please listen. It's... important."

"I'm listening," I said, coming down the steps slowly.

"The forest... charcoal burners...", gasped Tom.

"Ah...so that *was* where you went."

"Sir... I found.... Tom shivered. "They are all dead, sir."

"Who are?"

"The charcoal men."

Hal came out of the stable where he'd gone to stow away Grafton.

"What's this?" he said. "You back, Tom?"

"Master Hal. I went to the old house. The one my father...."

"Yes, we guessed that's where you'd go, lad."

Tom turned back to me. "M'lord. I thought just to go there for a while to think," he panted.

"Aye and what happened?"

"Nothing happened whilst I was there."

"Tom, you aren't making much sense."

I shouted to the folk who were now crowding into the courtyard behind Thomas.

"Go back to your homes...Tom is back and let it be known it is of his own free will."

My voice bounced around the walls and muttering, the folk, disappeared to their various homes and workplaces.

"Tom, come up to the hall."

Wearily, the young man, who was sweat stained and pink in the face from running, took the steps one by one. His face was grim and set.

Hal put a mug of ale in front of him.

"Now tell us from the beginning. You ran when the coroner came."

"Aye, sir. I was...."

"Yes, we know how it was, Tom. So you went to your father's old place close by the charcoal burners' huts?"

"Yes. I always have to go through their little cluster of houses to get to my da's old place. Oh it's nothing much since he died but I like to go there now and again."

"And...?"

"It was the smoke I smelled first."

"Smoke from their charcoal fires—their kilns?"

"No, sir, from their burning houses."

Tom's eyes were large and frightened.

"Their houses were alight?"

"No, sir... no longer alight. They had been though."

"So what 'ad 'appened and when?" asked Hal.

"When I can't say Master Hal, except that the embers were still warm and there were still some smaller fires alight."

"What happened then?"

"I saw that every house had been either torched or pulled apart in some way or both. Most of them were just blackened frameworks."

"There's about fifteen people working the kilns there."

"Aye there are... were."

Thomas looked down at his hands. I saw that in addition to their normal rusty pallor, they were black with soot. And shaking.

"I ran about calling. No one answered. I went into a half destroyed house and there was one man just alive...."

"You mean to tell me, Tom, that they are all dead? All fifteen?"

"Yes sir and their wives and children too."

His hand began to shake seriously as he lifted the ale pot to his lips.

"Burntwine, Hal," I said.

"Aye, I'll get some," answered my man at arms. He disappeared through the buttery door.

Tom's eyes filled with tears.

"It was awful... awful. Just littluns, sir. One little one had been spitted through the middle with a spear. It was still there... just... there, sticking up. It pinned him to the ground."

He put down the pot and covered his eyes with his hands.

"So all the charcoal burners have been murdered and their families and their houses...."

47

"And their kilns...."

"Destroyed?"

"Aye, sir. Every one." He took his hands from his face and I saw that he now had teary black streaks across his cheeks.

"You said you spoke with a survivor?"

"Ah well...he did speak to me but he didn't last long, sir."

"Never mind. What did he say?"

"Of course I asked him who did this thing? He shook his head as if he didn't know. He said 'ten of them'. I thought he meant ten charcoal men but on reflection I think he meant there were ten attackers."

"Ten men against what...?"

Hal came back through the hall door. "Hal. How many charcoal burners *are* there at the Le Broyle site—exactly?"

Hal looked up to the rafters and counted, "Eighteen."

"So eighteen men couldn't fight off ten?"

"They aren't fighting men, sir. They could just about give clout for clout with a quarterstaff but... and some of the men are but boys, sir, if you see what I mean," said Tom.

"Youngsters, yes. Go on."

Tom wiped his hands over his face again.

"The man said most were on horseback. There were a few sword wounds from what I could see. I asked him if he knew any of the people who did this. He didn't. And then he died, sir."

Tom took a swig of the burntwine and coughed.

"I found seven children. Most of them were wounded in the back. Struck down running away. Some were just babies sir. There were some women who had been...."

"Raped, Tom?" asked Hal at a whisper.

"Yes. And then killed." He threw his hands onto his face again, "Oh God! It was awful. All dead. Every one," he sobbed.

"No one was to survive to make it to Durley to tell us of the attack, Tom," I said, patting him ineffectually on the back. "Six miles through the forest. Probably ten by the road. A very isolated spot. No village nearby. It might have been weeks before anyone knew if you hadn't...."

I stood and looked up at the rafters. I tapped my fingers on the table in anger and frustration.

"Right Tom. Do I have your word that you will not try to escape again?"

Tom drew his sleeve across his nose and spluttered "Aye, sir. I'm so sorry."

"No, Tom. These things happen for a reason."

I paced up the hall and then back again. Both Hal and Tom watched me.

"There is nothing we can do for the poor souls today. It will be dark soon. We can't go almost all the way to Hungerford in the dark and return today. We must be away first light tomorrow. We shall take all the best trackers from the forest. Hal, can I leave that to you?"

"Right you are sir."

"Tom, will you be up to coming with us tomorrow, to show us what you found?"

Tom straightened up. "Aye sir. I must."

"Good man. Get what rest you can. Stay here in the hall. The men shall muster in the courtyard just after dawn."

"Yes, sir." He drew a shaky breath.

"And the woman's death sir?"

I sighed. "Tom, you must still answer to the coroner and we must continue to investigate her death but until we have understood how more than twenty of my workers could have met their deaths at the hands of a band of murderers and why... we shall have to put her death away for a while."

"What can they have been after, sir?"

"I truly don't know, Tom. They are the poorest of my people, these charcoal burners. They own very little, well you know that. You've seen them. They are secretive and quiet. They never stray outside the forest. They have no riches. They can have nothing that a man might want."

"Except charcoal, sir," said Hal.

"Aye Hal. Just charcoal."

*****

The next morning I took twelve men with me, most of them my paid foresters whose job it was to patrol Savernake and keep order and report infringements. We rode for Le Broyle, the eastern most bailiwick of the forest. This extended from just beyond Bedwyn village to the Hungerford Road and up to the town itself. Here the trees petered out and downland took over.

The charcoal burners of this bailiwick lived about two miles from the King's Road and two miles from the main road to Hungerford. There was another group who lived and worked in Hippenscombe on the Vernham Dean side of the forest. Again their camp was very isolated. I sent foresters to make sure that they had also not been attacked and told them to be on their guard.

We skirted the small village of Bedwyn and rode on the track which met the main road a few miles on.

We smelled the results of the burning long before we reached the clearing.

A short distance before the glade in which the houses lay, John dismounted and began to search the ground. Edgar Canty and Rob Hartshorn, two of my foresters, started to beat the brush either side of the track.

"Gently now. We don't want any evidence destroyed by being overzealous," I shouted.

Crispin Darrell, our priest of Durley, had also travelled with us. He now dismounted and ran to the roadside as one of the men shouted that there was a body.

Indeed there was. A woman lay twisted on her side. A huge bloodied rent disfigured her front. She had curled up, her knees to her chin, and died.

Crispin was down on one knee in a flash and he began the rites for her soul. I saw him pull down her kirtle and settle it about her ankles. This was obviously one of the women who had been raped.

50

Hal came over as I trotted into the centre of the small camp and dismounted.

"Sword stab to the middle. She won't have died immediately."

I shook my head.

"Can we collect together the bodies and put them in that house there, the one still partially standing?"

I looked around for someone to send to the coroner. "Bird, take Bill with you and ride to the coroner. He's in his Ramsbury house so not too far away. Tell him what's happened."

"Aye, sir."

"Keep your wits about you. Should you meet trouble...don't let yourselves be seen. Hide."

"Yes, sir."

"Tell Sir Hugo to bring men with him for safety too."

Bird nodded and was gone into the trees.

"Many of the bodies are here, sir," said Tom Potter striding over the grass.

"Hmm."

I followed and looked around. Ten men had died here. Flung about like so much rubbish. Most suffered sword wounds, others had stab wounds from spears. One had his head crushed by what must have been a very heavy cudgel.

"They were completely taken by surprise. All at their work with the kilns."

There were some rakes lying on the ground and two men still held them in their hands. I hoped they'd had enough time to use them to mark their murderers.

Two more, older women were found by the remains of a large house. The place where they cooked and did those daily chores required for such a life as the charcoal burners lived.

Two older girls, perhaps twelve and thirteen, were at the back of the hut. Both it seemed to me had been held against the wall and raped, then stabbed.

Thomas looked away, tears in his eyes. "The little lad lies over there sir. I cannot go...."

"No, Thomas. It's all right. Hal will find him."

Crispin passed me shaking his head.

"Such ferocity, Aumary. Why?"

I too shook my head. I had no answer.

Slowly we located all the bodies.

Eighteen males, fourteen older and four under eighteen. The rest were women. There were children too, as Tom had said. Three small children under five and four ranging from five to twelve.

We laid them reverently in the small space under what was left of the thatch of a partially burned house and Crispin went amongst them at a whisper.

John came up shaking his head.

"Horses. Maybe as many as seven or eight. A confusion of footprints and marks. Problem is the ground is hard. We've had no rain of late. Nothing to tell us much and the place is well trodden as it is."

"From which direction did they arrive?"

He motioned for me to follow. We stood at the edge of the clearing, close by one of the kilns which still smouldered.

"They came thundering in from here I think. Round the kiln. The two or three kilns here would have masked them until they were right on top of the men who were working here."

"That's why so many lay here. They were surprised and felled before they could retaliate, before they could do anything?"

"Then I think the band of murderers dismounted and went for the women and children and any other man they could find who was not at the kilns."

"Two men were found at the back where the stores of charcoal are kept. Working there loading the stores I suppose."

John nodded solemnly.

"It can't have taken long. Then they fired the buildings, slashed at the kilns bringing them down and destroyed anything else and were off back into the forest. For some reason a few holes have been dug at the back of the longhouse. Is that digging part of the process of charcoal making?"

"I don't think so," said Hal stroking his long beard.

"Why would our malefactors dig holes, sir? They are recently dug."

"I don't know John. Which way do you think they went?"

"Towards Inkpen I think."

"Can we track them?"

"It's doubtful but we can try."

*****

Leaving three men with the bodies, the rest of us mounted and rode out of the clearing in an easterly direction. The forest was still with us in fits and starts for I think I have told you that Savernake was a huge place and made up of trees, both close planted and spread out; meadows, glades such as the one we'd left, scrubby heath and commons.

It was about midday when we reached Inkpen. The trees were thinning here for we were right at the limit of the eastern edge of the forest.

John rose in his stirrups and surveyed the territory.

"Looks peaceful enough, sir."

We rode on into the village: few people were about. I knew no one here. This wasn't my domain and no longer the forest proper; it was an entirely different county. Berkshire.

An elderly man with a thin, flag tailed dog looked up from under a ragged thatch of white hair.

"Aw m'lord," he tugged on his forelock. "It's a quiet place 'ere. I in't seen no men on 'orseback but yous," he said in answer to my question.

"The tracks of several horses seem to lead us here."

"No, sir. I din' think so."

"All right. Where is the lord of your demesne?"

"The lord, sir?"

"Yes… I believe he's a Beaumont isn't he?"

"Please you, sir. He in't ever 'ere."

"Never mind." I could see I wasn't going to get anywhere with this recalcitrant

53

villein.

"Where's the manor?"

"At Eddington, sir."

"Not here?"

"Nothin' but sheep 'ere."

"In't that a true word," said Hal, scouting round. Sheep were beginning to crowd in around us from all sides. Bayard whinnied and tossed his head.

"All right ol' lad." I patted his nose.

"So Inkpen is governed from Eddington?"

"'Ungerford mostly."

"Who is there?"

"The Lord Beaumont but he i'n't...."

"There...yes I know." I sighed and rubbed my forehead.

"Be on your guard shepherd. There's a band of murdering men roving around the countryside. We have no idea if and when they'll strike again. Or where."

"Pass the word," added Hal.

The old man laughed. "We i'n't 'ad no great lots of masterless men since young Belvoir threw them outta the forest many years ago."

"Yes, my good man. I did."

The shepherd's eyes grew round as platters.

"That was in 1199 when I last had a sweep of the forest to rid us of outlaws. If I have to do it again, I shall."

The man bowed as low as his old bones would manage. "Aw m'lord I di'n't...I mean... it tweren't... I di'n't..."

We wheeled away with his protestations in our ears.

*****

That evening I sat in my office and listened to the sleet which hissed as it fell in the courtyard. I loaded my brazier with more charcoal and thought of the poor souls who had laboured to make it out in my forest. Now there was only one source, at Hippenscombe.

I wrote a letter to the priest at Froxfield, the nearest church to the charcoal burners' camp, asking that the bodies be interred in his ancient churchyard. I would arrange for them to be taken there by cart.

I also wrote to the sheriff of the county of Herefordshire, asking that he make inquiries about Cille of Hereford, a possible worker in the potteries there. For good measure, I duplicated that letter to the constable of the county; one of them might bear fruit.

Later that evening, before I made my way to bed in the upper chamber, I gathered together all those who slept in the hall and asked again about Thomas. Had he been seen here about midnight? Was he already here and asleep when the kitchen staff came in? Were Hubert Alder the farrier and Alfred Woodsmith aware of him arriving as they slept?

All shook their heads. No one had taken much notice. All were intent on their own rest. No one could tell me if he was already in the hall or not. It was dark, save for the very few candles and rushlights which burned at night on the table and they were doused before folk settled to sleep; they stumbled about tired themselves and fell into bed. Tom's bed place was by the wall at the right of the fire by the chapel steps; no one made a study of who lay there. I saw Hubert and Alfred look sidelong at each other as if they might be planning on a lie but no, they remained silent.

Thomas had allowed Hal to take him to Marlborough, to the castle. I gave instructions that he not be confined but that he have the free range of the castle ward. Andrew Merriman, my friend and main man at the castle, was given the task of making sure that Tom appeared before the coroner, when he at last got round to visiting. Tom promised me on oath that he would stay within the castle grounds. His friends and fellow villagers were responsible for him under the Frankpledge— the old Anglo Saxon oath, more commonly called the tithing, which bound men together and made each responsible for his neighbour. If he didn't behave or didn't turn up to face the coroner, his whole tithing would face a fine.

Hal billeted at the castle that night. It was too late and too dark to return with any safety. I went to my rest, if rest I could call it, fretting about the murderers loose in my forest and about Tom, accused of a murder I'm sure he didn't commit.

Yes, you have guessed Paul, my scribe, I slept poorly that night.

Chapter Four

"Well, that's done it!"

"What's that Hal?" I asked as I saw him come into the courtyard the next morning

"Old de Devil...he's back at the castle."

"Damnation." I looked up at Hal as he dismounted from Grafton and gave him to Edward, one of the grooms.

"What happened?"

"He weren't best pleased I can tell you."

"No, I suppose he wouldn't be."

"Especially when tubby ol' Hugo came in and demanded to see Tom."

"Tom was there I hope?"

"Oh aye, he was there. Ol' de Devil then had 'im locked up on the coroner's say-so and they stuck some leg irons on 'im."

"Damn!"

"He asked that you go back to the castle straight away and, ahem, account for your actions sir, de Devil did."

"Thanks Hal."

"Same old de Devil. 'E don't get any better."

"Is Hugo absolutely convinced that Tom is our culprit?"

"I don't think 'e rightly cares. It's just one more name to 'im and one more success on 'is list. 'Es nothing like the old coroner. What we wouldn't do to 'ave the old one back again eh sir?"

"Yes, indeed Hal. A much better man. I'd better get going and see if I can retrieve the situation."

"I'll come back with you. What with all this murderin' in the forest, I don't think it's safe for anyone to be out alone. I think it'd be best if we took a few more with us, just in case."

57

We were mustering a few of the men in the courtyard when in through the gate came a hard ridden pony. Flecks of foam speckled his mouth. His eye was wild, his ears were back. He snorted as he pulled up, sidled and backed and Cedric gentled his flank until he could get near enough to pick up the reins.

"There boy...you're all right now."

Hal looked up. "There's blood on his back, sir."

Peter Brenthall came running in the gate. "Sir Aumary... m'lord quick!" and he dashed out again crying, "A man fell from that beast, sir. Here."

I followed him out of the gate to where a knot of village folk had gathered just before the manor walls.

I saw Jonathan Reeve kneeling by a man, propping him up by the shoulder.

"Croker!" I yelled and ran the short distance to the injured man.

He grimaced and then clenched his teeth. "M'lord. Thank Almighty God."

"What's happened?" There was a very uncomfortable feeling in the pit of my stomach.

"A band of men. Attacked us...."

"At your workplace?"

"Aye..." the man coughed and blood came into his mouth. He swallowed.

I turned, "Peter. Take Fitz...ride for the doctor. Take Wilfrid, Rob Hungerford and Hartshorn with you for safety."

Peter ran off.

"I managed to get away. They were... killing everyone... just...."

"Some water! Quickly."

The man Croker's eyes filled with tears, "Just killing... for no reason... just going about and killing."

Alice Reeve came up with a beaker of water. Reginald Croker sipped it gratefully.

"I took a sword cut but played dead and then managed to get to a horse and unseen I slipped away but..." He grabbed the stuff of my cotte. "I don't think many will have survived. My Lord...what...?" He started to sob. "Why sir...? Why?"

"Get him into the small room on the south wall. Find Janet Peddler."

This lady was the person in the village whom we especially trusted with wounds of this nature, if Johannes was not present.

Croker carried on speaking, reiterating what he'd told me.

"Yes, we'll go and look. Yes, we shall catch them," I said in a placatory tone as I watched three of the village lads carry him into the courtyard. Hal ran on a few steps and opened the door. This was the same bare room which had housed the woman Cille only a few days before. Croker was borne inside. Janet came up a moment later carrying her cloth bag and bustled in.

I stood at the door staring into space.

"What the hell is happening, Hal?" I asked.

Hal's face was thunderous. "Almost as if someone is trying to destroy all the industry in the forest sir. First the charcoal men, then the potters.... Who's next?"

"We have cattle men, sheep herders, farmers, woodsmen... spread about the forest. Are they all of them at risk Hal?"

I opened the door. Master Croker was lying on his front. Janet Pedlar was wiping the blood from a long gash in his back and another along his flank.

"Croker...these men who attacked you. Did they take anything?"

Croker turned his head. Through his teeth he said "They were looting what they could from the houses further down the hill as I left...but I didn't look back. I just rode."

"Of course. Did you know any of them? Recognise them?"

He shook his head. The sweat stood out on his forehead. Then suddenly he opened his eyes wider.

"Yes… damn him! Damn his eyes...!"

"Who Croker, who?"

But before he could answer me, he had swooned and could say no more.

*****

The men we had mustered to travel to the castle were now gathered together

59

again and we made for the Ramsbury road and Cock a Troop Lane.

Once more we smelled the burning as we reached the place.

We heard raised voices and I cautioned quiet as we approached. However when we rounded the bend in the road and were able to see, we found the noise came from a few survivors; a pitiful few but these men, aided by a few womenfolk were salving the wounds of their friends, trying to put out the fires and make some order of the chaos into which the raid had thrown them. The bodies of their dead had been laid out in front of the largest building and one injured man was attempting to cover them with a large cloth.

Hal jumped down from Grafton and ran to his aid. He laid the cloth down and caught the man as he stumbled. Blood had trickled down his head from a wound in his scalp and he was very unsteady. I saw Hal duck and take him on his shoulder.

Hubert and Cedric were running to help others try to put out the fires. I jumped down and made my way to the row of bodies. I noticed my other men went to help where they could.

A man leaning on a stick was staring down at the humps under the cloth.

"How many, good man?" I asked. The man looked up and I saw he had a huge bruise which disfigured his face and closed his right eye. His left leg bore a stab wound from a spear.

"Ten m'lord. Some managed to get away. I expect they'll trickle back in a while."

"Master Croker rode for Durley to tell us."

"Aye, I saw him go. Thank God he reached you."

"What happened?"

"A party of men came up from the Ramsbury Road." The man swayed, probably faint with loss of blood. I caught him by the arm and sat him on a fallen piece of log then hunkered down in front of him.

"Thank you, sir."

"Water, Hartshorn."

"Aye, sir."

"They looked peaceful enough...just the four of them...nice as you like."

"Four?"

"Aye but then as they approached they made for the store sheds at a gallop and we saw that another six or eight were following fast on their heels."

"Water, sir," said Rob Hartshorn, holding it out.

I gave the cup into the shaking hand of the potter, whose name I remembered was Bartholomew and folded his fingers around it. He thanked me and drained it in one gulp.

"They were out with their swords, this first few and slashing about them before we knew what was happening."

"No provocation...no warnin'?" asked Hal.

"No, sir. Then the rest came up. Some of them had spears. We fought with what we could grab." Bartholomew swallowed painfully. "I think we wounded a couple but nothing much."

"What were these men doing besides going after the potters?"

"Nothing, sir."

"Go on."

"Well, some of us as I say, managed to get into the trees and melt away. Then these attackers made off down the hill towards the houses."

"Where the womenfolk were?"

"Yessir. Some of us followed. We did our best to protect them but...." Bartholomew's head slumped onto his chest and he began to sob. "There are more bodies down the hill sir."

"We shall recover them. They shall be buried with honour." I would have the bodies taken to the nearest church at Mildenhall.

"We saw that they were looting and felt it best to let them get off with what they wanted and get the women and children to safety." Bartholomew wiped his hand across his nose.

"You did a better job of that than our charcoal burners did."

"Sir?"

"This is the second raid by this group of murderers in two days. They made for the charcoal men at Le Broyle and no one survived there."

Bartholomew crossed himself. "Dear God!"

I stood. "We must get you seen and your hurts tended. You have no place to work but I expect some of your houses down by the river are still whole."

"Aye sir, we can all gather together in one of the houses. For the while."

"Whilst this threat is present in the forest, I shall send you some soldiers from the castle to make sure you are not attacked again."

"Surely my lord, they'll not be back," said the man with horror in his voice.

"Sir, m'lord Aumary," shouted John from up the hill.

I threw up my hand in acknowledgement.

"They may be back. You are a danger to them—you can identify them. Did you recognise any of them at all?"

"No sir. I didn't. Not a one. But one of them was as huge as a house, sir."

I nodded. People always exaggerated the size of their attackers. Especially those on foot looking up at those on horseback.

"Forgive me, my woodward wants me." I jogged up to meet John

"What is it?"

John beckoned me to follow him around to the back of the largest building at the workings, the workshop where much of the potting was completed. It was a rectangular wooden structure with a thatched roof about fifteen feet by ten and almost open fronted.

"Here sir. The same. Diggings. Pits hastily dug in the ground, not too deep. The same as we found at Le Broyle."

My brow furrowed in puzzlement.

"We wondered if this was some arcane practice of the charcoal men but now we find the same at the potters."

I came out from behind the building and shouted down to Bartholomew.

"Do you dig holes behind your work shop, for any particular reason Bartholomew?"

"Holes, sir?"

"Aye holes...not deep, about three feet wide."

"Our latrines are further down, sir."

"No not that kind of hole."

"Then no, we don't need holes. No, no holes for what we do here."

I went back to look at these small diggings.

Each one had begun at about two feet from the wall and they were all in a line; all hastily and scrappily dug at intervals of about three feet.

"Then what the hell were they looking for?"

Hal joined us. "Some of them go about with fire and sword, distractin', killin' and maimin' and the others come up here and dig?"

He scratched his grey locks. "I'm blowed if I know why."

"They seem to be looking for something but they don't know where they are to find it."

"Damn fine way to go about it. Kill everyone, then dig summat up."

"But here they weren't able to kill everyone. Too much resistance and not enough time."

I sighed.

"Must I protect every single forest industry and trade from these madmen?"

"I tell you what, sir," said Hal pursing his lips. "Ol' de Devil int goin'a like it one bit, when you take the castle soldiers and plant 'em down out 'ere in the forest."

"No, I don't suppose he will, Hal."

I looked up at the row of bodies under its cover.

"Might we get a list of the dead, please?" I said to a passing potter whose head was bound with a linen strip. "For the coroner. He will have to come and view the bodies."

"A list?" He looked at me with glassy eyes. "None of us can write, sir."

"Ah yes."

"We always got Thomas Potter to do any writing we needed but he's...."

"Yes, thank you."

"Want me to make a list, sir?" asked Hal.

I looked at him and smiled. "Your lessons with Hawise have gone into that thick skull and stuck then, Hal?"

63

"Aye, sir. I think I can make a passable job of a few names now," said Hal, puffing out his chest.

For years now my man at arms had accompanied my daughter at her reading and writing lessons, when his duties allowed. He had not had the opportunity to learn as a child or young man, but it seemed he had now made up for lost time.

"There's plenty of charcoal about with the burnin' timbers and I just 'appens to 'ave a wee bitty birch bark paper in me gambeson."

I smiled at him.

"Go ahead then, Hal. And can you make a list too, of all things which they can tell you might have been stolen from here?"

The man we had asked took Hal to the pile of bodies and uncovered it. The wounds the men bore were various. Sword cuts and stabs, spear thrusts. One man had almost lost a shoulder and arm with a downward swipe of a very sharp sword, no doubt executed from horseback. Some had horrendous head wounds.

"Jared Copper, Brayne Jewel, Henry Potts, Sigerd Potts, Henry Slip, Kaspar Faber, Anthony Wright...."

I looked down. There lay Thomas Potter's young friend, a man of no more than twenty summers. An axe swipe had practically severed his head from his body.

I looked up at the winter sky with a lump in my throat.

'We shall find them and they shall pay…,' I said to myself.

*****

It was the next day before I made my way to the castle. Hal argued with me but I made it clear I wanted to go alone. He stayed in Durley and fumed. I gave Bayard to an ostler and turned to go to my office. Peterkin Gayle, the man responsible for the gaol and for the royal treasury situated at the castle, came out of the gatehouse and caught hold of my sleeve.

"I'm sorry Aumary," he said. "There was nothing I could do." He tipped his head in the direction of de Neville's room. "You are to go in to him."

I patted him on the arm. "I understand Pete. You must do as the constable tells you."

I pulled down my cotte, settled my sword at my hip and marched off in the direction of the constable's office.

He was sitting behind his table with a smug expression on his face. He looked up at the rafters as I entered.

"No, it can't be. My eyes deceive me. Belvoir. It really *is* you? So nice of you to drop in to see us. AT LAST."

"I came as soon as I could m'lord, we have had a deal of trouble in the forest."

"I hear we have wolfsheads in the forest again disturbing the King's peace. The forest which *you* should be looking to, Belvoir."

"I'm not sure if they are masterless men but they have most assuredly disturbed the King's peace. Twice." And I told him of the two attacks on the potters and charcoal men. I then voiced my disquiet about the other trades in the forest and my worries for their safety.

"Let them take care of themselves, Belvoir. Take a party of men and comb the forest...get rid of these pests."

"I'm not sure they are residing in the forest like outlaws, sir. They seem to be mounted, for one thing."

"Wherever they are living, get rid of them. I don't want to have to see them in my gaol. Dispense justice. Hang the lot of them or put them to the sword, it's all the same to me. Just get rid of them."

"My Lord de Neville, the law says..."

"Hang the law Belvoir!" he shouted. "You have a bloody warrant you tell me. Use it. Find them and dispense with them."

"My warrant allows me to detain a man, to question him, not to put him to the sword without trial, m'lord."

"And on that matter what the hell were you doing allowing that felon of yours freedom of the castle? I've had him locked up where he belongs, in irons."

"I have yet to be convinced of his guilt. I am still making inquiries. He may yet be cleared of the charge of murder. I trusted him to stay within the castle pale. He did...."

"Ah, but he absconded before the coroner could get to him didn't he?" said de Neville sarcastically.

"He came back of his own free will."

"With several men chasing him I hear."

"It was Thomas who led us to the site of the first attack on the charcoal men. He returned to tell us...."

"Belvoir...have you gone soft?"

"I believe him, my lord. I've known him for many years. There will be another explan..."

"You *have* gone bloody soft." He stood up and pointed a finger at me.

In the slight silence of the room, I realised that the noises from the bailey had dwindled. All were listening to our raised voices.

"My God Belvoir. Of course the man professes his innocence. Pah! Like they all do. There's no doubt he's lying."

"He does, sir. I think him innocent."

"*I'm* not inclined to believe him."

"Sir, there is very little evidence to suggest...."

"You and your damn evidence. He was there. He was seen. His name was on the girl's lips. I want this sorted out before too long. She was a villein I take it from another county...."

"We do not know, sir, if she was a free woman or...."

"Do NOT interrupt me, Belvoir," de Neville was breathing hard. "Tip her into a grave. Make a spectacle of this Thomas man. They are but little people, Belvoir. Of no consequence. Deal with it. We've bigger animals to wrangle with."

I was very angry now but even so I do not know what made me be so bold.

"Tip her into a grave, sir? Oh yes. Take no notice of truth or evidence. Don't let it worry you. But I *do* worry. I am concerned that the right person hangs for the deed, not the first person whom the coroner claps eyes on or takes into his head to accuse. Oh don't worry, Lord de Neville, it won't bother you, much as the terrible death of your only daughter didn't bother you those years ago...."

The man's face grew puce and his teeth clenched. I knew I had gone too far but I could not unsay the words.

I had referred to an incident of 1204 when the Lord de Neville's daughter had been murdered in a room at the top of the keep at Marlborough castle. Only four people knew the truth of that murder. Johannes and I were sworn to secrecy. The other person murdered there was the Lady Matilda de Neville's bridegroom and his father too knew the secret and would keep it to his grave.

De Neville had, at that time, seemed more concerned for the amount of money he had spent on her aborted wedding than on the untimely death of the girl herself.

We stared at each other. The chief forester sat down slowly. His colour returned to normal. He wiped his hands over his face.

"Do it Belvoir," he said quietly.

"I will take a party of men into the forest and we shall attempt to discover who these men are. As to Thomas, I'd like him to stay in the gaol until...."

"This is MY castle, Belvoir. I say what happens when I am here."

He stood up again. "And I say he'll be tried by fire...."

"SIR!"

"We shall have it over and done with. The people want justice. They shall have it. With spectacle. They shall have their entertainment...I always find that after something like this, the country calms down. Quietens. We'll have order restored. I WILL have order restored, even if you can't be bothered. Am I making myself clear?"

"An innocent man's life is not for the public's entertainment. That isn't justice."

The constable's chin came up pugnaciously.

"I will not have you argue with me, Belvoir."

"No sir. You will not. I forthwith resign my constableship of the castle. You may do as you damn well please."

"The King...."

"Will hear of the circumstances surrounding my resignation." I bowed my

67

head swiftly in an irritated nod, "Good day my Lord de Neville."

I turned on my heel.

I'd barely reached the door when I heard the constable exhale and say... "Belvoir, don't be so hasty."

"No sir. My mind is made up. You may do without my contribution. Govern this castle as you see fit, without my help. I've had a belly full of it."

I reached for the handle.

"Aumary."

Ah, here we go, I thought. Now appealing to me sweetly by using my first name which he rarely did.

I didn't turn back.

"I will govern as *I* see fit and gather evidence as the King wishes me to do. I will adhere to the letter of the law but I *will* temper that letter with the spirit of the law, sir."

De Neville was seated again.

"I will have him submitted to a trial by fire. You will organise it."

I turned back.

"No sir. I will not. I resign my constableship. Now." And I passed through the door saying, "I'll find someone else to organise it."

*****

I stood in the darkness of the gate, the portcullis hanging above me. I looked up.

There it was, tons of spiked metal poised above me; held up only by rope and chain. It could so easily have come crashing down onto me.

I put my hands over my face. What had I done?

When I released my eyes, Gayle was looking at me under his bushy white eyebrows, from the gatehouse doorway.

"That didn't go well."

68

"It never could Pete," I said. "He and I are as unlike as rock and river."

"But the one wears down the other," he said smiling.

"Aye Pete... the rock funnels the river and it takes the river years to break the rock."

"Humph!"

I sighed and turned to my office. I took out my key. "I shall clear my things and then...."

"Aumary... don't go."

Andrew Merriman, my friend and captain of the guard who was on duty that day, came pushing through the jumble of men and carts in the bailey.

"Aumary! What the hell was all that about?"

"You didn't hear?"

"No, only the yelling. I take it it's something to do with your letting Thomas Potter free in the castle."

"That and a few other things."

"He's given up the castle, Andrew," said Gayle.

Andrew put his hand on his hip and stared at Peterkin. "No, he can't do that."

"I can and I have."

"The King will have something to say about that," said Merriman with a slight laugh.

"I expect de Neville will write to him and tell him how useless I have been."

"Well, John will know *that* isn't true."

"You'll have to write and tell him, Aumary," said Pete. "Tell him what has really happened."

"What really happened? What happened to turn my mind Pete, Andrew, was that de Neville wanted me to supervise a trial by fire...for Thomas."

"We haven't had one of those for...," began Andrew.

"I don't know how long and you know how long I've been here," said Pete.

I reached over and took Andrew's arm in my hand and squeezed. "Can you put it in motion. I know that the constable will be having the authorisation written as we stand here."

Andrew took his bottom lip in his teeth and nodded. "Aye. I'll do my best..."

"For Tom...do your best for him."

"You really think he isn't guilty don't you?"

"I do."

Peterkin Gayle looked up at the sky and crossed himself.

"God will know. God will decide," he said.

*****

After I cleared my office, I strode up the High Street at a pace and my feet led me to Johannes' house behind the High Cross. I stomped into the back yard and entered the kitchen.

Johannes was there before his fire, prodding it with a poker. He turned.

"Oh dear. I heard that the constable was back. Spoken to him have you?"

"*He* has spoken to *me*. I have resigned my post at the castle. I cannot stand the man any longer. His insufferable arrogance, his...."

"He's hardly ever there Aumary," said Johannes with a chuckle.

"But when he is, he damn near alienates the whole town and castle. I try to temper his vicious excesses...."

"You and I think the world is vicious, Aumary, people like de Neville know no better. To them, it's just—the way to do things. They have no compassion for their fellow men."

I thumped down on a bench. "He would hang an innocent man just because he happened to be there around the time of the murder and he'd do it just to tidy things up. PAH! He'll allow me no time to investigate properly."

"Whatever he says, he must allow the prisoner a trial. That's the law."

"Oh no! There's to be no proper trial. Here am I trying to bring some order into the system of catching criminals and de Neville thwarts me at every turn. He is the law and the law says if de Neville wishes it, Tom is to be subjected to trial by fire.

Johannes blinked. "Trial by fire?"

"I know... it's a little outdated when I am trying to gather information and proof and be much more factual about it, empirical as the King tasked me to be." I threw down my riding gloves.

Johannes came to sit close to me. "So, Tom will have to carry an iron bar nine feet measured by his own foot's length, an iron bar of one pound I believe, which has been heated to red hot in a brazier."

"The same."

"Hmmm. Then his hand will be examined for burns. If he is burned he's guilty, if not....

"And how can he not be?" I spat.

"You don't trust God to protect him?"

"No, I'm sorry Johannes, I don't."

Johannes laughed. "Neither do I my friend. However, I think *I* might be able to."

I looked up in puzzlement.

"I might be able to help."

"How?"

Johannes jumped up and fetched two cups and a jug of wine. As he poured he told me that he had seen something done when he was in Oxford and it had saved a young man's life.

"We must be able to get in to see Tom every day. We must try to postpone the ordeal for, let's say a week. Then we'll have a chance to do something."

"Andrew is to organise it...I'll get him to stall somehow. I doubt that de Neville will be at the castle long. If we can delay long enough for him to be gone...?"

"Can we enlist Peterkin Gayle's help?

"I'm sure."

"Then, this is what we do...."

71

Chapter Five

I returned to my castle office in a much better mood and called for Peterkin and Andrew. Andrew came in immediately.

"Have you thought about it, Aumary? Changed your mind?"

"No, Andrew, I haven't. I have been to Johannes and discussed what we might do."

"Do? Do about what?"

"About making it certain that Thomas Potter doesn't hang."

"That is for God to decide, Aumary. If Tom is innocent, God will stretch out his hand over him and not allow the fire to burn him."

"And you believe he will?"

Andrew narrowed his eyes.

"You are up to something."

"Johannes and I are up to something, yes."

"What?"

"I need for you to try to postpone the trial..."

"How can I do that when de Neville is watching my every move?"

"You're resourceful. You'll think of something," I chuckled.

"I'll lose my post!"

"A week... we need a week."

"We shall have three days where Potter will fast and pray anyway. It's the rule. Why do you need a week?"

At that moment Gayle's head poked around the door. "You wanted to see me, Aumary?"

"Ah yes. Now I can explain to you both at once."

I guided Peterkin to a seat.

"I need the trial by fire for Thomas postponed by a week."

"Aye, I heard that's what Sir Hugh had ordered," said Gayle. "He wants everything over and done with by the end of November."

"Why?"

"He says he needs to have the castle in order for when the King arrives. All prisoners out of the gaol."

"When is that likely to be?"

"I think he said the third week. Next week. De Neville will be here until the first week in December I've heard but before this he is commanded to go to Malmesbury to meet John."

"Better and better. So we may have time to do what's necessary."

Peterkin tilted his head in surprise. "Necessary for what, Aumary?"

"Aumary and Johannes have hatched a plan to save Thomas Potter from the noose."

"I know you're convinced your man isn't guilty, Aumary, but we must let the law take its course," said Pete.

"If that happens, Tom is dead."

"God will not allow...."

"I do not have your complete faith in God to stretch his hand over Thomas, Pete, and take the heat out of that iron bar. I have more faith in the ability of Johannes to prevent his hand from being too burned."

Yes, Paul, I know that saying this sort of thing is frowned upon by the church. I'm not worried. I'm an old man.

Peterkin looked up at me in horror. Andrew chuckled.

"And how will he do this? I will have to make sure that the brazier is good and hot, the iron bar glowing when he picks it up. I can't avoid that. It will be examined by others."

"No, there will be no blame attached to you. Tom will pick up the bar and he will walk with it."

"And after three days his hand will be examined for burns," said Pete. "We can't avoid that."

"No, Pete. We are going to give God a helping hand... hahaha... sorry."

Peterkin looked affronted. Andrew folded his arms.

"So what must we do?"

"For a week Pete, if you can do it I want you to go in to see Tom twice a day."

"I can do that. I take him his meals...."

"And then Johannes will tell you what to do. I'll get him to come and explain it to you."

*****

My two friends left my office shaking their heads but I had convinced them that our plan would work. Andrew would feign sickness for a while and Pete would go in to see Tom every day. Andrew would recover and then the trial would be organised for the end of the week.

I turned to lock my door.

A party of men came clattering over the drawbridge. I saw the gate guard Bunce lift his hand in acknowledgement. About ten horses passed me and I flattened myself to the wall as they went by.

"Bunce! Who are they?" I yelled as I jogged over to the guard room.

"Ah, sir. They are some of the men who came in with the Lord de Neville."

"I've never seen any of them before. At least, I don't recognise them."

"No sir. They are some of the King's Flemings."

"Ah. His famous mercenaries?"

"That's right. It seems he has more and more of 'em lately and Sir 'Ugh goes everywhere with 'em now."

"They'll fight for the King loyally as long as he pays them."

"Not like us proper soldiers though, eh sir?"

"They're tough men Bunce. They'd make ten of us."

Bunce laughed and disappeared into the guard room.

I stood staring up at the whitewashed keep on its mound. I was not looking forward to striding up those steps into the gaol and delivering the news I had to impart. The keep dominated both town and castle yard. The moat ran round its lower slope and in the bowels of the structure lay the gaol. Four stone lined and whitewashed rooms dug out of the base of the unnatural hill.

I climbed the thirty or so steps, ducked under the lintel and descended the few shallow stairs to the antechamber of the prison. Peterkin Gayle was there before me unlocking the cell where they had put Thomas Potter.

"Thank you Pete. Good morrow, Tom."

The door clanged behind me.

"My Lord Belvoir."

Thomas struggled upright, "God keep you, sir."

"No, no sit. It can't be comfortable in those irons. Take the weight of them from your legs."

I sat down. "I am so sorry it had to come to this, Tom."

In the half light flickering through the elevated grille set into the wall of the gaol, I saw a rueful smile cross Tom's face.

"We were unlucky that the constable arrived in the middle of our investigation. We might have been able to come to a conclusion and had you out of here and home before...."

"I know, sir. I can't hold you responsible. I know it's the law that a suspected murderer must be held securely."

"The Lord de Neville...,"

"Does not understand our agreement, sir."

"No, he doesn't."

I shifted uncomfortably on the stone plinth which ran around the wall of the cell and provided both seat and bed for the prisoners.

"Tom, I have some news for you. If there was any way I could soften the blow of this, I would but...."

"Sir?"

"The charcoal men were not the only people to fall foul of this band of murdering raiders in the forest. The potters at Cock a Troop Lane have also had a visit."

I turned to look Tom in the eye.

"I am so sorry but many of them have been killed, murdered. Your friend Anthony Wright was amongst them. I'm so sorry, Tom."

"Anthony?"

"He's dead, Tom."

I watched his face drain of colour. He closed his eyes. When he opened them again they were huge, dark and shocked.

"How?" he asked shakily.

"I can only guess that he died defending the womenfolk further down the hill. Master Bartholomew says Anthony went with him down to the houses to help when the raiders made for the dwelling places and the things stored there. He must have died quickly for he bore a wound which was a swipe to the neck with a sword."

Tears welled up in Tom's eyes and spilled over his dark, long girl-like lashes.

"It would be like him. He cared for the womenfolk, even though...." He dropped his head into his hands and began to cry quietly. "Oh, Anthony, Anthony."

It took all my will power for me not to join him in his tears. I too had lost loved ones. I knew how it hurt. I patted him on the arm.

"We will do everything we can to find these butchers, Tom."

"I can do nothing to help tied up in here, can I?" he said bitterly, lifting his head and wiping his nose on his hand. "I'm for the hempen necklace aren't I, sir?"

"Not if I have anything to do with it...."

Tom lifted his chin and shouted up furiously to the barrel roof of the gaol. "Oh God! Anthony... Anthony... maybe I shall follow you soon. Yes. Perhaps that *is* for the best."

I watched the anger gather on his face as the tears coursed down his cheeks. "Be best if they do hang me. Even though I've done nothing. Nothing at all. I don't want to stay in this God forsaken world. Not without Anthony."

"Tom." I took hold of his arm. "Tell me... is it as I suspect? Was Anthony your lover... no, no, don't look at me like that."

"No, sir.... No."

"I know that to admit it puts you in peril. But this is *me* Tom.... *Me*, the Lord Aumary, a friend. You have lived with me on my manor for eight years. You know me well as I like to think I know you. Do you think I would ask you something like this to trick you or to then pour censure into your ears?

"No sir. I cannot...."

"Listen. I care not if you loved Anthony as many a man loves a woman, Tom. I understand that it's possible. Believe me when I say that if God had not wanted men to love each other then he would not have made them as they are."

"Sir... the law...."

"The law was made by men, Tom. Fallible, ignorant men."

"They tell us it is...such men are the work of the devil."

I shook my head. "It's not what I think."

"A sickness, an evil malformation of the soul."

Tom wiped his eyes with the back of his hand.

"No. I think not. Tell me, for if this is true and you were Anthony's lover then I know for certain you are not guilty, for you would not be attracted to a woman and could not have fathered a child upon Cille of Hereford."

"How sir... how did you...?"

I smiled "I have known you, as I said Tom, for eight years. I think I understand you. Then something Anthony said when I visited the potters looking for you, made me think. He said, 'It cannot be true, it simply cannot.' I watched his face as he said it. He knew for you to be the father of Cille's child was an impossibility, not because he could not conceive of it, as others who denied this rumour did but that he knew, beyond all doubt, it could not be true. It was not in your nature."

Tom smiled.

"And your reaction too...you have lost a dear, dear loved one who cared for you deeply and you grieve for one whom you loved in return. Your tears are not for a workmate or a friend, Tom, they are for a lover. "

Slowly Tom's face came up to meet mine. The chestnut curtain of his hair swung back to his cheeks.

"Aye sir. I loved him. I cannot deny it."

I nodded and stood looking down at him.

"I must not deny it to myself. It would demean what Anthony and I had together."

"Aye, it would. It would. I now know, beyond all doubt that you are not guilty of the murder of Cille of Hereford but you must go through the formalities of a trial by fire, Tom."

His mouth dropped open. "Oh God!"

"No...listen. Have no fear. Doctor Johannes of Salerno and I have a plan."

"I am going to die... I am...." Once again, Tom put his hands to his face.

I hunkered down before him.

"Listen. You will not die. You will go to this trial by fire, prepared. Master Gayle and Sir Andrew Merriman are going to help us.

I took his hands from his face. "You will not die. You will be proven innocent."

"How, sir... how?"

I smiled and stood once more. "Listen and I will tell you."

*****

The following day dawned cold and grey. The starlings who roosted high up on the downs in the outlying shrubs of the forest came streaming into the town looking for food in the green spaces and banks down by the river serenading us with their tuneless calls. They were excellent mimics, those birds. One, I swear, had been hatched within the sound of the castle smithy, for his call sounded like the striking of a hammer on an anvil. I looked up at him, perched on the roof of the gatehouse. His head up, his throat rippling, he called and called until a few of his mates joined him and then they all flew off to the keep to prod their long beaks onto the grassy knoll of the mound.

My eyes followed them. I saw Peterkin labouring up the steps of the keep and opening the door to the gaol. I made for the southernmost wall and the room where Andrew had lodgings. I scraped at the door and a quiet voice asked me to enter.

There was Andrew wrapped up in blankets, leaning back in his bed. I shut the door.

"A very bad throat, Aumary. So bad I am almost suffocating. Doctor Johannes has been and has prescribed rest, warmth and a soothing medicine," whispered my friend.

"Good man."

"He'll come every day, he says."

"Aye and bring you the liquid that Pete will collect from you to take up to Tom along with his food."

"That's right."

"No one should suspect what is really happening."

"God willing."

Andrew shifted further up the bed. "Do you really think it will work?"

"I trust Johannes. I only hope we have enough time to achieve the result we need."

"If Tom is able to keep using the stuff, Johannes says that six days will be enough." whispered Andrew. " He won't be entirely free of some burning but sufficient for those who look at him to consider him innocent."

"And you'll be well in about five days you think?" I said chuckling.

"I will and I will praise the ministrations of Doctor Johannes of Salerno to the skies. How I was so ill and how he cured me of this affliction in just five days!"

"Can't do his reputation any harm."

Andrew snuggled down again. "I must say, I could quite get used to this life of leisure and comfort."

"Ah... just one thing...," I said as I made for the door once more.

"Hmm?"

"If your throat is so bad, you'll hardly be able to eat will you. Your throat has closed up. You won't be able to swallow. No solid food for you."

"Damn. I hadn't thought of that."

"I had my friend. Best we keep up appearances."

A pillow came flying through the air as I closed the door.

"I shall send you some of Mistress Brewster's best ale, Andrew. It's very good for sore throats and I'll order you a posset and soup from the kitchens," I chuckled.

*****

I returned home that afternoon knowing that my plan was in place and that Johannes, Peterkin and Andrew would play their part. I would return on Saturday for the trial by fire.

Hal met me by the hall door and I told him about the plan to rescue Tom from the gallows.

"You're really convinced i'n't you, of Tom's innocence?"

"I am, Hal." I took off my cloak and went to warm my hands at the fire burning cheerily in the grate.

"Then I doubt you'll want to 'ear what Master Croker told me."

"How is he, Hal?"

"Mendin' both in body and mind."

"Good... so what news is this?"

"I think it's best you 'ear it from 'im."

I trudged across the courtyard to the room on the southern wall. The skies were leaden and heavy, though I didn't think it meant snow. Snow for us usually came in February or perhaps late January, if it came at all. However the air was cold and my breath steamed out like a dragon's fire. I looked up at the sky. More starlings were streaming about looking for food. I heard their feet scrabbling as they searched for hidden grubs on the thatched roof of the room as I entered.

"God keep you Master Croker. How goes it?"

Reginald Croker lay on his side, propped up on an elbow. His torso was bandaged and for modesty his lower body was covered but his injured flank lay bare. Someone had stitched him very competently.

81

"I mend, my lord. Thank you. Your woman Janet is the best of nurses," he smiled.

I nodded to Janet Peddler who gathered her things and scurried to the door.

"Thank you, Janet, for your care of Master Croker."

She curtsied and was gone, this quiet, shy woman.

"Is there anything else you might tell me about the men who attacked you?"

"Aye... aye there is."

"Can you tell me from which direction they came?"

"Aye, from the river, up the hill."

"From Mildenhall?"

"Maybe the other way."

"The town?"

"Somewhere along there. Up from the common at the top of town maybe. They'd miss the population then go round and strike the Ramsbury road past St. Martin's, at Tin Pits. Then they'd ride up for us."

"If that's the case, Reginald, then they're running a great risk of being seen."

"I can only tell you what I think."

"Hal tells me you have remembered something. Something important."

Croker's face grew grave.

"I don't like to say it, sir but I feel I must. I'm sure if you go to Cock a Troop Lane and ask the others, they too will bear me out, those that live and are able to speak. Those that saw."

"Saw what Reginald?"

"Saw the men who attacked us."

"You said you did not recognise anyone. You knew no one."

"Aye. That I did say. The most of them, nay the greater part of them, I don't know. They are as strange to me as is a man from the moon, sir."

"But...?"

"But there was one I knew."

"Who, man?"

"Thomas Potter. Damn his eyes."

82

I felt as if I'd been punched and sat down swiftly on a stool.

"Reginald, why would Thomas Potter attack you? You are all his friends, his workmates?"

"That I can't say, sir. But there he was laying about him with a huge cudgel with nails a poking from the end."

I shook my head. "No, you're mistaken Reginald."

"It was him, I tell you, sir, as large as life. I do know him. I know him well."

"Then you would know that he would never attack his friends. And why should he be helping these men who, we think, are not from around here? These wolfsheads, if that's what they are?"

Croker shook his head. "I don't know, sir. He was with them. He was shouting at them. He knew where things were located, of course he did."

"No, I cannot believe it."

"I'm not lying, sir. Upon the wounds I received at the hands of these monsters. I don't lie."

"No, Reginald. I don't say you do. I just think you're mistaken, that's all."

"Humph. I know what I saw."

"Describe him, this Tom."

"Describe him? Why you know what he's like. Wavy brown hair to the shoulders, straight nose. Eyes as dark as the woods in winter. His mouth was all a grimace as he struck out here and there but it was him with his handsome face all the same."

"What did he wear?"

"Wear?"

"Yes, how was he dressed?"

"I...." Reginald Croker lay back carefully on his pallet. He took in a sharp breath as his wound hit the material below. "Green jerkin. Brown hood. Black chausses gartered with pale rags."

I thought back to the day when I'd seen Tom at the manor.

"When last I saw him, he wore a brown jerkin with a brown hood. Yes, I give you, his lower limbs were encased in leggings which were black and they were

83

gartered in strips of black cloth. His ankle boots were black."

"There you are then, sir."

"You were attacked on the Tuesday."

"Aye, sir."

"Then Tom could not have been in the forest for he came back on the Monday and spent the night in the hall."

"No, sir. He must have slipped out, for I saw him. As plain as day."

"All right Reginald. Thank you for this information. I shall think on it."

I made for the door. "Take all the time you need to recover. When you are fit to go home, we shall ferry you there in a cart."

"Thank you, m'lord."

I opened the door and was about to exit. Croker's parting shot followed me out. "It was him sir. On my oath. It was Thomas Potter and I saw him kill, sir. I saw him kill."

I closed the door.

*****

I sat in my office and brooded. I scribbled then scrubbed out the writing with a pumice and started again. Eventually I threw the holed parchment in the brazier, wasteful I know, but I was angry.

I went into supper and all gave me a wide berth for I was short with them and quiet. Eventually men came to me in groups, to ask how Thomas was faring in the gaol. He had many friends here on the manor and they were, there was no doubt, worried for him. I told them nothing of our plan but allowed them to think that Thomas would be tried by fire and that I was convinced of his innocence.

I returned to my office and wrote again. This time I was a little more organised in my thoughts.

I ran down to the gatehouse where Wyot Gatekeeper was just finishing his evening meal... which was in truth breakfast for him.

"Wyot...."

"M'lord?"

I fondled the ears of Wyot's huge mastiff, Thibault, who was as soft as butter but who appeared as fierce as a basilisk.

"The night Thomas returned to the manor...."

"After he'd run, you mean, sir?"

"Yes."

"And came back in again?"

I nodded. "Did he leave in the night? Might he have been out until the late morning of that next day?"

Wyot scratched his bristly chin. "No, m'lord. I don't reckon he did."

"He couldn't have slipped out and then come back into the yard, say just before midday? Before we brought in the injured potter from the crokerers?"

"Been out all night you think, sir?"

"Yes."

"Well, there 'ave bin times when 'e's bin out all night an 'asn't come 'ome. I just thought he was out with some lady friend... if you know what I mean, sir."

"Yes, I see. But that night?"

"No sir. I think I saw a light on till a little after dark in his pot room and then he went to supper and his bed in the hall as normal. Hubert and Alfred will be able to tell you, I think."

"I shall ask them."

I walked slowly back to the hall. Did Thomas have time to go out to Cock a Troop Lane, take part in the raid and get back here before midday?"

"No sir...of course he didn't," said Hubert when I asked him the same question.

This time Thomas had several witnesses. They had all been talking in the hall late into the evening.

"He was here, sir," affirmed Phil Wheelwright. "We were asking him about the charcoal men and he was telling us the tale of how he found them and we were all talking about what we saw when...."

"And you went to your beds at what time?"

The three men who worked in my courtyard, the wheelwright, the farrier and the woodsmith, looked at one another.

"I reckon it was about the fourth hour of night sir," said Alfred.

"And he didn't leave at all?"

"I can't say he didn't go to the privy, sir...," started Hubert.

"No, Hubert. Hal was sleeping out in his room on the south wall that night. The door was locked" said Phil.

"What does Wyot say, sir?"

"No one slipped out."

They nodded.

"So tell me boys. How can he be seen by Master Croker, before midday at Cock a Troop Lane, wielding a cudgel and striking at defenceless potters?"

They all exclaimed then. "No, it can't be!"

"Why should he do that?"

"He works there and has friends there," said Alf. "If he was there, he'd be helping to fight off the attackers, not striking his friends. No, it's unthinkable."

"But he can't have been there... and here too, sir," added Phil.

"And then of course Master Hal took him off to Marlborough sir," said the elder wheelwright, also called Philip; Old Phil to distinguish him from his son.

"And they left about the second hour of light, sir."

"So there was no time for him to get there and back." I stopped. "Unseen," I added.

"Aye, sir. Even if he ran all the way."

"And yet Master Croker swears upon his wounds and no doubt upon the Holy Bible were we to ask him, that Tom was there and killing."

"No, sir. He's mistaken."

"If he was injured sir, perhaps a knock to the head made him see things...," ventured Alf.

"Hmmm. I suppose that is one possibility," said Old Phil.

"Thank you lads. God keep you. Sweet dreams."

"Blessed be, sir," said Hubert.

*****

The day of the trial came round at last. Hal and I, accompanied by John Brenthall, made our way down to the town.

The fog had come down at dawn, thick, cold, quiet and eerie.

We clopped along the chalk and flint of the road to the town, seeing only a few feet in front of our horses' noses. No birds chirruped as normal. It was deathly quiet but for the echoing step of our mounts.

"Jus' the right kinda day fer sumthin' as 'orrible as a trial by fire eh, sir?" said Hal gloomily.

I think I grunted.

"The fog may thin out in the town."

However it didn't. The High Street was wreathed in swirling white as we made our way down to the castle. From the east we couldn't see the tower of the church of St. Peter at the western end.

"Sir Andrew says sir, that they 'ave managed to get it organised so that the trial is done in the bailey in front of the castle smithy."

I nodded. "Good, the chill of the day will help to cool the iron."

We turned in at the castle gate just visible in the thick fog.

Peterkin was waiting for us.

"Is de Neville here, Pete?"

"Praise Heaven, no," smiled Gayle. "He went out yesterday to Malmesbury to meet the King."

"Praise Heaven indeed," I smiled. "How fares our prisoner?"

"Well, I think, under the circumstances. Johannes of course has not been to see him but the castle doctor...."

"James...."

" Aye... he pronounced Tom fit for the trial and he is all set to do the

87

inspection of Tom's hands. Along with Andrew and Father Columba. FitzAlan will be there too"

I coughed. "And Andrew? Is he recovered?"

"Oh it was tag and go," said Pete smirking. "He's been very ill, but Johannes has managed to bring him round."

I nodded, smiling to myself.

I looked round the bailey, what I was able to see of it.

"We have no crowd yet?"

"Andrew won't allow them in. Says it compromises the security of the castle."

"Ha, ha. If de Neville were here, he'd have the whole show out on the street and make a spectacle of it."

"Aye, I know."

"Best shut the gate then."

Pete shouted to Bunce and his companion to close and bar the gate. Those outside who had business here would have to wait. I heard the gate clang and the locking bar slide home but owing to the fog, I could see nothing. I gave Bayard to an ostler.

"I will not take part in any way. I am no longer the constable of the castle," I said. "Who has de Neville appointed to take my place, Pete?"

Gayle scratched his ear.

"Well, no one really. He hasn't replaced you. Don't think he dare until the King is made aware. Andrew, Fitz and I are running things. But Sir Hugh did leave one of the Flemings behind to keep an eye on things. I think he's here just to make a report to Sir Hugh, to make sure all is done in the way he requires."

"The rest have gone with him to Malmesbury to the King?"

"Aye."

"Who do we have then?"

"A man called Cornelis Clijster. Great bear of a man with a shaggy beard and some of his company."

"Hmm" said Hal under his breath. "I 'ope it's a well-cared for beast."

"Well...." said Pete laughing, " it's not as fine as yours, Hal."

"Humph!" said my man at arms, his chin jutting.

"Where is this bear then?"

"He's in the forge, supervising the deploying of the brazier."

"Hmm. I'll search out Andrew. Pete, you'll fetch out Tom?"

"I will. I'll get the say so from Andrew. He's in charge of all this isn't he?"

"Aye, he is," I chuckled.

We approached the forge where a small group of castle people were gathered. Andrew heard us arrive and took me aside.

"We are all ready, Aumary."

I whispered, "How goes it?"

"Pete says that Tom's hands are still a bit soft but better than they were. He will still be a little burned but if we can influence the inspection party, we should prevail."

Johannes came up behind me. "Andrew...? How are you?"

"Never fitter doctor, thanks to you," and he winked.

"And our other patient?"

"We think he'll do."

"Good."

"So, we'll have him out shall we, Pete?" said Andrew.

*****

The fog was swirling around the bailey mixing with the smoke from the charcoal brazier which had been brought out from the forge into the open air.

John Munday the forge master, plunged an iron bar about eight inches long into the fired coals and left it there for a while. The farrier in charge of heating it, kept glancing at its glowing embers, treating it to a few passes of the bellows bag.

The white fog swirled around us again and in a gap in the screen, blown by a slight breeze, I saw Thomas emerge from the keep, blink and stretch his arms.

Down from the keep came Thomas, walking carefully on the steps for the incarceration had made him stiff. He walked with Peterkin Gayle the gaol master behind him and Maurice FitzAlan, our other captain of the guard before. The Flemish mercenary Cornelis Clijster met them at the foot of the steps. They disappeared for a moment in the opening of the wall which led to the moat around the keep and the fog swallowed them.

Then they reappeared and walked to the place in front of the forge. Tom's gyves had been struck off and he stood shivering in the cold of the day, his arms around his body.

Father Columba approached him and in a loud voice gave him a blessing. Tom crossed himself as did several others. The priest then led him to the space in the bailey which had been cleared for the trial. I saw Tom cast around for friendly faces. He found mine and smiled. I winked at him and his smile broadened a little. I saw Peterkin touch him gently on the shoulder as he left him. They took off his tunic and Tom shivered violently as he stood in his bare feet wearing just his braies.

Andrew Merriman took a deep breath.

"Thomas Potter of Salisbury lately of Durley you are charged with the murder of Cille of Hereford at Durley village in the county of Wiltshire. You plead your innocence of this crime. You cannot produce an oath taker for you have no witnesses to your innocence and none can take an oath that they know without doubt that you are indeed innocent of this crime. The Lord de Neville has ordered that you undergo a trial by fire. Will you submit to this trial by fire?"

I held my breath. It was commonly believed that felons who knew themselves guilty would at this point decline the trial, thus indicating their guilt. Those who knew themselves innocent would submit.

The premise upon which this rested was known as iudicium Dei, judgments of God. Those who were guilty of the crime knew beyond all doubt that God would find them out and were afraid to submit. Those who were blameless would put themselves in God's hands, for he would deliver them from any evil.

That belief seems naive to me Paul, my scribe but that is how it is. I can't expect you to understand how foolish I think this form of trial was, for you are a man of

God and must wholly put your trust in him. I am merely a simple sinner with too much time to sit nowadays and think. Anyway, it's all been stopped now. The church fully outlawed the practice in 1216.

Then of course there was often an intervention by priest or lord and the tried person would not be so badly burned for the iron bar would not be so avidly heated.

Yes, yes I know it was supposed to be up to God but even he needs a little help now and again Paul.

The iron bar would still be fiendishly hot but not quite as hot as the accused expected.

Thomas Potter lifted his head and in a confident voice cried out. "God will be my witness, I did not murder Cille of Hereford. I will submit."

I saw Father Columba and Andrew exchange glances. Andrew nodded and went to the brazier to speak to the forge master.

Maurice FitzAlan now took over.

"Thomas Potter you will walk from this line drawn in the dust of the earth to a place nine paces forward. At your normal pace and with your usual tread, walk in a straight line."

Thomas thrust up his chin, unwrapped his arms from his body and stared ahead. He walked slowly and confidently nine paces in a straight line and stood looking up at the sky.

FitzAlan came up to him and drew his sword and scored another line in the dust of the bailey floor.

"You will walk this distance, holding the bar. You must not drop nor hurl it away. You must not stop."

"Yes, sir," said Tom weakly.

Maurice took Tom's arm and led him back to the starting place.

There was absolute silence in the castle grounds as Maurice FitzAlan's voice

91

rose up to give instruction.

"Is the bar ready, Sir Andrew?"

"Aye, it is."

"Then may God be at your side Thomas Potter."

Father Columba then came up and, dressed in his ecclesiastical robes, began to intone a prayer. He would walk by the side of Thomas as he travelled his nine paces, for God must be seen to be present in the body of the priest and be working through his prayers, to prove Thomas' guilt or innocence.

The forge master took a pair of pincers and lifted out the bar. It was glowing red hot. Slowly, very slowly he approached the defendant. The bar was losing colour by the moment.

Master Munday showed the iron bar to the gathered men. There was a collective intake of breath.

"Grasp the bar," said FitzAlan authoritatively.

The forge master swung round and brandished the bar, taking a little more heat from it and tentatively Thomas reached out with his right hand.

He seemed to stall for a moment then I saw him take a deep breath and lean forward.

His right hand clasped around it. The forge master released his pincers quickly and stepped back.

"Go, Thomas...go!" I said to myself, "do not tarry."

I heard an in-drawn breath as Thomas' hand felt the heat of the bar. There was a hissing and I realised that it was my own breath being taken.

I saw Andrew at the other end of the nine paces brush his mouth with his hand as if he too felt the heat.

Thomas set off, a grimace of pain on his face. He groaned once as he walked purposefully but not too fast towards the line where stood Andrew. Father Columba kept pace with him for the nine steps, the Latin of his prayer covering the moan that escaped from Tom's lips as he reached the fifth step. Thomas drew back his lips across his teeth as if to scream but no sound escaped his mouth.

Sweat stood out on his forehead but he kept walking. He faltered a little on step eight and then when he reached the line which Fitz had scored in the earth, he dropped the bar and fell to his knees sobbing in pain and relief.

The farriers, stable men and soldiers who inhabited the castle bailey and its buildings watched and were silent.

In that silence I heard a shrill neigh from one of the horses penned in the stable. A small child on the road beyond the wall of the castle started to cry. A disgruntled crowd of people left outside the gate muttered and cried out that they didn't wish to be kept waiting much longer and banged on the gate. I heard Bunce answering them with an expletive or two.

Father Columba finished his prayer and reached down to touch Tom on the shoulder. Tom had now cradled his injured hand under his armpit and he struggled to his feet.

"Sir Maurice!" cried Father Columba. "Doctor, Master Clijster, might we now bind the man's hand for three days?"

Andrew came up to Tom and looked him in the eye.

"Thomas, give us your hand."

The castle doctor had now drawn near and Johannes was not too far away. Slowly Thomas lifted his hand from his armpit and shakily he held it out.

FitzAlan came up behind him. Clijster came up to his right hand.

All three men leaned in. Johannes stood on tip toe. He was a tall man and could see over the heads of the three bending judges.

Thomas turned over his hand.

There was a red mark all along his palm and across the middle joint of his fingers and thumb.

"God will deliver a verdict!" shouted Father Columba when the three men who were to pronounce on Thomas' injuries had conferred. "The hand will be bound and in three days examined. If the hand is mending or has no burning, Thomas Potter is innocent. If there is suppuration or blistering, Thomas Potter is guilty."

Suddenly the bailey became a hive of industry once more and Bunce pulled back the locking bars of the castle gate with a thwack.

*****

We endured three days of agonising over the verdict. How much worse was it for poor Thomas languishing in the confines of his prison, I thought. Johannes was confident of a good result. I did not know what to think.

Again the fog swirled around us; it had lifted in the afternoons to return in the evening and through the night, lingering long into the mornings. Again we clopped the chalk road to the castle and Tom was brought from the gaol.

The wrappings were taken from his hand.

Johannes grinned at me. I grimaced. Andrew peered carefully at the palm before him. He nodded to Father Columba.

"God has revealed the truth. The hand is healing. Thomas Potter of Salisbury is innocent of the murder of Cille of Hereford. Praise be to God," he shouted.

The onlookers raised such a cheer as made the birds in the trees on the Manton Road rise up in one large flock.

Thomas thrust his hand into his armpit again and fell to his knees, his eyes closed.

Johannes leapt across the ground.

"Quickly Thomas. If we are to prevent too much damage we must get your hand salved now. And we must make sure that the shock of all this does not make you ill, for it can you know."

He grabbed Thomas by the shoulder and shook him.

A tear stained face looked up at him through a curtain of lank chestnut hair.

"Thank you, sir."

Thomas struggled to his feet and Johannes and then Hal, who had been slinking around the perimeter of the proceedings, walked briskly with the young man to Andrew's lodging where Andrew himself opened the door. After a few paces they were lost in the swirling fog.

I sought the priest's face and found it. I nodded to him. He returned the nod.

Peterkin came up to me, his thumbs thrust into his belt.

"Satisfactory, Sir Aumary?"

"Very satisfactory, Master Gayle." I said, smiling gleefully.

Chapter Six

I made my way to Andrew's lodging and ducked through the door-hole, closing the wood behind me.

"Well done, Thomas."

Thomas looked up pink faced and shining.

"Thank you my lord for everything you did. All of you."

Johannes was fiddling in his medical bag and out came a small pot with a waxed lid.

"Ah, I know this stuff Tom," I said smiling "This saved my skin when I burned my hand badly in 1204. Marvelous stuff. We shall have you right in no time."

Johannes began to gently massage the burned hand with a soft yellow paste, a salve especially for burns, which smelled of summer, of herbs and flowers and a touch of some sort of pine resin.

Thomas grimaced but submitted to the doctor's treatment with some flinching and did not pull his hand away.

"You knew, didn't you, sir?" said Tom, suddenly looking up at me.

"Yes, Tom. I knew that once you had submitted to the fire they would take the heat, so to speak, out of the trial. They let the bar cool a little but I knew that it could still hurt you, so we, the four of us, played out a little game of our own to make you fit to carry the bar the nine steps."

"You believed me innocent, you said."

"I did. But those who submit are often hurt by the heat, Tom, even though they're acquitted of the crime of which they are accused. We did not want lasting damage to your hands, for after all, they are your livelihood."

"And so you had Master Gayle bring me some foul smelling stuff which hardened my hand. Thanks to you too, sir. What was it m'lord, he fetched me?"

"I cannot answer you Tom, for it's a substance of Doctor Johannes' making."

"Oh no, Sir Aumary. I can't make it. I..."

"What is it, Johannes?" I asked.

"Our own dear Gabriel Gallipot makes such stuff and only he knows how to do it. I believe it's a mixture of plant liquids exuded from the trees of far off lands. Gabriel tells me he distills it from several different ingredients. Naturally he won't reveal the secret to this humble doctor," chuckled Johannes.

Gabriel Gallipot was the town apothecary and a very learned man in his field.

"I believe he found out how to make it from our Jewish friends up on Silver Street."

"Another reason to be very glad of their presence in the town, Johannes," I said.

"I for one am eternally grateful to them and to Master Gallipot," said Tom smiling.

"And you must be grateful too, to Andrew here. He managed to postpone the trial by almost a week so that the stuff Johannes procured would work on hardening the palm of your hand, Tom. I'll have you know he went without solid food for almost that length of time, so that it would appear he had a terrible throat soreness and fever."

Andrew laughed.

"Such a sacrifice for a man who likes his food...even castle food," he said.

"A sacrifice indeed."

"Never fear Aumary. I smuggled in a little of my cousin's fare now and again. Good food. He didn't starve," said Gayle.

"We are very lucky in our friends, Tom," I said, smiling. I turned again to Johannes. "Will you bind the hand?"

"Only for a while, whilst the ointment does its work. Then the best thing for it is the open air."

"Can you ride back to Durley, Tom, with one hand on the reins? We have brought Athena, she is a good docile beast. She'll follow Grafton's tail."

"Aye, sir. I think I can. I'll be very pleased to come home."

*****

The horses saddled, we walked them out of the gate and stood in the foggy air of the drawbridge. Andrew came out to see us off. Thomas mounted Athena with difficulty and turned her for the road.

As I was about to mount and head for home, a burly figure appeared in the swirling mist of the gap in the walls. It looked like a fabled monster of Viking myth. The silhouette he made in the darkness of the gatehouse tower and the silver wreathing of the fog, made me think of tales our peddler in Durley told, about creatures from the wastes of the northern lands and their predilection for human flesh.

I watched as the figure approached and became more solid.

"My Lord Belvoir?"

Hal turned in the act of putting boot to stirrup.

"The hairy bear, sir," he said under his breath and stood down again.

"Cornelis Clijster, my lord," he bowed his head. The voice was deep and resonant.

"Ah yes. Pleased to make your acquaintance, Master Clijster."

I am a tall man but this man topped me and Johannes by a good few inches. He must have been at least six foot four. The beard was a dirty blond and although it was probably clean and combed it looked none too savoury. I saw Hal finger his own grey facial hair and watched as his eyes narrowed in disapproval. Hal was as fastidious about cleanliness as was Doctor Johannes.

A pair of blue eyes set in creases of tanned skin under bushy blond eyebrows fixed themselves on me.

"We have not been formally introduced."

"No, I'm sorry. That is an oversight but I am no longer the under custodian of this castle and so..."

"My Lord de Neville said that I was to be under your guidance and yet you return home, sir?"

"I have reluctantly given the Lord Hugh de Neville my resignation from the post as constable here, Master Clijster. If he chooses not to accept it, that is his affair."

"He is with the King in..."

"Malmesbury. Yes, I know. The King will now be in receipt of a letter from me informing him of my giving up the constableship of the castle and the reasons for it."

"I do not think that Sir Hugh will let you go, sir."

"He has no choice. I was appointed by the King not by Sir Hugh. If the King wishes me to stay on, I will consider it but it will be with certain... provisos."

Cornelis Clijster took a deep breath, creased his face and sneezed violently. I stepped back quickly so as not to be showered.

He then wiped his nose on his sleeve.

I saw Hal grimace and turn away.

"Master Clijster, you may defer to Sir Andrew here and to Sir Maurice FitzAlan and to Master Peterkin Gayle now I am not here."

The big man sneezed again. He inhaled noisily through his nose.

"The Lord Hugh returns with my lord the King in a few days, sir," he sniffed. "He will be here for some of Advent but travels to Windsor for the days of Christmas."

"Thank you for letting me know. The King often visits us at Durley at Christmastide. Do you yourself stay here or ride on to Windsor?"

"That depends on the King, sir."

"Well, then, perhaps we shall see you again."

I turned and mounted, hearing Hal say under his breath, "Not if I can 'elp it."

Clijster sneezed yet again and blew his nose on his fingers. He wiped it on his jerkin. I saw Hal grimace.

"That was well done, my Lord Belvoir," said the big man.

I turned to him again in the action of securing Bayard's reins.

"Master Clijster?"

"The fire trial. You got the result you wanted. I don't know how you did it but you did."

I did not let him see me smile.

"Best you get into the warmth Master Clijster," I said to him as I turned Bayard's head for home. "This fog will do you no good."

"Aye...I seem to have developed a soreness of the gullet," said the Fleming, wrapping his huge hand around his throat. He hawked and spat out onto the roadway. "And a cough."

I saw Andrew frown and glance at me.

"Well, don't look at me!" he said pointedly.

*****

The fog spiralled around us as we journeyed home at a slow clop. Thomas, who wasn't a good rider for he had little need to ride and not much practice, could barely keep his seat despite the slow pace, was almost asleep in the saddle. I suspected he'd slept poorly on his cold, hard stone bench last night.

The fog clung to our clothing like cobwebs, dampening cloaks and beards with pearly droplets.

The coldness returned and as we rode into Durley we were very glad to see the lamps lit by the manor gate, though it was barely past midday. Hartshorn was manning the gate.

The light went some way to cheering us and banishing the gloom of the dark day.

Lydia got up slowly from a comfortable seat by the fire and stretched out her hand to me as I strode up the hall.

"Have you brought him home? Is he acquitted?" I took her hand.

"Aye he is. He's gone to his workshop. Hal is with him."

"No doubt he'll be speaking to his friends there."

"Aye, Hubert and Phil, Bevis and the rest." I kissed her cheek.

"Thank Heavens he has been found innocent. Was his hand...?"

"Not too badly burned. It will mend. Johannes will treat it with his special unguents."

"Of course you know this means that you must now apply yourself to finding out who really *did* kill the girl, Cille?"

I threw off my gloves and swung my cloak over my shoulder, releasing the droplets trapped in the nap of the wool. They fell into the fire and hissed. I stretched out my hands to the flames.

"I have no idea. No idea at all. Do I yet have an answer from Salisbury do you know? Or perhaps from Hereford?"

"You have no letters waiting for you," said Lydia.

"Hmm." I sat down. "I will be happier when I have an answer to my questions. Although I believe Tom innocent of her murder, there is still the matter of him being seen...."

"If indeed the man *really* saw him."

"Yes. Seen at the Crokerers. Why would he lie?"

"I think the pottery man is mistaken."

"He must be. But there are others, he tells me, who also saw him. Are they all mistaken?"

We both stared into the fire for a moment.

"And I need to find out about this group of men terrorising my forest. Though now I'm loath to use men from the castle to do so. After de Neville's behaviour."

"Forest folk will help you I'm sure," said Lydia. "You have your verderers and agisters.

My daughter Hawise came down the stairs.

"Dada, you're back."

"I am sweetling, and how is my favourite girl?"

"Oh, you know... busy...."

"Busy with what?" I chuckled.

"Show your father what you've been doing, Hawise. I'm sure he'll be very proud of you."

Hawise ran back up the stairs to the solar and I looked at Lydia, my eyebrow raised quizzically.

"No, I shall not spoil her surprise. She has been working very hard on it."

Lydia eased herself into the chair again and rubbed the area of her stomach above the bump which was our future child.

"Indigestion again?"

"Yes. It's quite painful even though Johannes' medicine goes some way to relieving it. I almost feel as if I never want to eat another morsel," she chuckled.

"That will never do."

"Here we are Dada."

A few years ago, Hal of Potterne had made my daughter a doll for her birthday. Her mother had later encased the jointed wooden doll in a stuffed calico body. Now I noticed that Thomasina, as she had become known, had some new clothes.

I took the proffered doll from my daughter's outstretched hand.

"My Thomasina, you do look the great lady!"

A smart bliaut of thin blue wool covered a shift of white linen. There was a line of perfect stitching around the neck and hem of the bliaut. I recognised the wool material as one of my wife's old dresses.

"And you did this with your own hand, Hawise?"

"I had help from Mama but yes...I sewed it. It was a practice for something else."

"She doesn't like sewing do you, Hawise?" asked Lydia.

"No madam, I get bored with it."

"But this project was one which pleased her," said her proud mother. "And she made a good job of it."

"What have you behind your back, Hawise?" I asked, craning my neck.

"Ah...," said Lydia. "This is another task."

"One which pleases her?"

"I hope it will please you, Dada," said Hawise.

She brought out her other hand.

"It's a present for you."

I took the material and stretched it out. Pristine white linen glowed in the

103

firelight and the light of the candles and flares around the hall.

"My... goodness! Hawise! This is... as good as a professional seamstress." I sat down on my chair and smoothed the shirt, for shirt it was, out onto my knee. From the corner of my eye I saw my daughter flick a glance at Lydia and smile.

"All her own work."

"Though mama cut it out and told me what to sew, when and where."

I brought one of the seams to my eye. "Such tiny stitches. I remember Hawise when you could barely get a needle through a piece of material without sticking it in your finger."

"Hemming sheets is no fun, Dada" she said.

"But hemming a shirt for your old father is more fun?"

"Much more fun," she giggled.

"I shall keep this shirt for very best."

"But you *will* wear it, won't you?"

"Indeed I shall wear it to church on Sunday..."

Hawise laughed out loud. "No one will see it because it's so cold, you'll have your cotte over it and a robe."

"Well, I will have to go to church without."

Hawise chuckled and Lydia joined her with her high tinkling laugh.

"Oh Dada you'll catch a cold if you just wear your shirt."

"Ah well...I will just have to be cold. I must show off my lovely new shirt."

"Your father is teasing you, Hawise," said Lydia. "He will wear it and all will know that it's your handiwork. Maybe when the weather gets warmer and he can wear a cotte over it."

Hawise shrugged. "I don't care. I will know it when I see him in it won't I?"

"No one else will have such a superbly sewn shirt," I said, laying it reverently on the hall table and folding the sleeves over the body. "No one else will look as good as I do."

As I spoke those words a strange feeling came over me. Sometimes, we have a feeling that we have said something before, been somewhere where we cannot possibly have been before, seen things before in the exactly the same way we are seeing them now. We know without a doubt this cannot be true and it puzzles and unsettles us.

I stared at the fire. Something had indeed unsettled me but when I tried to grasp it, it disappeared like the smoke up the chimney.

"Thank you, Hawise, for this very special gift." I said, rising and planting a kiss on my daughter's cheek. "So where is your little brother, the rascal?"

Hawise's eyes rose to Heaven. "You'll never believe what he did, Dada," she said.

*****

I took a small meal of bread and cheese with some meat and ale and then went down to the yard to find Hal of Potterne.

He was standing by the brazier of Hubert's forge warming his backside, with a leather cup of ale in his hand. All the lads from the courtyard were there and a few from the village. As I approached, the village men melted away to their work and Hubert, Hal, Tom and Alf were left chewing over the cud of the day's happenings.

"Thomas, how is the hand?"

"It is devilish sore sir, I don't mind saying and I must put some more paste onto it. The doctor tells me I need to keep doing it."

"Yes, you do. Until it has all gone into the skin."

"How did you burn yourself so badly, sir?" asked Thomas with wide eyes. "That you needed to use Dr. Johannes' salve?"

It was almost as if he couldn't conceive of his Lord handling something hot enough to burn him.

"Ah... that's a long story," I said. "And concerns a beautiful woman, a slickstone and a plaintive song, Tom."

Tom's head skewed sideways in disbelief.

"Ask Martyn Peddler. He knows the story of it," I chuckled. "Meanwhile I need to ask you. Did you leave the manor at all the night before you went to the castle?"

Behind me I heard Hubert sigh. He was obviously put out that I hadn't believed him.

"No, sir. I stayed here all night. I had no reason to go out."

"Hal, you went to Marlborough with him?"

"Aye, I fetched 'im out of the 'all at the second hour roughly and we went to town right then."

"Thank you."

"Why, sir?" asked Thomas Potter.

"Because I have a sworn statement saying that you were seen, Tom, at the crokerers at Cock a Troop Lane that morning."

Tom's face creased in puzzlement.

"No, sir. I wasn't there that day. Saturday was the last day I went there... the last time I saw Ant...."

"Yes. I am going down to the potters now. Hal, will you come? Let's see if we can lay this rumour to rest."

"In the fog sir?"

"Aye Hal... in the fog. We know the way."

*****

John joined us on his mount, Fire as we left the courtyard and made for the forest trees. We had gone but a half a mile in the billowing fog when we heard footsteps approaching us and the tap, tap of a stick on the chalk road.

"Sir Aumary, my Lord Belvoir!"

The fog thinned and one of my deer men came into view.

"Alan. How goes it?"

Alan Hart was a forester with special responsibility for the deer in the local woods, their health, numbers and breeding. All men looked out for the deer of course but Alan was the senior man amongst them. As all my woodsmen, he also kept an eye out for poachers.

"F-fine m'lord," stammered Alan who had a slight speech impediment.

"I was c-coming to see you. I heard you were b-back from Marlborough."

"Well, you have found me."

The whole of him now came into view.

"You're walking Alan?"

"Aye, m'lord."

"And limping," added John.

I provided all the officers of my deer men with sturdy rounceys with which to patrol the forest.

"Humble was stolen two nights ago, sir."

"Stolen?" spluttered Hal. "Why would anyone want to steal your 'orse?"

It was then I noticed that Alan sported a huge black eye and a bruise to the chin.

I dismounted. "What happened?

"I heard a c-commotion about the fifth hour of the night sir. I went out meaning t-to go to the stable. You know that's only a stone's throw from the house."

"And inside your thick thorn hedge" said John.

"They m-managed to get through that."

"Beezulbubs bubbies!" said Hal.

"And they rode off with Humble sir. I t-tried to stop them but got k-kicked in the face for my p-pains and trampled a b-bit."

" 'Ow many were there?" asked Hal again.

"Just the one, sir. It was the old d-dog alerted me."

"Just one you say?" I asked in a surprised tone.

"Aye, sir. I d-didn't see or hear anyone else."

My deer man dwelt deep in the forest in an area known to us as Haw Wood. He lived with his wife and two young sons of ten and eight.

"No one else hurt?"

"No, sir. The wife came out and p-picked me up. I was pretty shaken but thought I'd better walk up to you sir and let you kn-know. It took me a while to c-come round, sir and feel like walking."

"Good man. The lads?"

"Slept through it till the last m-minute sir," he raised his eyes to Heaven. "The thief seemed to know where to g-go. It was all over in a t-twinklin'. He was up and mounted and g-gone, kicking me down for good measure, on his way out."

"He knew where you lived and knew you had a horse."

"Aye sir, and was determined to have her."

"'T'was no opportunistic stealin' then," said Hal, stroking his beard.

"Someone who knows the forest and who maybe lives in it. Did you see anything which might tell us who the man was, Alan?"

Alan frowned. "He was a g-good rider. He didn't take the saddle and t-tack. Just rode off b-bare. It was too dark to see much. I had a flare but lost it when I was k-kicked. But...," he looked down at his feet.

"Yes, Alan?"

"I got a look at his face before I d-dropped the flare and it looked like that p-potter from Cock a Troop Lane."

I felt Hal sit up straighter in his saddle.

"Thomas Potter, d'you mean?"

"Yes sir. The fella that lives in your courtyard. Though what he'd be d-doing..."

"Anything else you noticed?"

"Aye sir, as he grinned at me, I noticed he had a gurt b-bruise on his forehead." I nodded.

"Your dog?"

"B -Bramble? He'd been locked in the shed. He b-barked when the man came into the c-compound but somehow the thief managed to g-get him away."

"Unhurt?"

"Aye G-God be praised, sir. I would'a bin right sorry if anything had happened to B-Bramble."

"Someone you know then Alan...or rather Bramble knows maybe? Or someone with a way with dogs."

"L-looks like it sir. Though he doesn't know Thomas well."

"Hmmm. Thank you Alan. If you can walk to Durley, go and get another horse from Richard Marshall. We'll see if we can recover Humble."

"This b-blasted fog doesn't help, sir."

"No, it doesn't help anyone."

With a slap to the back I tried to send Alan Hart off in the direction of the Durley Road.

He turned back to me "And furthermore sir...."

"There's more, Alan?"

"Aye sir. There's been a d-deal of d-deer taken." Alan was speaking about the roe or fallow deer which abounded in Savernake.

"When?"

"Over the past ten days. Though n-nothing I think since Wednesday...day before yesterday."

"We've had no widespread poaching in the forest that we know of for two years or so. Besides the odd one that is."

"No sir. I found the remains of the fires where they prepared the c-corpus. Seems as if there was a c-camp or two. Feeding many men and...."

"Where?"

"First one c-close by Charcoal B-Burners Lane at Wooton sir, where the road splits and the next at Chisbury. The folk there all gone, sir. Many d-dead. The village is devastated."

"The camp? The old earthworks?" I groaned.

"Yessir."

"That'll be our wolfsheads, sir," said John.

"Four of our royal stags were t-taken, sir."

"Twelve point?"

"Aye and even one imperial."

"We have only four or five of those don't we? Stags with more than fourteen tines?"

"Yes, sir. We have one less n-now."

I chewed my lip. "Thank you Alan. Take care... these men have already killed."

"Aye sir. I know. Forest folk are a little jumpy. There d-doesn't seem any rhyme nor reason to the attacks."

"We shall sweep the forest when the fog goes, Alan. We'll find them."

Alan backed off. "Good day m'lord. If there's anything else, I'll see one of the forest lads. God keep you." And with a wave of his hand he limped off and the mist closed around him again.

John leaned over his saddle bow. "Just one man sir? That doesn't make sense."

"No John, it doesn't. Neither does it make sense that it was Tom. Perhaps this man's nothing to do with the rest of the raiders."

"I can't believe that," said Hal. "We got folk out in the forest every day. Loadsa folk live here, scattered about. Someone musta've seen them, these men. Someone must know this one man too."

"No one left behind to point the finger," said John.

"We must search these temporary camps. There may be something they've left behind which might tell us what is going on."

"Chisbury and Wooton copse," said John.

"First, Cock a Troop Lane."

*****

We approached the potters' village slowly and when we felt we were near enough called out so they shouldn't think us the enemy, for the fog was very thick here.

I heard Master Bartholomew Ollam shout up the hill.

"Aye sir, we hear you."

We rode down into the cleared land, the purlieu at the forest edge, land granted to the potters.

The site had been tidied since we had last seen it and many of the men were labouring at repairing the working sheds. A pile of broken crockery was heaped up at the edge of the clearing. People were going about quietly in the fog, preparing to begin working again.

Some folk still wore the bandages on their wounds, like badges of honour. Some were scarred, others still leaned on sticks as they walked.

I slowed in front of Bartholomew.

"God's greetings to you all."

"And to you, sir."

"How goes the recovery?"

"Slow and painful sir, but we shall be back at work late tomorrow. Our kiln has been rebuilt." He nodded towards a structure set a little way from the workshop. It was an oblong of what looked to me, like hard packed mud with an opening at the front and a vent in the top.

These potters were self-sufficient here. Potters part of the time and working the agricultural land the rest. Freemen all.

"It will take us a day to get it up to heat. Twelve hours to fire our work and twelve to lose the heat."

"It was destroyed then, in the raid?"

"It was. Hacked at by swords. We have no idea why."

I sighed. "Master Croker continues to improve, Bartholomew. We shall send him back to you when he's able to travel."

The potter nodded.

"Thank you, sir, for your care of him. He's amongst the most skilled of us all."

Many others were now gathered around us.

"Have you found the bastards who did this to us, sir?" asked one young man.

"When the fog is gone, I shall sweep the forest and locate the den of these animals. I hear that they have been seen at Wootton and at Chisbury. Does anyone have anything to add to the information you gave me before?"

They looked quizzically at each other.

"We did hear from a man who came up from Axford...."

Axford was a small village in the river valley.

A man who wore his arm bandaged to his shoulder gesticulated in the direction of the river. "That a party of riders was seen coming from Briary woods."

"When was this?"

"Day before we were attacked, sir."

"Do we know where they were headed?"

"Man said they were laughing and joking and quite open about riding through. He said they frightened the life out of the villagers and then just disappeared up the road to Mildenhall."

"Can it have been the same group?"

The man shrugged. "Two lots of ruffians, sir?"

"You say they rode. Were they all mounted?"

"Aye, they were and with an array of weapons on display. People scurried for their homes pretty quick I'm told. Dead scared they were."

"They made no attempt then to attack the village?"

Heads were shaken.

"And still not one of you recognised any of your attackers? Could this man from Axford not place anyone?"

A few of the men looked large eyed at each other as if weighing whether to speak up or no.

Hal fingered his cheek with a gentle, scratchy, stroking movement "I reckon as some of you don't wanna' speak out eh?"

There was a quiet disgruntled muttering, then the young man who had first spoken stepped forward.

"I will speak out for I am an honest man sir, and cannot hold back."

"Speak."

The others in the group shifted their feet and mumbled under their breath.

"It's said that Thomas Potter was amongst the attackers."

"I saw him with my own eyes!" shouted one man from the back of the group. "I was close enough for him to give me a blow with his club." He lifted his fringe of hair and showed a purple bruise with scratches along his forehead.

The young man turned to the accuser.

"And why would he give you a blow, Harkin Clay, when all he's ever been to you is a friend and helper?"

112

"It was him."

Another man now joined his voice to the throng.

"He was accused of another murder, so we know he's capable of it."

"He has been acquitted, good man," I said. "He underwent trial by fire in the castle and was proven innocent by God's good grace." I did not add *and the intervention of the town doctor.*

There was more loud mumbling.

"I saw him fell and kill Jonas Beech," said another older man with a mop of dirty grey hair.

"You will swear on your immortal soul that it was Thomas Potter of Salisbury?"

The man shifted his feet and looked up at me, perched on Bayard.

His eyes narrowed. "Aye. I would."

The first young man tutted and shook his head. "Never, Aldred Clay. It was not Tom."

"Did you see this man they claim is Thomas Potter... what are you called?"

"Alban sir. Alban Thrower. Yes, I did."

Voices rose to drown him out. "Yes, I did!" he exclaimed. "I saw him close to. Close enough to trade a blow with him before he reeled off."

"And you say it was not him."

"It was, I tell you!" shouted a few men.

"Quiet!" My voice rode over the clamour made by those who disagreed with Alban Thrower.

"Why do you say it wasn't him, when other folk here are no doubt willing to swear on the Bible that it was Thomas?"

Thrower licked his lips.

"I saw Tom last Saturday. He wore his faded brown jerkin that day. This man wore green."

"A man may change his clothes, however poor he may be. A man usually has one change of clothing if none else."

"No sir. Tom never wears colours. He...." A fleeting smile crossed his face,

113

"He never wears anything but brown sir. It's just his way. I don't know why, but he doesn't."

I pictured Thomas Potter in my mind's eye. Crossing the courtyard; on the village green, at our village celebrations and in church and today in the castle courtyard.

"I have never seen him in green either, Master Thrower," I said smiling. "You're right. It's just his way."

There was an unsettled muttering.

"Sir," said John. "A man might wear a different set of clothes as a disguise."

"Yes. He might. Have you ever known our Tom wear another colour, John?"

John shifted in his saddle. "No, I haven't."

"You, Hal?"

Hal harrumphed. "I always thought 'im a funnyosity. There's so many lovely colours to be worn and 'e 'as to go and pick brown."

My man at arms had a taste in clothes as colourful as a pheasant's.

"And what's more."

"Yes, Master Thrower?"

"It looked like him...yes...but I would swear in front of the throne of Almighty God, that it wasn't him."

"Why?"

"It was he slew poor Anthony Wright, sir. This man."

"Ah."

"I saw him pick up an axe from his belt and he swiped Anthony almost severing his head."

"Aye… aye he did!" shouted the older man with the grey hair. "The bastard!"

"Tom would never have done this, sir," said Thrower. "He could never have hurt Anthony."

Alban Thrower looked up at me with an open face. His eyes met mine. He neither blinked nor looked away. "They were like brothers, sir."

'He knows,' I thought. 'He knows what Tom and Anthony were to each other and he understands it.'

114

"If it's any consolation to you, Master Thrower, I do not believe it either," I said.

The group erupted in shouting and Hal had to bellow at them for quiet. Silence descended once more.

"No sir. It was not Tom. It looked like him but this man had an old scratch and a bruise on his forehead." He pointed to his own head. Last I saw Tom his head was unblemished," said Alban Thrower.

Chapter Seven

As I rode back to Durley I thought over the words of both Alban the potter and of Alan my deer man.

Two things leapt out at me.

The man who had stolen Alan Hart's horse was a good rider. Thomas Potter was unused to riding and was most unsteady in the saddle. That fact I knew. It was extremely unlikely Thomas Potter could ride without a saddle. And as I'd seen him in his pottery today, and at the castle grimacing with the heat of the iron rod he was carrying, Thomas had a perfectly smooth forehead. Not even a scar.

As we turned into the lane which led to the village, Grafton, Hal's big grey, bucked and neighed.

"What's the matter with 'im then?" said Hal. "C'mon ol' thing, we're nearly 'ome now. Come on. Walk on then."

But the horse wouldn't be budged.

"I'll lead Bayard on, maybe Grafton will follow."

We stood on the ground for a moment listening to the sounds of the foggy woods.

"Can you hear anything?" I asked my man at arms.

Hal threw up his head. "Nope. Nothin'."

"You John?"

He shook his head

I took hold of Bayard's reins and walked him forward. Grafton reluctantly followed, snorting, whickering and sidling, Hal leading and encouraging him. John followed with Fire.

We had perhaps gone twenty paces when something reared up in the middle of the road as the fog swirled and eddied. We stopped. Bayard neighed. Grafton backed. Fire stopped dead.

"What the 'eaven and 'ell is that?" said Hal, peering into the distance.

We caught hold of our reins more fiercely and cautiously approached the strange thing in the road.

It stood about nine feet tall with horns and a thin body. Hal crossed himself.

The fog obscured it again. It made no movement or noise.

We walked on cautiously.

As we approached it, the fog opened out and we saw that the bottom half was formed of a spear shaft sunken into the road surface.

On the top was the decapitated head of my Emperor stag. A noble beast of fourteen tines, fourteen points to his antlers.

The spear head had been driven into the neck.

A magpie cackled loudly close by and flew through the underbrush, making us all jump.

We took Bayard and then Grafton past with difficulty, Fire following quickly and we stood them further on in the road. Hal and I walked back to the gruesome offering.

"A warning do you think?" asked Hal.

"Defiance, more like." I answered. "Look at the tongue. The beast's tongue had been pulled out and a stick inserted which made the mouth gape."

"Planted where we are bound to find it and saying, 'Here I can do as I please.' "

"One of the deer Alan spoke of, taken by the poachers. 'Oo'ever they are. Are we watched do you think?"

"The fog is so thick, I doubt anyone could hide in the bushes and see us with any clarity."

Hal took the deer's head with both hands and pulled hard. The neck came away from the spike with a sucking sound. "It's quite fresh."

"Leave it here. I'll tell one of the lads to come and fetch it later. The horn will be good for some working, I think. The beast won't go to waste. The poor may have the flesh."

"If the foxes and birds don't have it first."

"Aye, if they do, they're welcome to it. Bird will enjoy carving that."

My forester Bird liked to carve bone and horn in his spare time (when he

118

could get it legally).

Hal laid the head at the side of the road. I pulled up the spear with some difficulty for it had been jammed hard into the packed chalk of the road.

"This can come home with us."

"That was put there after we passed earlier," said Hal with a shiver. "I'd swear it wasn't there when we went out."

"No, it wasn't," shouted John.

"Someone was watching us then."

"Knew we were going out on this road."

"Who knew? Knew we were goin' out to Cock a Troop Lane?"

"The lads in the courtyard heard me say that was where we were going."

"Hubert, Alf, Phil...."

"Yes."

"And Tom," added Hal, his eyes side sweeping me a look.

"Aye...Tom."

We rode on in silence.

*****

The light was fading as we rode into the courtyard. I handed Bayard to Cedric and turned back to Hal as he dismounted.

"Of course, the grooms did. Knew we were off there. I mentioned it to Richard as we collected our mounts. Aelfnod was there too, wasn't he? I always like to think that someone knows where we are when we go out. Just in case."

"Aye... aye, they did."

The young lad called Aelfnod, Nod to his friends, came out from the stable. I'd taken him for a trainee groom as a thank you, in January of that year. He had been a little young at ten years of age but was proving a willing helper and good with the horses.

"Nod... can you stow this away in the stable?" I handed the spear to him. His eyes grew large and round as he saw the gore on the spear tip.

"Yessir."

"I'll come and fetch it tomorrow."

"Yessir."

"Nod, you knew we were going out to the potters at Cock a Troop Lane today, didn't you?"

"Aye, sir. You told me, when you took Bayard out earlier."

"Did you tell anyone else?"

His young brow creased.

"Only Master Tom, he asked me where you were goin'. Why, sir?"

"Tom?"

"Master Richard sent me home to Mistress Marshall on an errand and...."

"Home to their house?"

"By the river, sir, yes. And I met Tom Potter and he asked me where I was off to. I told him..."

"Outside the gates...?"

"Down by the salleys, sir." Nod looked puzzled. "Did I do wrong, m'lord?"

"No, Nod. Nothing." My eyes sought out Hal's face. He looked at me under his eyebrows. John folded his arms and cleared his throat.

"Then he asked me where you were? I told him you were off to the potters. I thought it was all right since he was one of 'em, sir."

"Tell me Nod...," I said catching hold of his shoulder lightly. "What was Tom wearing?"

"Wearing sir? Ah yes. That was funny... he was wearing a green tunic sir."

"Green?"

"Aye." Nod giggled, "I said to him, 'Oh Tom, what're you doin' wearing that? You always wear brown'. "

"Nod, you are most observant." I squeezed his shoulder and let go.

The young lad preened himself. "I laughed 'cos, he blended into the bank by the river, what with all the fog and that. He made me jump."

"I'm sure he did."

"Did 'e say what 'e was doing down there, lad?" asked Hal.

"I didn't ask him but I 'spect he was by the river looking for a bit of water for his potting an' all."

"Hmm," harrumphed Hal.

"Was his hand still bandaged, as it was when he came home?"

Nod screwed up his eyes. "Ermmmm.... No. It wasn't. It was all right, sir."

"Thank you Nod, you have been very helpful."

We turned to walk up to the manor steps. It was becoming quite dark now.

"Tom again?" said Hal.

I stopped on the top step and faced him. "Why did he need to ask Nod; he knew. He already knew where we were headed."

"'E musta' 'eard us. So why did he ask again?"

"He didn't."

"Ah no.... It wasn't 'im."

"No."

"'E's gettin' awful plucky this person in a green tunic," said Hal as we entered the hall, suddenly understanding what I was saying.

"Bold in the extreme, Hal."

John just shook his head.

*****

The following day, the fog receding, I went to the stables to recover the spear. Hal and I pored over it but it told us nothing.

I gathered everyone together.

"We need as many men as we can muster, Hal and we shall go out to Chisbury and to Wootton. Rouse Stephen and Peter will you? We shall need their help today."

These were my two further local men at arms whom I usually kept at the castle. These soldiers accompanied me on longer journeys and were my paid men, owing me loyalty and service, if my monarch were to summon me to fight on his behalf.

"All trackers to be out in the forest. Send to Nathan and his team to meet us at Chisbury. We'll see what he has to say about his part of Savernake and we'll get him to comb the eastern-most baily. Send messages out to the agisters and verderers. Get their teams out looking.

"John. Can you go to Wootton? Look around this camp that Alan was on about, see what you can find. Meet us at midday at Big Bellied Oak. Wilfrid. Take your gang and go out to West Woods. Drive anyone you find backwards from there to Cadley. Search the forest for signs of our men. We'll see you too at Big Belly. Tostig. Take as many men as you can muster and patrol the Southgrove baily. Then go to Hippenscombe. We'll see you back here this afternoon."

I looked round for more men.

"Johnathan, you and your brothers go up to the river north of the King's way. Take any villagers you can. Search the Briary Woods for marks of our marauders. We shall see you back here this afternoon."

"Aye sir." Johnathan Reeve stepped forward. "Sir...do we need weapons? Over and above the usual things we carry, sir?"

I looked to the back of the crowded courtyard. "Henry!"

"Aye, sir?"

My steward came pushing through the gathering of men.

"Break out the spears and bows."

"Yessir."

"And listen lads....We are searching for a particularly evil group of killers. If you must—then defend yourselves. If not, don't engage them unless you know that, without doubt, you are superior in numbers and have a chance to subdue them. These aren't the usual sorts of wolfsheads we have in the forest. Displaced men, dangerous because they are desperate. These men are murderers first and foremost. They don't think twice about spitting a small child on a spear...."

"What do we do if we find them, sir?"

"Take note of them, where they are going and then run and hide, Bird!" I said.

*****

The sun came out as we left the village and Hal and my group moved up the road towards Bedwyn. More men joined us as we travelled through the forest; those who lived in the outlying farms and cotts; the men whose job it was to guard the forest and report to me.

They brought weapons with them, bows and spears and others in the form of scythes and wicked looking hay rakes, cudgels and staves. I moved them about until we were a line strung out into the trees and were combing the ground towards Chisbury.

Chisbury was a hill fort encompassing some fourteen acres looking out over the forest and surrounding countryside from a high vantage point. I was told that it had been a Burh under the Saxon kings but it was a very degraded place now.

The lower slopes of the fort's mounded exterior were wooded with scanty birch and ash. As we approached and I drove Bayard through the gap into the compound which comprised the hill fort, I smelled the burning which signalled that thatch had been alight fairly recently.

We milled around in the middle of the compound and I dismounted, ordering the men to fan out and search. I knew that here had been a small farmstead of a few families who had raised pigs in the surrounding lands. Not one pig did we find. Not alive. In the centre of the fort, we found the remains of a fire, as we'd heard from Alan Hart. Animals had been slaughtered and cooked here and their bones were scattered about the hilltop. We also found the relics of our poached deer.

As we explored further we found the remains of the farming families. Not one left alive. Their small houses had been fired and destroyed. Hal came back from the tiny chapel of St. Martins which clung to the edge of the vallum on the western bank, with a thunderous face.

"No one left. All dead or fled."

"It's a very isolated place Hal. I take it the priest of the chapel is...."

"Aye, dead too."

"Just fourteen folk."

"Aye."

"What about Sir John de Monceaux? His manor lies there." I pointed.

"He's away at his other manor. The staff are here but they fled when the raiders came. Some of them are dead," said one of my men.

Crispin, who had come with us, prepared to minister to the poor souls here who'd lost their lives.

The chapel was a small single storey building with a thatched roof. Previous lords of Chisbury had built this little place as a chapel of ease though I could find no document anywhere in Savernake which told me anything about it. There was no doubt it was old as was the Saxon manor house, now crumbling to ruins close by. The whole place had had no more than five households at its largest. Now it was empty and forlorn. I asked the men to place the bodies in the chapel.

"Hartshorn! Scout around and see what there is. See if anything can tell us aught about who has been here?"

"Aye sir." Hartshorn, one of my good trackers and wood wardens, loped off with his team of foresters.

We combed the place from top to bottom. Nothing told us anything.

Nathan Kennet, the forester of the fee for the eastern most baily arrived, with his men mid morning. I sent him back the way he'd come with instructions to fan out and comb the forest from here to Hungerford. He had already explored from the King's Road to us at the hill fort.

He sent a runner back to Durley late that day. No sign of any ruffians in the forest. He did find one elderly and witless beggar who was holed up in an old warren near Froxfield but he sent him packing out onto the road to Berkshire.

We met our other men by Big Bellied Oak and took stock. John had tracked the group of men who had camped near Wootton, to the edge of the hill at Pantawick, close by the town of Marlborough. There the signs had petered out as if the men had simply disappeared into the ground. Wilfrid's gang had met with John's group coming south and they had ridden together through Cadley village. There they had stopped to ask if there were any sightings of the murderers. Nothing.

The gang of killers had completely disappeared.

Frustrated I clomped up the steps of the manor later that afternoon as it was going dark. The men deputed to lead the groups of searchers came with me and shambled wearily into my office.

John, Hal, Johnathan, Wilfrid, Tostig, Stephen, Peter of Devizes and four of my senior agisters, ranged themselves in front of my table and shuffled their feet.

One by one they gave me their reports.

"It was hard to track them because it's been such a time since they went but the group of men, I'd say about eight horses...," said John, "either went down the Granham hill towards the town or doubled back and went west to Kennet. There, they're out of the forest and into open downland."

"Not safe to be seen."

"No, sir. I can't say truly which way they went. Tom Potter went a small way down the hill to see if he could see any marks but there was nothing."

"Tom was with you, John?" said Johnathan Reeve in a worried tone.

"Aye, he came to Cadley with us."

Stephen Dunn, my man at arms stood up straight. "He rode on my stirrup some of the way."

"Where did he join you?"

"At the edge of the village just as we left the road."

I saw Johnathan's dark head shaking. "No sir, that can't be. Tom was in our group."

I stood up slowly. "At Briary Wood?"

"Yes, sir. He came loping up the road from the direction of Cock a Troop Lane...we thought he...," his voice tailed off. "He asked if he might join the search."

I rubbed my forehead where a headache was just beginning.

"He cannot have been in Briary Wood *and* at Pantawick."

Hal folded his arms across his chest, "Our green man again, sir."

"Johnathan...was the man wearing green."

"No sir. Brown... like Tom always does."

"Thank you everyone." I said, sitting down slowly. "You may go."

I leaned back and stared at the rafters.

"Hal, can you go and see if you can find Tom? Ask him where he was this day? Which group did he go with?"

"Aye sir."

Hal shut the door with a click of the latch. A stabbing pain went across my brow. I reached for a beaker of water and sat and brooded until Hal returned.

"He was out at Pantawick."

"Then the man who was with Johnathan's group....was not Tom, Hal."

"Then who the devil is 'e?"

*****

I willed with all my might that our murdering wolfsheads, if outlaws they were, had moved on out of the forest. However, I was also angry, for if this was the case, I would be unable to hand them over to justice and vengeance for their wickedness.

I'd had to deal with a great amount of evil over the years but none had given me the overpowering sense of revulsion I felt then.

I saved my report for a verbatim account for I knew that the King was due in Marlborough castle on November 25th.

That morning I dressed with care in my best clothes, clipping my short dark beard, rubbing my teeth with salt and combing meticulously through my curly black locks and rode to town with Hal, Stephen and Peter in tow.

The King's retinue filled the bailey of the castle and the private buildings of the King's and Queen's house were full to bursting with servants and hangers on. The land around the castle was dotted with tents.

We negotiated the bailey with difficulty and found Peterkin Gayle talking to a small man with a round face and deeply sunken eyes whose silver hair hung either side of a completely bald pate.

He lifted his face and peered myopically at me.

"My Lord Belvoir! It's good to see you again."

Petit, John's personal servant who went everywhere with his master bowed from the waist. "The King will be extremely pleased to see you."

"I hope the fates have been kind to you, Petit?" I said smiling and embracing him warmly. I had last seen this man in 1204 in Rouen.

"The Lord God love you sir, the late foggy weather has... dampened our spirits a little but we soldier on... we soldier on." Petit always spoke of his master as if he spoke of himself. Indeed, the two were inseparable.

"How *is* our lord the King?"

"We are tired sir, if truth be known. We shall be glad to set our feet under a table for a few days and rest in the same room for more than one night."

I laughed, "Petit... you know full well, the King will have it no other way. He loves to travel his realm."

"Aye we do love it. But as we grow older...well...." Petit had spent most of his adult life as valet to John and was fiercely loyal.

I brushed his shoulder gently with my hand. "None of us are getting any younger."

Petit laughed. "Ah no, sir. That's true. Why I remember you as a young man barely up to my shoulder and now look at you. Over my head!"

I chuckled. "I have been over your head Petit, these seventeen years almost. You have been with the King so long."

The man crossed himself. "And hope to be with him another seventeen and beyond."

"Where is he?"

"He's with the Lord de Neville in his office. He asked me to let you know to go to him when you arrived."

I heard Hal clear his throat behind me.

Petit smiled at him, "The Lord Geoffrey is with him also."

My heart lurched. "The sheriff?"

This was another of Hugh de Neville's relations. The Lord of Raby and Sheriff of Wiltshire. We rarely saw *him* in Marlborough. So everyone had been drafted in to meet the King at the castle today.

"I shall go in to him." I said nodding to Hal, Stephen and Peter to stay put.

*****

The door was opened to me by a man standing outside whom I didn't recognise, a small weaselly-faced being with a pointed beard and a bandage on his hand. I was ushered into the office and immediately went down on one knee and bowed my head. Best to show some humility if I was to be castigated, I thought. I was in elevated company.

John was lounging behind the table with his feet on the board. He jumped up and reached for me the moment he saw me.

"Aumary!"

"My King."

I took the proffered hand and kissed the largest ring which he wore on the middle finger of his right hand.

He snatched it away and raised me up from my knee. Restless as ever, he embraced me and jerked me forward to a seat in one movement.

I staggered towards a stool. The other two had risen as the King had jumped to his feet, as was proper. Now they settled back on the bench as John re-seated himself.

"Of course, you know the Lord Hugh and here we have Sir Geoffrey, come down from his estates in the north."

Geoffrey de Neville nodded to me. "Ah my King...I wasn't *so* far away when you called for me. Only in Winchester."

"Ah yes... of course you were. Doing the job we set you to do...."

I never did find out what the job was.

John rubbed his hands together. "So here we are and here we shall stay until Wednesday. We shall hunt in the forest Aumary. Oh yes we shall. Every day!"

"As my lord wishes," I smiled.

I turned to the Lord Sheriff. "You have been with the Queen, sir?"

He nodded. I knew that the Queen had been in Winchester in readiness for the birth of John's child.

I turned back to the King. "I trust the Queen is in good health, my lord?"

John's face positively glowed. "She is...and why shouldn't she be for in October, she presented me with my son and heir." He grinned from ear to ear. "He's a lusty lad and just over a month old."

"God hold them to his bosom," I said. "Congratulations, my liege."

"And your little lad?"

"A mischievous two year old, sir."

John chuckled. "Simon isn't it? And the little Lady Hawise?"

John had, it seemed, forgotten nothing of my family. I knew that he and Hawise were special friends. It was known that John loved children.

"She sends her greetings and love to you as always and says, 'Hello King,'" I smiled.

John threw back his head and burst out laughing. This was a personal greeting which Hawise had, at the tender age of five, given her monarch and John had never forgotten it.

The other two occupants of the room fidgeted uncomfortably on their seats as this domestic conversation unfolded in front of them.

John beamed at me. "Perhaps we shall be able to visit and return the greeting to our little lady."

"Aye, sir. If you ride in the forest, Hawise will be there."

"And that uncommonly lovely wife of yours...?"

My heart gave a lurch. It was known that John coveted the wives of his noblemen and was often to be found in their beds. Indeed he'd once tried to wring a promise from me that I allow him to sleep with Lydia but it had come to nothing. I hoped he had forgotten.

129

"My lady shall, God willing and in the fullness of time my lord, give me another son. She has another two months to go before she will be brought to bed...."

"A brother for Simon and Hawise. That *is* good news, Aumary."

I nodded. Just a bow shot over his head to tell him that Lydia was out of bounds, were he thinking of another request.

"Is she well... does all go well with her?"

"Yes, mostly sire. She tires easily."

Now the de Nevilles were visibly irritated. I saw John flick a look at them both.

"Aumary and your King are old friends. We go back years, don't we Aumary?" he said.

"Indeed we do, my liege." I answered.

"And the welfare of himself and of his family is of great concern to us."

"Thank you my lord. That is most kind."

Hugh de Neville cleared his throat.

"Good to hear, Belvoir," he said gruffly, "that your lady will erm... give you... erm... will produce...." He tailed off as John's eye sought his face.

Geoffrey, the sheriff of Wiltshire, leaned back in his seat and folded his arms in silence.

"Can you stay with us, Aumary... yes stay with us here? We can all ride out together to the forest," said John. Where he thought I would sleep was open to conjecture for the castle was bursting at the seams.

"I would be honoured, my lord King."

"We hear there's been an amount of trouble in my forest? Shall we be hindered in our pleasures by these ruffians? We hear they have been picking off my loyal subjects, good hard working men about their lawful businesses. Our peace should be inviolably preserved, even if it were only granted a dog."

"I have combed the forest sire. We have found traces of these wolfsheads—if lordless men they are...and I am by no means sure they are."

"You say they are not outwith the law?"

"They go mounted. They appear to have some order to their depredations and yet they seem to kill purely for the pleasure of it. No sire, I don't think they are merely desperate outlaws, forced to live in the forest. I must admit I don't know where they live or where they come from. We have tracked them to the outskirts of the forest both east and north but they do not seem to have a camp."

"They must be there, Belvoir," said Hugh de Neville irritably.

"We have found no place we can call their permanent abode. Nowhere they have stayed for more than a few hours to cook and eat the deer they've poached or the other animals they've stolen."

John looked surprised.

"Then they are coming from the town or further afield?"

"They are brazen. They seem to have no fear of being seen, though they have managed to hide their tracks so far, by killing most men and women who have seen them. They leave no witnesses."

John's face grew thunderous. "By God's lights...."

"I have made extensive inquiries of my foresters from one end of Savernake to the other. I've sifted all the information, compared statements from this man or that. These murderers leave few clues."

"Then sift some more, examine further, inquire deeper. They must be caught," said Hugh de Neville.

"They will my lord. They *will* make a mistake and then I will be onto them, like the forest falcon to the sparrow."

There was a little silence.

John stood up. We all followed suit.

"And yet, my Lord Hugh tells us that you have been lax in your pursuit of these malefactors, Aumary. Are we to believe him? It's not like you to fail us."

"I shall not fail, sire. I just need a little more time."

I saw de Neville give me a piercing look.

"I have pursued every track with which I've been presented, sire. The Lord Hugh, forgive me, sir...," I nodded to the man in question, "does not know my methods, nor understand my ways of working as do you, my liege. You charged

131

me with the task of delving into crimes within this area. I do this, as you know, by sifting facts, comparing evidence, questioning folk and finally putting it all together."

John cocked an eye at Sir Hugh like an inquisitive blackbird.

"You yourself sire, have commended me on my methods, my thoroughness, in the past. My record speaks for itself, I think. I have done my very best with the resources at my disposal...."

"And what's this we hear about a potter?"

"The Lord de Neville is custodian of this castle, sire. When he is in residence...."

"He tells us that you disobeyed him. That your behaviour caused some difficulty in the running of the castle...."

"If you can find evidence to suggest, sire, that this is what happened, then...," I bowed my head, "then I shall be brought to account and admit my failures."

"This murdering potter...?"

"Acquitted sire. Thomas Potter is one of my tenant freemen. The Lord de Neville wished, when he was here, to try him for murder, though I attempted to explain that this was not going to be necessary for I was gathering information and evidence which suggested that Tom was not guilty. He would not countenance my 'interference', sire."

"He is your overlord Aumary, under your King," said John sternly.

"He is, sire, but unless you tell me otherwise, he is the constable of this castle and I am the—for want of a better word and one which you yourself and your justices used—the searcher for truth—in this county as is laid out in the warrant you most generously provided for me. I must be allowed, with your permission, my lord, to operate as I see fit to uncover that truth. I have never failed you."

John was seated again. We sat.

"We are told that your man underwent trial by fire?"

"That is correct, sir, and was found not guilty. It was not my wish but that of the Lord Chief Forest Warden...."

"A little behind the times... eh Hugh? Trial by fire?"

Hugh de Neville stared at his King.

"Something which might have been done in my father's reign."

"Yes my liege," he said tersely.

John left it there. Then he said, "We cannot have our officers at loggerheads, Aumary."

"No sire. That is why I resigned my custodianship and left the trial to others."

John rubbed his forehead distractedly, "We will not have our officers arguing amongst themselves," his voice was slightly raised.

"No sire."

"Hugh."

"Yes, my liege?"

"It seems the Lord Belvoir's… erm… methods rub against your grain now and again?"

Hugh de Neville glared at me. "He is too lenient, too lax and long winded, sire," he said. "I can achieve the same results without all the nonsense of…."

"Nonsense, Hugh?" said the King "You consider it nonsense, this role I have created for the Lord Belvoir?

"Sire… I…."

"And yet you have just exhorted Aumary to inquire more deeply, examine further and sift more thoroughly, have you not?" John chuckled. "Hugh…you cannot have it both ways. If the Lord Belvoir were to be removed from this office, we would be forced to find another to fill his boots. We might be forced to give the role to you. How would you fare, do you think?"

"My Lord King, may I speak…?"

This was the sheriff, Geoffrey de Neville.

John nodded slowly.

"Sire, the Lord Belvoir is well thought of in the town and surrounding area. His methods, as he called them, meet with the approval of town and county but I think that…."

"So *you* approve of Aumary's methodical sifting of facts to get at the truth then?" John chuckled to himself. "He saves you a job, for which you must be grateful. It's not Hugh's job to pursue felons as the constable of this castle, it's yours—in part, as sheriff of the county."

"Yes, sire," said the sheriff of Wiltshire. "But I simply do not have the men or the time to...."

"Yes... yes... yes... Geoffrey... I've heard it before. That's why we rarely see you isn't it, at this fair castle of mine."

Geofffrey de Neville turned pink.

"And yet we find that your returns for the farm of this county, Geoffrey, do include the monies for the fines and amercements which you have not the time to administer."

There was complete silence.

"Ah well...," said John. "At least the exchequer gets those monies... most of them."

John stood again.

We rose.

"We created this role in order to free the shrievalty from the task of apprehending felons, one in which they were singularly ineffectual. There are other tasks of course assigned to my constables but in the main, we require them to pursue lawbreakers and gather evidence for trial. Trial, gentlemen."

"The man had a trial," said Hugh, his chin jutting. "Sire, he's but a churl. He doesn't deserve...."

"Yes, from what I can gather, yes, he did have a trial," said John, coming round the table to perch the royal backside on its corner. "However, we are trying to introduce something—we believe, correct me my Lord Belvoir, if we're wrong—something we might call logic into the procedure. We are attempting to rid the system of unreliable practices like this trial by fire."

"You are quite right, sire," I said quickly.

Hugh de Neville rubbed his chin. "My King, I don't dispute that the Lord Belvoir is successful in what he does but he upsets the smooth running of my castle with his poking about and his interfering...."

"Nonsense Hugh."

"His crackpot ideas, a trial for a churl. Pah! Well, they...inflame the...."

"Thomas Potter is a freeman, my lord," I said.

"Whereas you, Hugh, antagonise the locals and make enemies of those we would cultivate as friends?" said John sternly.

Sir Hugh de Neville spluttered. "Firmness is what's required, sire. An unyielding hand at the whip. Make an example of wrongdoers."

"May I, my Lord King?" I asked.

John turned over his palm.

"Sir Hugh, this firm hand, does it, do you think, prevent further crime? Have you evidence to suggest that it does? Do we hear folk muttering that they dare not do ill for fear of the consequences? No sir. In my experience, a man may watch a gruesome hanging one day and yet kill his neighbour in a drunken brawl or stab his irritating wife, the next. But I cannot alter the law. If a man is proven guilty, after evidence has been sought and procured and weighed against him, then he must hang. What I cannot countenance is wanton cruelty and the haphazard apportioning of blame without the due process of the law as it stands. My liege lord has tasked me with the job of seeking the truth about a crime. I do not think I have been lax, or lenient. I have especially favoured no man...."

"Your tenant potter...," spluttered de Neville.

"No, sir. Even he, were he guilty, would have been led to the gallows by my inquiries. The law of habeas corpus sire," I turned and bowed to my King. "No free man shall be taken or imprisoned, or be disseized of his freehold, or liberties, or free customs, or be outlawed, or exiled, or any otherwise destroyed; nor will We not pass upon him, nor condemn him, but by lawful judgment of his peers, or by the law of the land."

John nodded, "The wise words of our father of blessed memory and his learned advisors."

"This law gives a free man the right to trial." I continued, "The writ of the lord my King issued to me in 1204 gives me the right to seek evidence to put that man to trial by our justices. Evidence sirs. When the evidence has been procured and the man apprehended, when we know beyond all reasonable doubt he is guilty, then I must give over the felon to your keeping, my Lord de Neville. Then begins your task."

John looked at me under his eyebrows.

"So what do you say to this, Hugh?"

De Neville spluttered a little more and then his face softened.

"It must be as my King wishes," he sighed dramatically.

I did not believe it for a moment.

John clapped his hands and the sudden movement and sound made us all jump.

"Good! We must not be made enemies over this," he said, jumping from the table top and circling behind us.

Yes, Paul...I know...in the light of what happened later on in John's reign and the accusations which were levelled at him, this is strange, but I can tell you without any prevarication, this is what happened.

What? Yes, I know that the great men of the day accused the King of just such terrible infringements of the law. Things did change, it's true. John himself changed. De Neville was accused as one of his 'henchmen' and evil advisors at the time but at that time and in that place, John was all for the rights of the little man. And yes, everyone seems to think that this was enshrined at the very first in The Great Charter, but I can tell you, it predates that document by quite a few years.

John stood behind the table and leaned on his knuckles. "The Lord Belvoir will continue in his capacity as constable of the county and search diligently for these murderers loose in our forest. He will continue to gather information about crimes committed in the area and he will bring these felons to the courts of justice with the evidence he has garnered. The justices will then make up their minds and pronounce. If they prove to be wolfsheads, their necks will be placed in a noose for they forfeit the right to a trial. I will have order in Wiltshire."

We all acquiesced.

Then Hugh de Neville folded his arms over his chest, "My Lord King, John...

I don't require Belvoir as my deputy here."

"I have resigned, my lord...I must admit I do find it difficult to...."

"Nonsense. You are acting like spoilt children." I saw de Neville bridle at that and his hands fell to his sides.

"We do not accept your resignation, Sir Aumary. Contrary to my Lord de Neville, we believe you good at the job we have appointed you to do. You'll just have to get along."

I bowed, "As my Lord King wishes."

We all watched the King carefully as he sat behind the table. None of us were reseated, expecting to be dismissed.

John played with a large ruby ring on his little finger.

"But since you have, both of you, my Lord de Neville and you, my Lord Belvoir, transgressed; you Hugh by hampering the Lord Belvoir in his duties as constable and you Aumary, for resigning your commission without our permission, I amerce you both, twenty marks each." He turned to his scribe who was sitting in the corner of the room. The man nodded.

John looked up, smiling.

Twenty marks was quite a considerable sum to me. Over two hundred shillings.

I bowed. Hugh de Neville sighed.

"And now...," the King bounced up from his seat all smiles.

"We hunt in the forest." He swept to the door. "C'mon gentlemen—we're wasting time!"

Chapter Eight

We hunted in the baily known as La Verme where I knew we had abundant game. The King was not disappointed. We were close to home at Durley but I didn't manage to get to my manor and John, contrary to his earlier mood and promise, seemed not to wish to visit the place now.

We feasted in the castle's hall that night. There was not an inch of spare space at the tables.

Hal, Peter, Stephen and I slept in my office on the floor on piled up blankets and it was a good thing it was a mild late November night.

Contrary to expectation, John did not sleep late that next morning but was up and about and busying himself around the castle. I heard his voice bellowing for his mercenary captain who went by the name of Louvrecaine.

After four days of hunting in the forest John departed with de Neville, leaving some of de Neville's routiers or mercenaries behind, promising to return on December the first before turning his feet to Windsor and Christmas at the castle there.

*****

Towards midday that fine November morning, we rode down the High Street and turned into the London Road to make our way home to Durley. As we began to trot up the hill we met a riderless and frightened horse coming down.

Hal jumped from the back of Grafton and caught the jumpy horse who screamed in fright and could not be subdued.

I dismounted and let Bayard go to the horse, hoping that his calm nature would help to pacify the beast.

Stephen looked the horse over whilst Hal held the reins and gentled his nose.

"We know this 'orse, sir. One of the glassblower's beasts, I think."

In the forest John had licensed a group of glassmakers. He had ordered that the King's and Queen's rooms, the chapel and the great hall windows at the castle, be glassed.

The men who worked the glass lived for the most part in the town but some lived in small bothies on the site in the West Baily where the glass was made. There was an abundance of the raw materials in the forest and the proximity of the river allowed for easy production. Work on the castle had finished but there was ample work in the vicinity for the men to continue working. I myself had employed them to glass the manor at Durley.

"It's Aldo's horse, I think," I said. "Aldo Swift."

Aldo was the glassmaster who lived in a house in Marlborough owned by the mistress of the trade, Juliana Glazer, the widow of the original owner.

"Where is 'e then?" asked Hal looking round.

"Turn the horse about and we shall ride to see," I said.

We laboured up the steep slope becoming known simply as Forest Hill, towing the errant horse.

Half a mile just off the chalk road we found the rider.

Just before the village of Cadley and another steep hill, a narrow lane ran off into the trees. Here the body of a man lay sprawled at the side of the track. His head had been dented by a blow from a club; his face was smashed.

"It's Archard White sir," said Hal sadly. "He's a stoker at the glass works."

"What was he doing with Swift's horse?

Hal shrugged. "Think we better go and take the beast back? Find out?"

Hal and Peter picked up the body and draped it over the back of the horse. He sidled but walked on obediently after a while.

We rode on through the trees on the small path which eventually led to the open glade where the glassblowers had their workings.

As we approached we heard raised voices, weeping and shouting but none of the customary sounds which we usually heard when the glass was being made.

We came upon a scene of devastation similar to that at the potters on Cock a Troop Lane. People were milling about, some injured. Some dead had been laid under the main open fronted building where folk would rest from their labours, shelter from the weather and take food. We counted four humped bodies under separate sheets.

I sought out Aldo, who was whole and uninjured.

Throwing my leg over Bayard's ears I jumped down quickly.

"Aldo... what goes on here?" Though a terrible feeling in the pit of my stomach told me I knew what had happened.

"We found your horse...and the man riding it."

"I sent him off as soon as I knew we were under attack m'lord."

"The man is dead... I'm sorry. Hal says it was Archard White, though his head was hardly recognisable he'd taken such a blow."

Swift grimaced as I pointed to the horse where lay the body. Two men were lifting him down. "Holy Mother of God...I sent my son...." He crossed himself and his face creased in grief.

"Osric?"

"...down the hill by Glass Lane, to fetch you as quickly as he could. Archard went the Cadley way."

"Then please God Osric has reached the town."

Aldo swayed on his feet. "He didn't meet you? I sent him to the castle."

"No."

"We gave as good as we got. We are not soft folk here who can't fend for ourselves."

I took the man by the elbow and led him to a three legged stool which was sitting by an open doored bothy.

"When did this happen?"

Aldo shook his head. "Not long...the sun was just over the trees there." He gestured.

"Less than the time it takes to get to the town?"

"Maybe."

"Where are the two soldiers usually deputed to stay with you?"

Aldo gestured to the dead bodies. "They were the first to be attacked."

"Knock out the professionals first then?" said Hal. "'Ow come they let themselves be so surprised?"

Aldo Swift shrugged. "They were on us so silently and so quickly. These men were mounted. Our soldiers were mown down as they stood."

"They knew you had soldiers here?"

Aldo nodded. "They did."

Someone gave him a beaker of what looked like mead and he sipped it gratefully.

"How many men were there?"

"We counted eight."

"From which direction did they come?"

"Granham Hill."

As I spoke to Aldo, my eye roved around the site. I counted almost twenty men still standing and walking.

"Seven men against twenty-odd with two soldiers...?"

"Aye sir. They bit off a trifle more than they could chew with us. We aren't soft potters." Word had gone round the forest about the attackers.

"The same group?"

"Aye m'lord. There's no doubt."

"Which way did they leave?"

"They followed Archard to the Salisbury Road."

"Did they stop to take anything? Did they pillage the huts and workplaces?"

"Not as far as I know m'lord. I was fending them off with a gathering of hot glass." He chuckled grimly. "They knew they were outnumbered and once they'd conferred with the man who seemed to be the leader, they were off pretty quickly."

"Did you manage to injure any?

Aldo laughed joylessly, "Oh yes...one or two bear burn marks. Harry there fought with a shard of broken glass wrapped in sheep's wool. Amazing what a good sword that may become."

"I've no doubt."

I continued to scan the site.

"Can you describe any of them? It would help greatly for we have no real description from any survivor."

"Aye, I expect between us we can make a fist of that, my Lord Belvoir."

"Good. Tell Hal here. I am riding down the hill by Glass Lane, I'll see how far young Osric managed to ride."

"He was on foot, m'lord. I told him to scarper as soon as I knew the danger."

"Good man."

"I told him if he was followed he was to scale a tree or lie flat in the undergrowth. Sir, I'll come with you!"

"I'll find him Aldo. You stay here."

I hollered for Hal to take charge and leaving Stephen and Peter with the glassblowers, mounted Bayard once more and rode swiftly down the track which was becoming known as Glass Lane. Here the laden carts had rutted a track from the glade in which the glassmen worked, to the main Newbury Road and thence over the town bridge to the castle.

A quarter of a mile down the track I started to yell Osric's name at the top of my voice.

No answer came back to me.

*****

Hal told me later that the men had been described but none knew them. They'd kept their faces covered. One interesting fact emerged though. As the murdering band approached the camp, they had yelled the names of the first men they struck down.

The two soldiers whose job it was to escort the glass cart to town and to the workshop there, were known to them, it seems.

What did that tell me?

I rode alone down the Granham Hill shouting for Osric Swift. I had almost reached the edge of the trees where the forest gave way to downs when I noticed

143

Osric's pale head facing up the hill, his body partly concealed by a furze bush.

"NO!"

I dismounted and, panting and struggling, lost my footing a couple of times as I slid down on the close cropped chalk. All around us, my sheep crunched on obliviously. I strove to stay upright and ran down to him. I caught his shoulder.

He groaned.

"Thanks be to God." He was alive though he wore a bloody gash on his head.

I eased his shoulders up against my knee.

"Osric! Speak to me lad. How are you hurt?"

"Sir! My lord. My father?"

"Is alive and well, Osric. Do not fear. He is worried about you too. Where do you hurt?"

"My head... I hurt my head."

I gently pushed back the blond hair from his forehead. The bleeding had ceased.

"You have been to the camp m'lord?" he mumbled.

"I have. I know what's happened there. Come...." I eased him up from his position on the chalk and unsteadily he gathered his strength and rose.

I helped Osric up the hill, mounted Bayard and held out my hand.

"Come up on Bayard and we shall ride back."

Setting his foot in the stirrup which I had left free for him I hauled him up. He settled behind me.

"Hold on tight." Tentatively Osric wound his arms around my waist.

"Good, up the hill we go!" The lad weighed very little for he was but twelve and thin and active.

My horse snorted his displeasure but started off at a good pace. Soon we gained the shelter of the trees and slowed a little.

"You didn't reach the castle looking for me?"

"No, my lord. I didn't know if you were at home or at the castle but I thought if I went to the castle someone there would know and someone would send soldiers to our aid," he said groggily.

"It seemed to me that you were hiding when you heard me coming down the hill?"

"Aye, sir, I was. Under a furze bush. But I was very fuddled. I fell and banged my head on a stone."

"You were not followed, Osric. Poor Archard White was followed by the marauders and I'm afraid they killed him."

Osric stifled a sob. "Oh poor Uncle Archie."

"Mother's brother?"

"Aye, sir."

"You were lucky they didn't split up and some follow you."

"They didn't see me go, sir. But I did see them again."

I looked over my shoulder at Osric's tearful face.

"Saw them?"

"Aye, sir. That's why I was hiding."

"But they rode the path to Cad...."

As I said this, I realised of course that if the gang had ridden the further path beyond where we'd found Archard White, we should have met them on the lane to Forest Hill. There were only two roads open to them this way, down the hill to Marlborough or towards Salisbury. No, I was wrong. There was a third. Through the forest.

"They must have gone down the hill on some other path."

"The only way they could have travelled, sir, is through the forest on the smaller paths."

"The horses would not have managed, Osric. The paths are too small for mounted men. I know this. When my men and I travel them, we must lead our mounts."

"Well, I know that's the way they went because I saw them."

I slewed in my saddle. "Where?"

"I was running down the hill and I lost my footing...."

"Aye it's quite steep in places."

"I slid down a few feet and when I got to my knees I could see them, all eight

145

of them. I ducked down behind a bush."

"How close were you?"

Almost at the bottom of the hill."

"Newbury Road?"

"Yessir."

"Where were they?"

"Riding on the road, sir."

"In full view of everyone? On the street...?"

"Aye sir. The road which leads to the castle bridge."

"Why ever would they be so brazen?"

"I don't know, sir. Folk were just watching them come and then scurrying for their houses."

There were few houses along this road. It led to the town bridge as Osric had reported and its other end joined the London to Salisbury Road where it forked and drove up the hill into the forest. Most houses were at one end or the other. In the middle were a few bothies and barns and an orchard.

There was nothing to prevent a group of men coming through the trees down the hill, past the cherry orchard held by the priory of St. Margaret of Antioch and debouching onto the main road.

"Which way did they ride?"

"Towards the bridge sir. I saw them and hid."

"The fact that they don't care about being seen is puzzling, Osric."

"Yessir."

"At one moment they're disposing of all witnesses and the next, riding boldly about town." I frowned as an idea came to me.

"Let's get you back to your father and get your head mended."

*****

Osric delivered and Hal, Stephen and Peter collected, we rode for Durley

146

at a gallop.

"John!" I bellowed as I entered the courtyard.

Peter came out of the smithy.

"Da's gone to Burbage, sir."

"Who is about?"

"A tracker like Da, sir?"

"Yes."

"Hartshorn is by the church sir. Bird's in his garden."

"Fetch them both. Peter, come out with us. We need to track a band of men down from Granham Hill."

"Aye, sir." Peter Brenthall ran off through the gate.

"Cedric!" I yelled. Cedric's rusty blond head poked itself around the stable door post.

"Saddle Fitz, Athena, Count and Fenrir. We ride in moments."

"All this ridin about'll be the death of me," said Hal grumpily.

*****

We straddled the hilltop, at the lane to the glassblowers' camp, the five of us. Bird Forester hunkered down and looked at the signs left by the eight riders. "Here sir."

Peter was striding about in the crackly brush. "And here m'lord. It's only a narrow path, made by badgers and such but a horse and rider came this way."

Hartshorn bent to look at the signs. "Aye lad...several horses. Well done."

We dismounted, Bird leading for he was on foot and did not ride. When travelling any distance, he usually rode pillion or stood on the stirrup.

We had gone just a quarter of a mile when the track petered out in a glade of oak, ash and beech.

Peter turned in circles.

"Where did they go?"

"Riding again," said Bird slightly ahead of us. "Open ground just there," he pointed; we followed him.

Our party came out suddenly into the sunlight of a winter's day. Below us the priory cherry orchard spread over the hill. No one was working there during this season.

Hartshorn dismounted and whistled Fenrir to follow him. Bent double, he and Bird scouted between the trees. Hal and I followed with Peter.

"Down to the road, sir," he said.

"Right. Mount and ride the road. Slowly. Keep your eyes open for anything... anything at all which might help us. If I stop to talk to anyone, walk on, I will meet you at the bridge. Wait for me there"

Two bothies lay at the side of the roadway. A man was gathering stones from his patch as we rode by. Recognising me, touched his forelock.

"M'lord."

"Good man, did you see a party of eight men, armed to the thigh with sword and club, pass this way a while ago...just as the sun was over the forest?"

The man put down his bucket. "Aye m'lord. Going that way," he gestured west. "I 'id."

"Why?"

"I've 'eard the rumours. I di'n't wanna be spitted like a 'og."

"They passed peaceably?"

"Aye they did. Praise be."

"Minding their own business, as were we," said his neighbour, an old crone of indeterminate age. Her lined and walnut brown face stared up at me with one white eye. "I took the goat in, quick."

"Where did they go?"

Both of them raised filthy hands and pointed with equally filthy fingers. "That way, sir."

"Thank you." I tossed a couple of halfpennies to them and rode on to catch up with my men.

"Still with them, Hartshorn?"

148

"Aye sir. Same men. Same horses."

We slowly quartered the ground as the road wound round to reach the recently rebuilt bridge. There the track joined the road coming down from Granham Hill. I could see the white shape of the keep rising above the town and hear the swish of the River Kennet as it bubbled under the new structure.

More houses lay at this end but there was no one about. It was, of course, market day.

"Ah...," said Bird. "One has gone off up the hill."

"Why?" I asked, perplexed. "Why come all this way and then go back the way they came?"

"Not quite, sir," said Peter. "Quickest way down the hill is the way they came. It's the quickest way to Pewsey and the Vale, with horses."

"I'll give you that Peter," I said, "but why come all this way just to come to the Pewsey Road when you could have gone straight across and come to the road at Pumphrey's Wood?"

"Stayed with his companions sir... for some reason. I dunno," said Rob Hartshorn, shrugging.

"The rest are away across the bridge, sir," said Bird, from the middle of the Town Bridge. He moved aside as an ox cart passed and turned to go up the Granham Hill, the driver swearing and cursing at his beasts.

"Here it will be impossible to track them, there will be far too much traffic and the signs will be fuddled. Do your best though."

"Aye sir."

The road went alongside the newly built King's garden which lay on Southfield, opposite the castle and its moat.

The encompassing wall was complete and the garden almost finished but building work was still carrying on. A large dovecote was rising in the middle and an observation tower at the northern end was rising, stone by stone to the Heavens. All so that the Queen could come and stay in the castle and have diversion.

Hartshorn, Bird and Peter Brenthall milled around in the space where the

High Street met the Pewsey Road.

"Gone sir," said Peter.

"Thank you lads. You may ride for home now."

I left Fitz with instructions to stay and wait for me, knowing that he would and he clopped across the road to begin to crop the meagre grass growing by the moat side.

I pushed open the gate of the King's garden.

Several pink faces lifted as I entered and closed the gate.

One man straightened, "My Lord Belvoir. It's good to see you again."

This was the King's gardener Master Jardine. I had met him whilst investigating a murder earlier in the year. Indeed his master, Oliver Green had been killed by our murderer and now Jardine had taken over from him.

"And I you, Master Jardine." I looked round. "My! You would never think that scant time ago, this was nothing but a scrubby and waterlogged field, fit for nothing but displays of archery."

"And the fair."

"Ah yes... the fair," I chuckled.

King John had given the town a fair to be held in August upon this field. When he appropriated the land for his garden, the fair had to be moved to the High Street.

"Tom, I know that there's a wall between you and the road and it's a very long shot I'm loosing here but, before Sext, did you hear a party of men come by from the town bridge, all mounted?"

"Before midday you say?"

"They came down the hill and over the bridge, from there we know not where they went."

"We would have been taking our meal then, in the shed."

"Ah yes. How foolish of me. You won't have heard them."

Tom Jardine shrugged. "Sorry we can't be of more help. What's it about?"

"The glassblowers in Savernake are the latest target of our wolfsheads, Tom. They were fought off and the malefactors made to ride down the hill past the priory's cherry orchard. We have tracked them thus far but cannot see where they went."

Tom Jardine crossed himself. "Jesus aid them. Many dead?"

"This time only four and two of them soldiers from the castle."

His eye brows flew up into his hair. "Soldiers. Unlucky then. How come trained soldiers can be killed so easily by mere outlaws?"

I shrugged. "The advantage of surprise and they were targeted it seems. I cannot think how they managed it."

Jardine was shaking his head "I'm sorry we can't help...." His brow cleared. "Wait...sir!"

He turned about and searched the space. His eye lit on a young man who was knocking a post into the ground with a hefty wooden mallet.

"Clynne... come here a moment."

The man put down his mallet and wiped his upper lip with his sleeve. "Aye, sir?"

"Clynne was out at the gate, weren't you, at midday? You took your dinner earlier, didn't you?"

"Aye, I was out at the gate repairing it from when that cart hit the post, master. Last week."

"Clynne...."

The man grabbed his coif and screwed it up in his hand when I addressed him directly.

"I am the Lord Belvoir, constable of the county. Can you tell me, as you were mending your post by the gate, did you see a party of mounted men ride by? Either to the High or to the Manton Road?"

The man bowed. "Men sir...?"

"All mounted, all armed."

"No m'lord. No men came past me around midday."

I sighed. "Thank you."

In anger I slapped my riding gloves on my thigh and swore. "Where the Hell did they go?"

151

Tom Jardine commiserated with me. "So much traffic hither and thither. It's hard to know where any man's going."

"Aye. There's the stone from the yard across the road destined for you here. There's men to-ing and fro-ing up the High Street with goods from one part of the town to another not to mention out of town. There's supplies for the castle. And it's market day."

"A course...!" said Clynne suddenly. "There was this load a men went out this morning about Lauds sir."

"Early this morning?"

"Yes m'lord. I was getting my stuff ready when they clattered out of the castle."

"You watched them? Which way did they go?"

"Up the road m'lord."

"Clynne..." said Tom in exasperation, "which way as in north, south...?"

"South." The man pointed in a vague way towards the wall which bounded the garden on the western side. "And north."

"How many? I'm looking for a party of seven or eight."

"Oooh, more than that, sir."

"Ah yes. That will have been the Lord de Neville riding out with his routiers. He followed the King out."

Jardine nodded. "Yes of course, it will have been the King's men."

I sighed.

"He dropped in here, didn't he, Clynne, just to see how we were getting on?"

The man's eyes positively glowed with pride. "Aye, he did. And he told me what a fine job I'd made of the scaffolding."

"The King?"

"Aye...himself. Large as life," he grinned.

I slapped him on the back "Good for you, Clynne."

I turned away to leave, thanking them both.

"Wait...." I retraced my steps. "The King was going to Faringdon I heard. He will have passed the gate and gone up the High Street."

"Aye, he did say he was headed that way," said Tom.

"Aye, the King did take his party that way," affirmed Clynne.

"And the rest?"

"They came out of the castle and split, some to the High and some to the bridge."

"Let me get this absolutely right, Clynne. You saw the men come out of the castle early this morning."

He nodded.

"A large party of mounted men?"

"And baggage and beds and all the servants and...."

"Yes. And soldiers?"

"Oh yes, sir. There were soldiers. Lots of them."

"Do you know the Lord de Neville, Clynne? How he seems?"

The gardener screwed up his coif even further.

"No sir. I don't know what he looks like. 'Twas the first time I met the King," he grinned.

I looked at Jardine. "The King didn't have de Neville with him when he came into the garden?"

"No, Sir Aumary. Just his man Petit and a few others. He was here scant moments. Enough to say a dozen Paternosters."

"Do you know where de Neville went?"

"Oh he followed the King sir. A few moments later. The King said as much to me, 'de Neville will follow and catch us up'," said Tom.

"Along the High?"

"I expect so. I didn't see or hear."

"So who went down to the bridge?"

The two men looked at each other.

I looked up to Heaven.

"Ah, no... it will have been *Geoffrey de Neville's* men returning to Winchester. Of course it will. They would go to the bridge, along Newbury Road and up the hill. They'd branch off the Salisbury Road at Ludgershall."

I sighed. "Well, thank you anyway. I think our search will founder now."

153

"God give you ease, my Lord Belvoir," said Tom Jardine as I went out through the gate.

"And you Tom. I for one am going to need it. Good day."

I went to reclaim Fitz from the moatside grasses and turned up the High Street. I had a hankering to visit my favourite town doctor.

*****

It was market day.

The High Street was groaning with folk at their purchasing and selling. I clopped slowly between carts and stalls and because progress was so slow, I dismounted and walked Fitz along the emptiest part of the roadway at the edge. The sidelong look he gave me under his long lashes said, 'What do you bring me here for? I was enjoying myself cropping those nice grasses.'

I crossed the road and wove carefully between a stall selling turnips and winter vegetables and the small priory entrance where lived my friend Gilbert, the cordwainer. His door opened and out he came, a smile on his rubicund face and a very smart robe of rust red on his back. He closed the door behind him.

"Ho Gilbert! How goes it with you and yours?"

"Oh, m'lord Belvoir. We mustn't complain, you know."

Gilbert was an especial friend of many years standing, despite the difference in our stations. He was a town councillor, a skilled artisan and a member of the guild of craftsmen which Henry, John's father, had allowed to be set up in Marlborough in 1163.

"I'm just on my way to the church." By this he meant St.Peter's at the western end of the town. I knew that he was a church reeve there.

"We are having a special dedication there this evening and I'm just off to make sure all is well."

"You're a busy man my friend."

"Ah well. Now Harry is come to his journeymanship...." This was his previous

154

apprentice Harry Glazer, "...I have a bit more free time to do those things which are good for the town...you know sir...being a councillor and all...."

"Have you another apprentice yet?"

"Aye I have. You know I still have Felix."

"Yes." This was the son of Castleman, one of the castle's garrison.

"And I have just taken the fourteen year old son of Edmund Darrell to apprentice. He should be a good lad, sir."

"The Chilton Darrells?"

"Aye the same. William."

"I know of them."

"And...," said Gilbert puffing out his chest. "I can afford now to take on another journeyman worker. With the town expanding, there's a lot more work."

"Good for you Gil!"

"So, my lord, what are you about this fine November morning? Or can you not tell this humble cordwainer of the town?"

I laughed. "Just pursuing my latest conundrum, Gil."

We moved further into the little alley which led to the door of the priory, to allow a large cart to pass without hindrance.

"Aye, I heard." Gil took my sleeve, "Saints preserve us from these beasts. They seem to have no mercy."

"None at all Gil. They'd spit you as soon as look at you, I know."

"Why sir...why? What on earth are they about? Have they no fear of God Almighty and his Heavenly angels?" He crossed himself quickly.

"I said to myself just yesterday Gil, how these fiends seem not to care about God's laws or commandments. I have never felt such a sense of revulsion at their crimes in all my years as constable."

"We've seen some nasty'uns sir. But this... there's no reason to any of it."

"No Gil... none it seems."

Gilbert tucked his rust red robe about his shoulders.

"Word is sir...." He leaned his head nearer to mine, "That they have been digging and looking for corpuses in these places they desecrate."

155

He crossed himself again. "Though what so many corpuses would be doing in the middle of the forest I have no notion."

"They have been digging Gil, but not for dead bodies, I think."

He straightened up and his jovial face grew perplexed. "Then why sir...what are they digging for?"

I shrugged.

"Buried treasure, I'll be bound."

"Treasure Gil?"

"Aye. Treasure. Buried church plate or some such stuff. Coins... buried by wicked thieves years ago perhaps?"

"How would they learn of this treasure?"

It was Gilbert's turn to shrug.

"I am off to church to make sure we have everything ready for our own treasure to be consecrated by the priest."

"Ah yes. I've heard that the new church plate is to be installed in the church today."

"The council, and that includes me of course, have thought that, should we ever be in the position of having to safeguard our treasure, that we would bury it in the churchyard."

"Would this not be the first place anyone would think to look, Gil?"

"They would hardly dig up God's earth, would they?"

"I'm sorry to say Gil, but it has been known. Some men have no fear of God's wrath. Like our present murderers."

He shrugged. "Nick suggested that we bury it by the mill somewhere. Somewhere there are always people working so that it could be watched."

"It will never come to it. I don't think these men are going to be so bold as to raid the town."

"I am glad to hear it, sir."

"Though they did ride mighty close to the town this morning."

"NO! I don't believe it!"

"Aye, they did. We lost them at the town bridge," I said.

"You saw them?" said Gilbert, his eyes as round as the full moon.

"No, young Osric Swift did. He tells us they rode down the hill through the cherry orchard and onto the Pewsey Road."

"Was he mistaking the King's men maybe?"

"No, *they* rode down the High from the castle."

"Aye, they did. I saw them from my window."

I took hold of Gilbert's rusty sleeve and towed him further into the darkness of the alley.

"What did you see Gil?"

"The King ride by with all his panoply of men."

"De Neville?"

"A moment later."

"The sheriff?"

"Geoffrey? He was riding with the King. My! He's a peacock of a man isn't he?"

"Aye, he loves display. So you saw Geoffrey and the King and then..."

"A heartbeat later... Hugh... yes."

"And all their men...?"

"I wasn't counting, Sir Aumary? There were, it seems, dozens of them."

"The routiers?"

"Those devils! Aye, they were there too... with their haughty faces and their belts stuffed with daggers and other weapons. Nasty lot they are."

"Hmmm. Thanks, Gil."

I mounted Fitzroy again.

"Good luck with your dedication."

I trotted off and threw over my shoulder. "And give my regards to the family."

*****

I made the further end of the High Street without incident and led Fitzroy

157

into the yard at the back of Johannes' house.

I left him with a bag of feed and some water and scratched at the back door.

Johannes's voice bid me enter.

"I thought it was you," he said.

"What *are* you doing?" I asked.

Johannes' face was screwed up tight as he tried to pass some thread through a needle.

"Sewing my hem."

"Leave it to Little Agnes."

Agnes was Johannes' little mute servant and housekeeper.

"She's busy and has gone out and I keep tripping up on it. It's driving me to distraction."

"Ah well, you're quite good at sewing," I chuckled.

I took the needle from him and threaded it in one, handing it back.

"Hmmmpf," he grumbled. "My eyes aren't what they were."

He began to tack up the hem of his robe without taking it off.

I sat down and put my boots onto a stool. Johannes pushed a beaker of wine towards me.

"I've had no dinner; I don't think I can stomach wine. Have you ale?"

"There. And there's bread and meat on the pot board."

I reached for the jug and a cup.

"So what's your news then? How's Thomas?"

"I have been so exercised by my murdering outlaws and by de Neville's antics, Johannes, I haven't had time to speak to him. Speak to him I must for I have a few little niggles which only he can answer."

"Niggles?"

I told him about the word that Tom had been seen with the outlaws and what had been said by the crokerers and my deerman, Hart.

Johannes put down his needle and cloth. "No. That doesn't make any sense at all."

"None." I swilled the ale round my mouth and swallowed.

"Has Tom made an enemy of these people that they might swear against him for some reason?" asked Johannes.

"I did think of that. As far as I can tell there's no bad blood between Tom and Master Croker. Nor has my deerman any reason to lie about Tom stealing his rouncey."

"Where would he keep such a beast?"

"He lives for the best part of the time at Durley. He visits Cock a Troop Lane. He comes to town with his wares once a week with a hand cart. His old father had a cott out in the forest. I suppose he might keep a horse there but, that's unlikely. How would he afford it? Tom doesn't ride well at all. He has no need to and has had little practice. When he does he invariably falls off," I chuckled.

"Must be someone who looks like him."

"Nod saw him. He was fooled into thinking that it was Tom. The man wore green. Tom always wears brown. After that day when this man was seen he wore brown too..."

"He's learned... he must know him, he's imitating Thomas?"

"Yes, but why?"

"Throw suspicion onto him."

"And so far...it's worked."

Johannes bit off the last of his thread. "There! That should hold until I can get it mended properly." He stood and settled further into his long ankle length robe.

"So, what's been happening with you?"

"Oh...the usual. A queue outside as long as de Neville's nose this morning. Market Day."

I chuckled. "You still swear that folk save up all their ailments until market day when you deal with every one of them?"

"I do," chortled the doctor.

"Haemorrhoids, boils, a broken nose... fell over a barrel in the cooper's yard!" Johannes threw his eyes to Heaven. "One of the apprentices."

"Ha ha...what was in the barrel, eh?"

He nodded. "Hmmm, exactly. Erm... what else? A stye of the eye... very

159

interesting. Two broken fingers...."

"How did those happen?"

"One man punched another at the Green Man. And the other was one of the mercenaries of de Neville."

I sat up. "What happened there?"

"Trapped his hand in a door, he said. Pah!"

"Why did you get him and not Dr. James at the castle?"

"Didn't want his lord to know."

"James wouldn't breathe a word."

"I know but...," Johannes shrugged.

"So he comes all the way up here with a broken finger?"

"Aye, he and his mate. He was burned quite badly on the forearm."

"His excuse for that?"

" A firebrand fell on him when he was up on the walls."

"A likely story."

"Same there. Didn't want his master to know," said Johannes.

"It's a dangerous place, the castle, for a foreign mercenary."

"Ah well...they've gone now. I saw them ride out with the King."

"Yes, so did Gilbert." I looked up.

"These two, they left this morning, you saw them all?"

"The whole town did."

"You're sure? Their wounds were received yesterday?"

Johannes nodded " So they say. They'll be back in December so I hear."

I sighed. "And that's too soon for some folk."

"Aye, they're very unpopular."

"They're unpopular in the town. It's said that theft from the shops goes up when they're here."

Johannes snorted.

I laughed. "You know, the mercenaries I've met, Hel Joosens, Angil Vermulen at Devizes and one or two others are good men, men who are loyal and true. I liked them."

"You've not met this current crop then?"

"Just one. Cornelis Cliijster."

"Hmm."

"Oh, he was polite enough but I have to say, I didn't take to him. I cannot say why."

"Hmm. Well, it seems the King is relying more and more upon them and less and less upon his English levies."

"It's a sad truth and it will not end well Johannes. I am sure there's trouble ahead."

"Oh damn!"

I sat up quickly, spilling the ale on my knee. "WHAT?"

"The other bloody side is coming down now!"

I sighed. "Give me the needle," I said.

*****

I rode leisurely home later that day musing on what I'd seen and heard. I rounded the church of St. Mary on its small grassy knoll and clopped gently down the lane past the lych-gate.

I stared up at the path remembering the very first day and how all this had started, with the girl Cille screeching at the gate by the graveyard's hedge. She now lay cocooned in our churchyard until the day of reckoning.

Suddenly, the shouting was repeated, though not from the graveyard this time but from inside the church.

Muffled but raised voices, though I could not tell what was said for the walls of the church were four feet thick and the door was closed. The windows were glassed and kept the noise in.

I stopped to listen and jumped down from Fitz' back, slapping him on the rump and telling him to go home to his stable. He cantered off obediently down the slight incline. I didn't like the tone of the altercation.

161

I jogged up the path and opened the south door of the church slowly and as silently as I could.

Our church was not large, nor was it a complicated building. It was a simple rectangle of stone with round pillars marching along each side of the nave holding up a high roof. The priest's room was a small room tacked on to the northern wall where an open door stood inviting entry. This part of the building had no external door but a small window. The west door, the door in the tower, used only for special occasions and liturgical processions, was usually locked by Father Crispin and the only other exit was that of the priest's door in the north wall of the chancel where he would enter the church to perform mass. The chancel was cut off from the nave and the worshippers who gathered there by a screen. This was not a great elaborate carved affair as in some churches but a simple stone panel either side of the break between the larger nave and the smaller chancel. It was just possible through this opening to see the altar.

Through this opening I saw Crispin struggling with a man of roughly his own height wearing brown.

As I turned into the nave the man struck Crispin on the head with one of our silver altar candlesticks.

I ran forward.

"Hey!" I cried, or I think I did Paul, for I was completely taken by surprise.

The attacker lifted his head.

I gasped.

There looking straight at me, was a man I knew. His shining chestnut hair parted in the middle, fell in waves to his shoulders. His brown eyes, glistening in the meagre light coming in through the glassed windows, fixed on me.

He pushed poor Crispin to the ground, tucked the candlestick under his arm and was gone through the priest's door.

It was Thomas Potter.

Chapter Nine

It seems as if all this, as I recount it Paul, lasted a long time. It was merely a heartbeat. It takes longer to tell than it did to happen but it was such a shock; I am sure that my senses were dulled by it.

I jumped forward and caught Crispin as he fell. His head was pouring blood and so I grabbed the altar cloth from the stone, pulled it off, murmuring an apology to God and pressed hard to our priest's head. He was still conscious but very groggy. The second silver candlestick fell to the flagstones with a metallic clang and rolled away.

"Hold this. I'll return," I said, letting him gently down to the floor and I leapt towards the north door.

I flung open the wood which Thomas had slammed and pelted out to the small path and thence to the lane which ran at the back of the church. This road went into the village centre at one end and out to the forest and towards the main road to Salisbury at the other.

Our villain ran for the open space known as church fields or the glebe, for this was the land given over to the priest for his upkeep. I followed. Thomas ran up the hill and into the small copse which spread out towards the main forest.

There was no escape this way for the deerpark was surrounded on all sides by an eight foot high barrier planted at the base of the main forest. On this side of the fence lay a deep ditch making the barrier, in effect, twelve foot at least. These fences were ostensibly to keep the deer penned within their own territory but they also prevented their incursion and that of other animals into the manor fields and into the villagers' strips. Under forest law, deer were allowed to roam freely and the villeins were not allowed to protect their crops but the fence was effective in keeping out the rabbit and badger.

Tom ran swiftly on clutching the candlestick to his side. He veered west and

163

ran along the deer fence. I saw where he was headed and drove myself across the tilled field to head him off. The ground was sticky and soil clung to my boots. I jumped from furrow to furrow, slipping and sliding and making little progress.

I risked a look behind and around me. Surely there was some villager who could see me? Surely someone had heard the shouting? Was there no one about today in the fields, on the roads, coming from the forest?

I shouted "Harrow, harrow, to me!" the customary cry when pursuing a felon. No one answered.

I was alone.

I ploughed on.

The man ran nimbly and quickly along the deer fence boundary and disappeared into a deep furrow along the Durley Road.

I ran on.

I was now just a hundred yards behind him, my lungs bursting, my legs growing tired trying to stay upright at speed on the sticky and uneven ground.

Suddenly he was gone. I stopped to listen, breathing loudly.

I heard the whinny of a horse and then the unmistakeable rapping of hooves on chalk and flint.

He had a horse. No doubt Humble, the beast he'd stolen from my deerman, Hart. The sounds of hooves receded.

He was away and riding for the Salisbury Road.

*****

I cursed. I cursed myself for a fool. I cursed Thomas Potter for the villain he was. I cursed fate for dealing me such a hand.

I ran back to the road, battered on John Brenthall's door as I passed and yelled that I wanted him at the church. I stopped very briefly to wipe the mud from my boots on a grassy bank and ran on, back up to the church.

John came out of his house and followed me, his cotte flying behind him as he shrugged it on whilst running.

"What's wrong sir?"

"Crispin… in the church."

I skidded around the corner and turned right into the churchyard from the lane. I leaped over the grave plots and back through the north door.

Crispin was where I'd left him. He sat on the altar step with his head down between his knees. He still held the cloth to his wound.

He turned his eyes to look at me as I came in but didn't lift his head or speak. I skidded to a halt and came down beside him.

"Let me see the damage."

"It's all right. Did you get him?"

"No. He had a horse. He'd left it by the main road. He's gone."

Crispin groaned.

"Come. Let's take you to Lydia and Agnes. They will see if they think your wound needs the attention of Doctor Johannes."

"I doubt it."

Crispin struggled up just as John Brenthall and Bird Forester came in through the north door.

Our priest wavered. "God's truth Aumary... I never thought... I tried to stop him. Reason with him."

"No. I know." I put my arm around him and John caught him under the arm on his other side.

"Come, can you walk or should we carry you?"

"I can walk."

We walked in silence out of the church, Bird holding the door open.

John's eyebrow was raised in a question. I moved my head in an infinitesimal shake.

"Later John," I whispered.

Crispin stumbled but Bird righted him. "It's all right now sir. We'll get you to help."

We came in through the manor gate. Edward, one of my grooms was just

165

leaving the stable.

"Oh sir... I was worried when Fitz came trotting up on his own...." He noticed the bloody state of his parish priest and stopped with his mouth open. "God's cods!" he said and then blushed up to the roots of his hair as he realised that his priest had heard him.

Crispin smiled and struggled on. His feet were dragging now.

Up the stairs we went, lifting and dragging poor Crispin.

We laid him on one of the wide benches at the side of the hall.

"John, fetch Agnes." He ran off down into the kitchen which was a building close by the side of the hall.

Hal, who had been lounging by the fire, got up with a puzzled expression.

"What in the name of...?"

"Hit over the head with one of our silver candlesticks. Fetch a blanket, Hal." I threw him the key to my office where there was always a pile of blankets folded on my day bed.

Crispin's eyes were closing but he snapped them open.

He grabbed my sleeve.

"Aumary... how could it be? I saw him... I *saw* him."

"Aye Crispin, so did I. You are not wrong, in case you thought your eyes deceived you."

"It was Thomas Potter, Aumary. Thomas."

"I know."

Hal turned back at the door.

"Well... I'll be bugg... buried in Burbage!"

*****

Agnes came clucking up the kitchen stairs fetching Janet Peddler with her. Once they had taken a look at the damage, Janet ran back down the stairs for some hot water and some more linen was fetched from the store. Lydia came carefully down the solar steps. I saw Hawise's head momentarily peek around the solar door which was then closed quickly by Felice, her nurse.

Lydia reached the group gathered around Crispin.

"What on earth has happened?"

Crispin was losing the battle for consciousness.

"We must keep him awake," said Agnes. "He mustn't be allowed to sleep."

"Should we fetch Johannes?" I asked.

We all looked at each other.

Lydia pushed through the throng.

"Let me see."

Crispin smiled feebly at her.

"It will need stitching. Perhaps we should fetch him."

"I can do it sir," said Janet. "I don't think we need to bother the doctor."

I nodded. "Do your best, Janet."

I took hold of Lydia's arm and moved her to the other side of the large table by the fire. I sat her down on the bench.

I perched on a stool at the further side and reached to pour some ale which always sat in a jug on the table.

"Aumary, you are caked in mud," said Lydia.

"Aye, I chased the felon over the fields but he escaped on horseback. Damn him."

"What happened?"

"I came upon an argument in the church between Crispin...," I nodded towards the party now gathered around the priest, "and Thomas Potter."

"Tom? Oh don't be foolish."

"Lydia, I swear it was him. He struck Crispin with our silver candlestick, I saw him and then he was out of the door in a flash. He then rode into the forest."

"Why should he?"

"Why should he do any of the things he's done? He took us all for fools."

Lydia was shaking and shaking her head.

"It can't be."

"It was, I tell you. Both Crispin and I saw him. He stole the candlestick."

"But it can't be. I saw Tom go out to Cock a Troop Lane just after noon. I saw him in the courtyard and he said he was going down to the crokerers to try to convince them that he hadn't been amongst the men who attacked them."

I shrugged. "That doesn't mean he didn't double back and go to the church."

"He was very upset that they thought him guilty. He couldn't bear it that his friends thought so very ill of him," she said.

"They aren't the only ones, Lydia."

"Oh no...Aumary. It can't be."

"Eight years I have known that man. Sheltered him in my manor, given him work. Eight years and this is how he repays me. He is the best dissembler I have ever met."

"No, Aumary. There must be some mistake."

I leaned forward and took her shoulder.

"I saw him, my love. Plain as the nose on my face. It was Thomas. So did Crispin. We were very close to him."

Lydia's eyes took on a far away look. "But he cannot ride Aumary. He is a terrible rider."

"Or the best of riders and has made fools of us all these eight years."

"You think then that all that nonsense at the castle, that trial...you think he was also guilty of the death of the girl Cille?"

"What else can I think?"

"Why would he submit to it knowing God would...?"

"But we gave him every bit of help we could, didn't we?"

Lydia looked down at her locked hands.

"Did you see his hand...this man's hand when you saw him strike Crispin?"

"I must admit, looking at his hand was the last thing I thought of."

"He must be a Godless creature Aumary... this man. For he doesn't seem to care who he kills or hurts."

"You keep saying... this man... it was Tom, Lydia."

"But Tom isn't a Godless man. He is as God fearing and as loving to his soul as are you or I."

I tossed back almost a full beaker of ale and coughed.

"He is the best liar I have ever met." 'Bar one' I thought.

Yes, Paul, you remember that story. The first of which started us off on our tales.

Lydia shook her head again.

"Why should he? Why kill the girl? Why join this band of marauding outlaws? Why steal the candlestick and attempt to wound a priest? A man he's known for nearly four years. It's a grave sin to strike a priest, Aumary. It makes no sense."

"He doesn't seem to care about sins, my love. And I don't know. Maybe his brain has been turned by some... some... Oh!" I threw up my hands in frustration. "I don't know."

Hal wandered over to us and coughed.

"Am I 'earin' this right? Tom Potter struck Crispin with one of his own candlesticks and fled the church?"

"Aye. That's it."

"An' you ran after him and couldn't catch 'im?"

I shook my head.

"Where d'you think he'll go?"

"Almighty God knows."

Hal looked up through the window at the sky. "Too dark to pursue now."

"I know...but upon reflection, tomorrow perhaps we'll visit this little cottage his father had by the charcoal burners' place."

"You think he may be there Aumary?" asked Lydia.

"It's a start."

*****

Crispin was helped to his house by Hal and John. Agnes said that she and Janet would look after him for a while.

No sooner had they gone than I went into my office and started to write down everything I'd learned that day. When at last I looked up from my writing it was quite dark and one candle was not enough to light the room. I had left the door open and could see into the hall. Henry was lighting the lamps on the walls and the space was beginning to become bright with candles and oil lamps. Lydia had gone back to the solar. All was quiet.

It was then I heard a slow tread coming up the manor steps outside and the main door opening and closing.

I didn't look up, for I thought it was Hal returning from Crispin's house.

"How is he? Is he conscious?"

Passing the open door, a figure, slightly slumped and with a hand to his head, shuffled by and then stopped. Meaning to enter the hall he turned.

"M-m-my lord?"

I looked up. The figure was back lit by the lights in the hall. The passageway was in semi darkness. It was hard to see who it was.

"Crispin? How is his head?"

"Better than mine my lord, I hope," said a quavering voice.

I hissed and stood.

Into the light came Thomas Potter and blood, now dried, had been pouring down his face from a wound to his forehead.

His eyes rolled up into their sockets and he measured his length on my office floor.

Chapter Ten

I stood and stared.

I was so taken aback I couldn't move.

Then I yelled for Henry in the hall and leapt round to the front of my table. Henry came running in.

"Merciful Heavens, what happened to him?"

We bent to make sure that Thomas was still alive and then between us manhandled him through the office door, the hall door and into the hall where we laid him on the wide bench.

Henry turned Tom's head to the burgeoning light of the wall lamps. "Tssooo, that's a nasty gash."

Henry had been in his office late afternoon and hadn't heard the news about Tom's flight.

"Can you go and fetch Hal, John and Agnes? If you can, run up to the Peddlers' place and ask Janet to come up here, if she's gone home, or send someone."

Janet and Martyn Peddler lived in almost the last cottage by the priest's glebe.

"Aye, sir."

Whilst I waited, I searched Tom's body for anything he might have with him. He had no weapon, save his eating knife and the candlestick was not concealed upon his person. His scrip contained just a few pennies. His brown clothes were muddy but not overly so and there was little caked mud on his boots.

He was out cold and moved not an inch as I searched him.

Hal came up first. "Well, well... this is gettin' a bit of an 'abit i'n't it?" he said.

"Why return, Hal? Why?"

"Did he think you 'adn't seen him? "

"Oh no, he knew that all right."

"Then all that clay he plays with has got into his brain."

I lifted one of Thomas' hands. The palms were a reddish brown. His right hand bore the scar of the recent fire trial.

"It's him all right."

Hal scratched his head. "If I were 'im, I'd be miles away now with that silver tucked in me saddle bag. There'd be someone somewhere willing to buy and no questions asked."

"It doesn't make sense."

John came in through the hall door.

"By all that's Holy!"

"Yes, John.... It was as much of a surprise to me as it is to you."

John walked forward slowly.

"Is he dead?"

"No, unconscious. He's taken a nasty bang on the head. He staggered in here and then fell unconscious on my office floor."

Hal bent over the prone man. "Looks a right ragged cut and a lot a' bruisin'."

"Hmmm."

Agnes followed her husband into the room. "Good Lord. As I live and breathe...."

"Agnes, see what you can do for him."

"Aye sir... but.... "

"No, we shall make no further judgement until the man can explain himself."

Hal and John took Tom by the feet and shoulders and got him to his place by the fire. Agnes unrolled his pallet. He was laid carefully on it and Agnes yet again ran down the kitchen steps for some hot water.

Soon Janet Peddler was ministering to the unconscious man.

"Two men, with 'ead wounds in one day, sir," said Hal. "I 'ope it's not to be three." He lifted his grey hair. "I already got mine thanks."

There on his left forehead was a white scar, the result of a wound sustained in 1203 when he had been hit by part of the regalia which belonged to me as the forest warden; an ivory horn which was decorated with silver, one of the symbols of the power of the warden given to us by the first Norman king, William.

"And I have mine." I added. Mine had been gained when I had been hit whilst wandering the forest at night searching for a ghost...

You remember that story Paul—the ghost which plagued the forest in 1206?

I sat down at the table and watched as Agnes and Janet bathed the wound on Tom's head. As they cleansed his head, a vertical and jagged cut became clear and it began to bleed again. There were also many bruises.

"More stitching, Janet?" I asked.

Janet Peddler smiled. "It's been a time for it, m'lord."

"Aye, first Master Croker... how is he by the way?"

"Gone back to Cock a Troop Lane," said John, "this morning. We sent him in a cart."

"And then poor Crispin, now Tom."

Tom's head thrashed from side to side and Hal came forward to hold him.

Tom cried out in delirium. "No! No! It's not true... you can't...!" He flailed about on his pallet.

His hands raised in defence of his head. Janet tried to pull them down.

"Now Tom," she said, "I have to look at your head if I am to help you."

He seemed to be reliving an attack for he moved as if fending off blows. "Ahhh!"

"Come now, 'elp the lady Tom," said Hal. "She can't 'elp you if you don't let 'er."

Tom groaned and at last lay still but he did not regain consciousness.

I stood and paced about the room, finally stopping before the fire and throwing on another log.

"Lady Lydia said that Tom went to Cock a Troop Lane this afternoon. She saw him leave. He told her he was upset at the way his friends disbelieved him."

"Then 'ow could he be in the church an' 'ittin Crispin over the 'ead an' stealin' the silver?" said Hal.

I sat down abruptly and ran my hands through my inky black locks. "I don't know. All I can say is that I saw him."

173

Agnes looked up from bathing Tom's head. She paused with a cloth in her hand.

"Sir... might it be...," she lowered her voice, "some sort of magic? The work of the devil?"

I laughed out loud. "Ah, no Agnes. I don't think so. The only devil we have here is the man who stole that silver and hit Crispin over the head. A flesh and blood man, Agnes."

"But I hear...," she struggled to her feet. "That the devil can make himself look like anyone he likes. He has the power, sir." Her eyes were huge in her face.

I shook my head. "I do not believe it. Wherever did you hear this Agnes? It won't be one of Crispin's Bible tales I'll be bound."

"Ah no sir.... It was Old Odo said...."

"Old Odo is a fool and wanting in wits, Agnes...and so will you be if you listen to him."

This was an old beggar man in Marlborough who stood on the street corners and shouted out about the devil and the end times, how we were all doomed. Many folk stood about and gossiped, half an ear to his tales. Others dismissed him and moved him on whenever they could. Some pelted him with dung and offal.

"It would be better if..."

Suddenly and without warning a new idea came to me. I stared at Thomas' prone body on his pallet. Was it possible? I thought it through but I'd had no experience of such a thing. I had no idea. It might be possible. I needed to speak to Joannes.

Thomas didn't regain consciousness all night nor the next morning.

*****

And on that next morning, Hal and I travelled to town and sought out the doctor.

He was in his workplace seeing a man who had a jagged cut to his forearm.

174

Once again stitching was taking place.

We made ourselves known and then waited in the kitchen.

Johannes came in shortly afterwards wiping his hands on a square of clean linen rag which he then dropped into his fire.

I told him about Tom's attempt to steal the candlestick and his wounding of Crispin.

He folded into a chair in absolute disbelief.

"No. It can't be."

"Unless I am seeing things, Johannes and I can assure you my eyes are perfectly good."

"Hmmm...," said Johannes with a tinge of disgust. "Better than mine."

"It was Thomas. Crispin will confirm that it was our potter who struck him and made off with the silver candlestick."

"Jesu defend us," he said. "Have we been so wrong all this time?"

"There's more."

And I brought him up to date about the felon's return to the manor and how he too had been wounded.

Johannes' brow furrowed.

"Why would he return?"

"Unless...it wasn't him. It was never him."

"But you just said...."

"I know. The man who lies in the hall at Durley is Thomas Potter. What if the man who has been murdering his way through the forest, stealing, maiming and causing mayhem, is not Thomas Potter."

"Aumary... you just said...."

"Aye, I know."

"You aren't making sense."

Then I asked him one question. The thing I had been pondering about during all the hours of darkness. The thing that had been exercising my brain through a sleepless and uncomfortable night.

Johannes listened intently.

Hal whistled through his teeth. "I i'n't never heard of it," he said.

Johannes got up and pulled a flagon of wine to him.

"I have *heard* of it. Never seen it, you understand. It's very rare. Folk can be quite upset by it and tend to ascribe unearthly, supernatural reasons to the phenomenon but yes. It happens. It might be the answer."

"Then only one person can tell us if this is true in this case," said Hal.

"Yes," I said. "Thomas himself."

Johannes jumped up. "I must come with you. This I cannot miss for all the jewels on Becket's casket!"

I laughed out loud. "I thought you might say that."

"And Thomas may need my doctoring help, may he not?"

"He's like our peddler, Johannes, gone deep inside himself whilst his head mends. He is still unconscious. With your help we may have him telling us the story and helping us to understand this deep mystery, within the day."

Martyn Peddler had been found in the lane to Durley with a terrible head wound. He had been unconscious for many days before he came to, with the loss of much of his memory. Thankfully, he had lived, regained his wits and his memory and stayed with us at Durley to marry Janet.

We desperately hoped Thomas would do the same.

Oh no Paul...not marry Janet!

*****

We waited whilst Johannes saddled Titus, his old horse, collected a saddlebag and threw a few things into it, took up his doctoring bag and told Agnes that he would be back within a couple of days.

We made good time to the forest and were to be in time for dinner at the manor, for we took our meal early in the village.

The sun was trying to shine feebly behind a screening of cloud but as we rode the fog came down again as deep as it had been the day of the trial.

Ghostly creatures came into view as we clopped along the road. Trees with stick-like arms and fingers reared up at us out of the fog and we could see neither the sky nor the ground under our horses' feet. We could just about see each other and the pale ovals of our faces, shining out from the darkness of our hoods which we'd put up against the damp.

A couple of pheasants whirred from the roadway as we approached and went clacking off into the trees of the West Baily, I heard the mew of a distant kite and wondered how he managed to see where he flew.

Apart from this the forest was silent.

We passed Cadley village and saw the shadows of a few folk about, working at their tasks, their shoulders wrapped in hessian sacks against the freezing cold fog. The church here had burned down in January 1207 and there were people shifting the debris of the old church, and moving in materials in order to begin building the new one. They seemed like lepers with their bodies and heads covered.

We rode down the steep hill, up the other side and passed the Big Bellied oak, that venerable old tree which was old when the Confessor was a babe.

The fog cleared a little as we took the road to Durley, then thickened and we were almost at the village when we heard a party of mounted men galloping as if all the Hounds of Hell were behind them.

We could see nothing. The fog disorientated us. The sounds first came from the east, then from the south.

"Better get 'ome, I think," said Hal, a worried expression on his face. "We might be followed."

"But why Hal?" said Johannes. "Why would anyone want to follow us?"

"I dunno, but I i'n't 'angin' about to find out," and he put his heel to old Grafton's side.

I followed him and Johannes brought up the rear.

Suddenly an arrow sped out of nowhere and brushed Fitzroy's nose.

"Ride!" I yelled and we put our heads down and urged our mounts to faster speeds.

177

Another arrow hit the ground in front of Hal. One arced over Johannes' head.

"Jesus, they're all around us!" cried Hal, pulling up his horse.

"But they can't see well and it's the same for us."

I wrenched Fitzroy round and made for the deeper forest at the side of the road, freeing my sword and sliding it out of the scabbard, in case I was impeded by an archer on foot hiding in the bushes.

As we approached the dried bracken and the waist high ferns of the verge I heard the whinny of a horse which was none of our own.

"Down!" I yelled. "Down."

Obediently, and with a tug on the reins Fitzroy lay down in a twofold movement, in the sparse grasses and crackly brush of the forest floor. Grafton followed a moment later. Of course Titus had not been taught this manoeuvre and so stood.

"Johannes! Get him into the further trees and dive for cover."

My friend nodded and ran off into the fog to be swallowed up a moment later.

I lay with my head poking up over Fitz' side. Hal sat, almost lying on Grafton, back to back.

The fog eddied around us. A blackbird flashed up a worried call and sped off over the roadway.

I whispered "Can you hear anything?"

"Nothin'," said Hal.

We sat in silence.

"They're still there. I know they are."

"This fella who's making scary figures out of deer 'eads and spears you think?"

"I don't know."

"Nah! There's a lot more of 'em."

"He may be amongst them."

"Bet you a shillin' 'e is."

I chuckled quietly. "Only you Hal could be making a wager at such a time."

He put his gloved finger to his lips.

Voices.

I risked a look at the road some way off, but sadly the fog was too thick to see. The voices seemed to be arguing.

I didn't recognise any voice nor anything said. It was all too indistinct.

Fitzroy shifted beneath me and I put a calming hand on his neck.

I whispered to him; his eyes swivelled and the look he gave me said, "I hope this isn't for much longer. I am a fine horse and I do not lie down in forests."

Horses milled around on the road. We heard the uncertain clip-clop of their hooves but could see very little. They were just grey shapes in the grey fog.

More voices. I recognised my name being spoken.

My ears stretched to their full limit but I could make nothing of it.

Then quite suddenly someone jumped down from their beast and I heard his feet strike and scuff the chalk of the roadway.

A sword was slid from a scabbard. I kept my hand on my own weapon.

Hal silently slid his weapon from his own scabbard and put his head close to mine. "Do we fight if we must?"

I nodded. "Have we a choice? We must try to pick them off one by one."

"The fog is our friend here."

"And theirs."

"How many do you think?"

I smiled, "Might there be ten of them, do you think?"

"I was wonderin', " said Hal wistfully. "Ah well... it won't be the first time I've had such odds. When we fought our way from...."

He was abruptly silent as a man approached, swishing the bracken and plants of the roadside with a wide arced movement of his sword.

Hal tensed. We were ready to spring.

The man passed within feet of us. His face was concealed in a linen muffler which wrapped his head and neck.

We held our breath.

'Please God,' I thought. 'Do not let Fitz suddenly decide he's had enough of this game and snort or move.'

But he was as still as the grave.

The man made a huge semi circle of the forest floor.

I heard him say what sounded like 'nets' and then his crackling footsteps came on.

His friends muttered amongst themselves.

Abruptly and without warning there was a loud rattling of undergrowth close by.

I looked up and behind me.

No… not Titus! 'Titus,' I said to myself. 'Stay put. Do not give us away.'

But it was not Johannes' horse.

A large fallow deer buck, his antlers bristling in the meagre light and the damp air, lifted his head and snorted.

Hal turned.

"Almighty God," he whispered.

I picked up a stone. One of those small flints which litter the forest floor here and there and threw it at the buck not more than eight paces from us.

He started. I realised that we were upwind and he'd had no idea that we were there.

As fluid as a bolt of lightning he was off in the direction of the road.

The poor beast came face to face with our hostile party of men and with a snorting of horses, a yelling of surprise and a scuffling of feet on the roadway, the men mounted and were off after him whooping with delight. The searcher made an about turn and ran for his horse.

The stag melted into the mists as did the men.

We let out our breath.

It was some time before we moved.

I struggled up and brushed my clothes of mud and leaves, moss and bits of dried grass.

I grasped Fitzroy's reins and eased him up, telling him what a wonderful horse he was and that he had served me proudly.

It was some time later when we began to tentatively and quietly call for Johannes who was further in the trees.

We were answered by a snort from Old Titus.

After a while Johannes came crunching through the bracken leading his horse.

"By the Old Gods... that was a close thing."

"Aye, and thank those Gods for the presence of Herne the Hunter. He saved us I think."

"Twelve points," said Hal, talking about the buck's tines. "I 'ope they don't get 'im."

Johannes, who was not a country creature, shook his head. "Hmm?"

"A great stag came close to us and bounded out into the road distracting our attackers," I said.

"Sent by 'Erne the 'Unter," said Hal.

"Who?"

"Otherwise known as Cerunnos" I answered. "An ancient British god."

"Patron saint of stags," said Hal.

"Not quite, Hal," I chuckled. "But he was certainly our friend this day."

"Don't know about you... but I'm goin' 'ome," said Hal. "I'm as dry as a Burbage bosom."

"Come on then," I said.

*****

We rode carefully and as quietly as we could, for the village. We passed John Brenthall's house, the first house in Durley, where a light flickered through the window. The daylight was so poor, one needed more than just firelight to engage in any tasks. However the fog was clearing a little here.

We came past the church and past Crispin's house. He was just coming from his door, his head bandaged, his face pale in the whiteness of the fog.

"Where are you off to?" I asked. "Shouldn't you be resting at home?"

I heard Johannes tutting behind me.

181

"The church. I can rest there as well as at home and be of some use at the same time."

Some folk were milling about at the lychgate as we passed. I noticed Walter Reeve with his long staff and his son Johnathan looking up at the roof of the small building. With them was Bevis Joiner, one of my carpenters.

I threw up my hand in greeting.

We turned onto the path, past the bothies which clung to the side of the manor wall. Old Joan was out doing something with a barrel at the side of her home.

Her great nephew Dysig, who was a simpleton, was leaning on the wall singing to himself.

I screwed up my eyes attempting to see who else was out and about at this time of the day. Little could be achieved in the fog and folk were engaged in tasks which might be accomplished in the comfort of their homes or in the confines of their gardens. In the light of what happened later, perhaps that was not so fortuitous.

Two small girls, daughters of Ackerman, one of my foresters, seemed to be playing some game of their own devising, despite the fog. They squealed and chased after each other.

My houndsman Plum came striding back from the village green to his house by the manor wall. Most of my dogs were with him, save little Holdfast, my gazehound who waited for me by the manor steps as we clattered under the gate house.

Folk were busy about the courtyard. I looked round as I dismounted. Cedric came to take Fitz from me.

Edward loped up to take Grafton from Hal.

"Extra feed for the lad Cedric," I said. "He served me well today."

"Aye, sir."

I heard the children arguing in the space before the manor gate.

It seemed that Dysig had tried to enter into the girls' game and was not being allowed to join in.

However, young Adam Forester, Bird's smallest child, was taken into the game and there was more laughter and squealing. They ran off towards the green.

I smiled.

A moment later, however, the smile fell from my face for their squeals of delight had turned to screams of horror. Their voices floated back over the fog into the courtyard where we stood.

"Alys... Alys...," cried her young sister Dorcas and her calling turned to hysterical screaming.

Then other screams and shouting joined them.

Hal was out of the gate in a flash and scanning the ground around.

"Horses...people...running."

I followed him out shouting, "Everyone into the manor yard NOW!"

I grabbed Dysig by the elbow as I passed him and bundled him into the gateway. Cedric came out after me followed by Edward. Stephen and Peter followed them.

Shortly after this I saw Richard Marshall and Tostig Frithson releasing their weapons and running for the village green.

Looking up the slight hill at the church I saw that Crispin had just reached the south door of St. Mary's.

"CRISPIN! Take folk into the church and bar the door," I yelled.

Two or three of my villagers came running up quickly from the direction of the green.

"Under attack sir," wailed Warin Safernoc, Walter Reeve's eldest son. "They're firing the thatches."

"Collect all the able bodied men you can find. Then, wait here."

"Horses Hal," I screamed, and we ran back into the yard to remount our beasts which had not yet been divested of their tack.

As I ran and climbed onto Fitz again, I yelled, "Anyone who can ride, get on a horse, unsaddled, if must be, and follow. Find weapons...anything."

Henry Steward who had anticipated my words had, a moment before, run for the armoury in the undercroft of the manor house and opened the door.

Some men dived in and emerged with spears and clubs and one or two bows.

Other men had their own weapons in the form of bill hooks and scythes, staves and clubs and we all streamed out of the gate.

"The green—follow..."

We all ran or rode as fast as we could go in the fog for the centre of the village.

Smoke was mixing with the swirling mists as we broke out into the open space. Walter's house roof was burning. John Kellog's outhouse was smoking and Rob Hartshorn's dwelling was well alight.

"Get the women and children to safety," I yelled as I spied a man on a dark horse, his trappings glinting in the light from the fires, standing up in the saddle to thrust a fiery brand into the roof of Mistress Giffard, our alewife's house.

She came out of the door and drove at him with a broom, screaming at the top of her lungs.

He swiped her with a sword. She ducked and stumbled. He rode off laughing.

"Cedric...go about and get folk to leave everything and go up to the manor. My orders."

"Aye sir. But sir...."

"Do it Cedric. Lives are worth more than things. Tell Wyot Gatekeeper to close the gate up so it can be finally shut when our horses are through."

"Yessir," he galloped off the way we'd come.

We looked round. There was some hand to hand fighting and I made for the nearest mounted man who was menacing Richard Marshall with a sword. Richard parried it with his quarterstaff and reeled off to help John Kellogg engage an attacker and stop him from carrying off his wife Aelsa.

I struck the man with my sword on the back and he turned in the saddle, an inane grin on his face. I didn't know him but I realised that under his surcoat, he went armoured in maille. He threw a back handed swipe at my head which I ducked and, disengaging from my stirrup, I pushed the man with my foot. He landed on the other side of his horse with an 'oomph'. He was up just as quickly and remounted, turning his horse for the nearest house and cover.

I rode on. Two of the raiders were rounding up the screaming children and herding them into the space around the village well.

Hal, Stephen and I made for them and laid about us.

"Go to the manor house!" I screamed and the children grabbed each other and ran.

We traded blows with a few of these men whom we realised were also, every one of them, well-armed and armoured. Some wore wrapping around their faces to conceal their features.

There was a confused mêlée as folk attempted to engage the attackers from all sides, both mounted manor folk and villagers on foot.

With every breath I could save I yelled, "To the manor house...Or to the church. Now—go!"

Folk didn't think twice, they turned and ran.

Some villagers were pursued and struck down. Hal and some of the others, who had managed to get themselves horses, followed and intervened as best they could, slipping between the attackers and their quarry.

I reached down and lifted a fleeing Janet Peddler onto Fitzroy as I passed, the ineffectual blow aimed at her by a man on a brown rouncey. She was looking about for her children, panic stricken.

"They are safe... go! I saw them with Peter."

I raced for the partly open gate and setting her down, pushed her towards the opening and turned in the same movement to return to the fighting which had now come to the banked space before the manor house.

Tostig was grappling with a man...the same man we had seen in the fog in the forest. He kneed him in the groin and the man went down howling.

"Well, done my lad!" I shouted. But his opponent was tough and staggered away to draw a sword and took a swipe at my groom.

I leapt from Fitzroy's back and took the blow on my own sword. My arm was momentarily numbed but the man, realising he was now at a disadvantage, without his mount, ran for the space before the church lych-gate.

I heard the church door clang shut and the locking bar go down.

Small clusters of resistance were taking place here and there as manor folk

185

banded together, both men and women, to defend each other from this threat.

I hit Fitzroy on the flank with the flat of my hand, "Go home, Fitz." I knew someone would take him in at the gate when he got there.

I took a deep breath "Belvoir...to me, to me!" I yelled. Our rallying cry.

The folk I could see broke off the fighting one by one and ran for the manor gate.

Hal and I were the last ones through before Wyot and a couple of the others pushed it shut and thrust the huge wooden bar across.

The wicket however remained open and, after ushering folk away from the gate, I stepped outside to scour the ground for attacker and villager alike.

Edward Groom came running as fast as he could, ducking down and weaving from side to side, from the vicinity of the poultry bothy, sheltering Annot Pierson under his arm. She had little Algar our orphan cradled to her bosom.

He thrust her at me and disappeared into the fog.

"Ed... come back!"

He came back almost immediately tugging a reluctant Alice Reeve by the sleeve.

"No... no… my house! I must go and save my house...," she whimpered.

"Save yourself Alice," cried Edward. "Your house can be rebuilt..."

"No, no...," she pulled away. Edward's grip strengthened. He pushed her towards the open wicket.

He was about to turn and leave again when an arrow came speeding out of the gloom and caught him smack, into his right side.

He gasped and went limp.

I caught him and lifted him up, passing him quickly to Johannes who was standing behind me.

I ducked out under the wicket once more, scanning the ground before the gate.

A mounted man, a hundred paces in front of me and momentarily clear in the break in the smoke, lowered his bow. He bowed from the waist, laughed and reeled away into the fog.

186

"Henry, organise the tithings. Find out who, if anyone, is missing."

"Aye, sir."

I turned about and bounded up the stairs of the gatehouse. There I stood and waited; this was the highest point, all save the church tower, and looked out along the street of the village to the green.

I could see two bodies. They lay, not moving. Perhaps there were others.

I looked towards the church tower where I could just make out the white bandaged head of our priest and four others clustered together looking down. One was a woman; Agnes Brenthall.

The attackers were not to be seen but they hadn't, I knew, disappeared. They were waiting for something.

Hal followed me up the steps.

"Edward?"

"Johannes is with him now." He shook his head. "Not sure 'e'll make it."

I slapped my thigh in anger. "Stupid boy...why did he?"

"You know 'ow 'e is. Always carin' about everyone else."

I looked Hal in the eye. "I know. It was a brave thing to do… but still...."

Suddenly there was a flurry of skirts. Lydia came scurrying up out of breath.

"Aumary, what in the name of the Almighty is happening? People say the village...."

"Aye… attackers. About ten. Heavily armed and all mounted."

I turned and took her by the shoulders.

"Go back to the manor. Get everyone you can into the hall. There are wounded. Do what you can. Lock the doors...all of them, behind you. Get Wyot to lock the postern and mount a guard there. Muster the tithing, help Henry."

"But Aumary...."

"DO IT LYDIA!"

She looked up at me with a white, tearful face. I pecked her on the cheek.

"It is too dangerous here. I'd not have you in danger. Go and help and look after our children."

She nodded.

187

With a swish of her skirt, she was gone down the steps.

The manor courtyard began to empty of folk, all but those able bodied men who thought they might fight if need be.

Phil Wheelwright the younger, armed with a wicked looking knife, no doubt something he'd picked up from his workshop in the courtyard, pointed as he came up beside me.

"Sir... there...."

In a break in the fog, the ten men... damn, there were still many of them despite our best efforts to wound or maim some of them... cantered in a group up to the space a distance away from the gate. Thankfully I saw we had blooded some of them.

Haha! I thought... not too close, for a bow might be able to wound them from here, maille or no maille and they suspected we might try it.

Under the arm of one of the mounted men was a small wriggling girl.

"Dorcas!" cried Ackerman, her father, as he came up beside me from the courtyard.

"Oh my God! Dorcas...!"

He was all for turning and running down the steps and forcing his way out of the wicket but Hal and Tostig took hold of him.

I gathered my strength and took a deep breath.

"What can you possibly want with a small girl? She is but four. Let her go."

There was a burst of laughter. Dorcas screamed again. Her father grimaced, "If they hurt her I swear...."

I squeezed his arm.

"I will pay you to let the child go."

"No, sir," said Hal quietly. "That i'n't the way."

"What then?"

Hal subsided into mutters.

"If they want to 'ave some fun, let me go out there and I'll exchange myself fer 'er."

I shook my head.

"I will pay, I say," I reiterated in a louder voice.

Ackerman groaned.

The first horseman nodded to the man who held Dorcas.

He struggled with her and eventually set her down on her feet. She wobbled momentarily and then ran, picking up speed as she saw the open wicket gate in front of her. She stumbled once or twice.

The first man leisurely unbuckled the strap which secured his lance to his saddle. He lifted it, took aim and let it fly.

"Dorcas!" I yelled "lie flat...lie down!"

The little girl tripped and flattened herself to the ground.

I had seen the trajectory of the spear and knew it would only pass over her body if she were prone.

Out from the wicket came Hal of Potterne. I hadn't realised he'd left my side. As quick as I had ever seen Hal move, he scurried to Dorcas, grabbed her hair, lifted her waist, dropped her over his shoulder, turned and ran back.

The spear had clattered uselessly on the packed earth of the road.

People on the roof of the gatehouse cheered.

The attackers milled around on their horses and conferred. The fog thinned a little.

I counted them

There were nine.

Where was our man on the rouncey who kept his face concealed?

John, who had been monitoring the group on the church tower, for his wife and son were sheltering there, took a hissed in-breath.

"Sir." He pointed.

Round the corner of the hay barn came the man on the brown rouncey.

John growled under his breath, "Humble, sir."

"Aye John, I see."

Our man with the scarf around his lower face came slowly clopping around the corner. Far enough away from our bows, close enough for us to see who he had roped to his horse's tail.

189

"God damn you!" said Johnathan Reeve, suddenly at my elbow.

The man dismounted and made his way on foot to the rest of the group, dragging his prisoner behind him.

He turned and located me on the top of the gatehouse.

He bowed.

His voice rang out with strength, confidence and good diction, behind his concealing muffler.

"You were willing to pay for a small girl child of no consequence...."

I looked back to where the family of Ackerman had been reunited in the middle of the courtyard.

"What would you pay for a valued member of your household?"

Johnathan pushed in front of me. "I have four brothers you scum! If you harm him, it will be a blood feud. We shall hunt you down."

I moved him aside. "Johnathan."

I stepped forward.

"Careful sir," said Tostig, nocking his bow and aiming. "They aren't to be trusted."

"Put down your weapon Tostig," I said

"I will pay," I shouted again.

"How much?"

I thought of the amercement I had to pay into the King's coffers for the transgression of which he had accused me.

"Five marks."

Poor Walter Reeve looked up at me with his rheumy eyes, "NO, sir! I'm not worth it."

"You are to us, Walt," I shouted.

"Not enough!" yelled the man who held the rope which tethered Walter.

"Eight marks and no more."

The man pushed Walter to his knees.

I felt a soft presence beside me.

"Walter!" It was Alice Reeve, his wife, mother of the five sons and one daughter, Janet who was now the wife of Martyn Peddler.

"Go wife... go and do not look. I order you," shouted Walter in a choked voice.

"You are in no state to order anyone!" said his captor who kicked him viciously in the side.

Walter toppled over in pain and because his arms were pinioned by the rope he fell heavily.

"Ten marks," said the man, "and he's yours again."

"I don't trust them," said Hal, who'd come up once more to the gate house tower.

"Let the man walk to the gate and we shall exchange the man for the money then."

"Go and get it."

I mentally worked out how much money we had in the manor coffer plus the money saved for the poor and then that in my private chest in my office. The amount they asked for added to almost one hundred and thirty shillings. I didn't have this amount here in Durley.

"I will have to get it. I don't have that amount with me here at Durley"

"Aw come, come... master forest warden. The constable is not so poorly paid, I'm sure."

I snapped back "He is not paid at all churl! He does it for the honour."

"Something you'd know nothing about!" yelled Johnathan.

The man laughed. A pitiless and high pitched wail.

"Ha...no... there must be monies. Silver plate, wine, food, horses. That's a fine horse you ride my Lord Belvoir. He must be worth eight pounds in himself."

I wiped my hand over my forehead.

"The horse for the man?" said Walter's captor.

"No sir...NO!" shouted Walter.

"And whatever monies you have here at the manor."

"I will get it."

I looked back, "Henry."

Henry looked shocked.

191

"All of it, sir?"

"All of it...and Fitz please, Richard."

Richard sighed.

"You sure, sir?"

I nodded and then smiled weakly. "He's only a horse… whereas Walter is...."

I looked back down into the space before the gate. They had now righted Walter and he stood weakly but with great haughtiness, before them.

"Walter is a friend."

"You will not beggar my lord Belvoir," he said lifting his chin. "No sir, do not pay for me. I'm not afraid to die. I'm an old man, I've had my life."

"Shut up old man," spat his captor.

"This old man is the great grandson of a Saxon thegn, churl," said Walter with great dignity. "A lord in his own right before the conquest. A great lord, when you and your predecessors were crawling on your bellies in the mud!"

I saw Johnathan smile weakly.

He looked at me, "It's true, sir."

"I've no doubt of it, Johnnie," I said.

I leaned out over the parapet. "This will take some time."

"No sir...do not do it," said Walter with a catch in his voice.

"I said shut up, old man," said the veiled attacker.

Walter took a deep breath, let it out and suddenly pushed hard on his bonds. He pushed them up and struggled.

"Belvoir, to me, to me!" he cried.

His captor was taken by surprise. He had assumed this old man had no strength; that he was a weakling, that he would just stand there and take whatever was meted out to him. I knew that Walter had been a very strong young man. I'd known him all my life and I remembered him as a brawny, muscle armed farm worker able to lift a sheep over his shoulders.

He stepped back as Walter launched himself at the villain.

There was a hissing of metal and a swish.

Alice screamed and turned into my chest to hide her eyes.

Warin, Athel, Paul, Harold and Johnathan, the sons of Walter Reeve, all shouted at once.

With the Belvoir name on his lips, Walter toppled on to his knees and his head rolled a few feet, coming to rest at last, with his eyes up to Heaven and to his family staring down at him, from the gate tower.

With one swipe, the man had severed poor Walter's head from his body.

Chapter Eleven

Time seemed to come to an end.

We all stood transfixed, like a fly caught in amber, horrified at the thing happening in front of the gate.

Then Alice Reeve screamed. A huge, high pitched, painful sound which hurt the ears. I thrust her at her youngest son who was whiter than the sheet on my bed place, and stepped forward, leaning out over the parapet.

"It *is* the blood feud then!" I shouted.

The murdering villain made for his horse again and was in the saddle at a leap. He pulled hard on the poor beast's mouth and then the ten men clattered into the fog across the village green and disappeared.

He made no reply to my shout and did not look back.

Henry came up the steps of the gatehouse, two at a time. "Sir, we are missing Hervey Kellog, Stephen Hawknose and John Chalkhill. Walter is also...."

His gaze strayed over the parapet and caught sight of the eyes of Walter Reeve staring up at him. He had been too busy counting money in the office to take notice of the tragedy being enacted in the space before the gate.

"Oh...," he said, turning pale.

"We have no need of the money now. We have some folk in the church, Henry. John, Stephen and Hervey may be there. How many wounded do we have?"

"Seven, sir," said Henry dragging his eyes from the terrible sight on the roadway.

"Any dead that we know of?"

He shook his head. "Not yet, sir." He screwed up his eyes and gazed out over the green. "Except...."

His sad eyes met mine, "But that looks like Stephen and Hervey there, sir."

I nodded and turned to face the church tower. There was a small space which allowed a free view of the roof and gazing past the apex of the hay barn I yelled,

"Crispin, who have you there?"

Crispin waved. "Eleven. All fit. Mostly women and children."

"The devils have gone. We need your help."

He threw up his hand and disappeared down the steps. A moment later the south door of the church opened and he exited, carrying the requisite items to save the souls of the poor Durley folk who may have lost their lives.

Eleven folk streamed out after him and ran rapidly for the manor gate, skirting the severed head of my village reeve.

John Brenthall was reunited with his wife and son and Agnes immediately took charge of a blubbering Alice Reeve. Janet came up, tears streaming down her face. Her husband was away in the countryside at his peddling and she had none to comfort her. She clung to her mother and all three women staggered up to the hall, weeping. Annot Pierson followed them, leading Janet's toddling twins and holding little Algar, our orphan.

"Go in your tithings about the village," I yelled down into the yard. "Discover who is wounded or dead and bring them back here. Go armed in case these murderers are still about. I also want a report of the damage to buildings."

Men organised themselves into groups of ten and streamed out of the gate which Wyot had now reopened.

Women began to collect themselves and their children into groups; all were accounted for. Only one woman was missing. Mistress Giffard, the alewife whom I'd last seen grappling with the man who'd tried to fire her thatch. Her son Rob ran rapidly out of the gate yelling,

"I thought she was behind me. Oh God! She was behind me!"

I came down into the courtyard passing through the gate and stooped to pick up with two hands the head of Walter, my loyal reeve and good friend of many years, and reunited it with his body, closing his eyes. Crispin came up quietly behind me.

"Someone will pay, Crispin," I said quietly as he began the prayers for the dead.

196

*****

We went gently about the village that afternoon as the light faded and the smoke from the burning thatches billowed out over the green. No house beyond the green had been fired. The thatch of Walter and Alice's house was still alight but parties of folk with water from the well and the river, managed to contain it.

Rob Hartshorn's house was a smouldering pile of ashes and beyond redemption.

We found Mistress Giffard in her yard frantically drawing the ale from her barrels in a bucket, to dampen the flaming thatch of her outhouse and her neighbour's house roof.

There would be no ale this night for it had all but been used up.

I went about my people congratulating, commiserating, praising, for they had all behaved impeccably and bravely.

I found the small lass, Dorcas, grasped hold of her, threw her in the air and caught her, telling her what a brave and clever girl she had been to obey me so swiftly. She had no idea she had been in such danger. She giggled and screeched with delight. Her father looked on smiling.

I would allow no man or woman back into their homes this night for I feared a return by the murdering band. All stayed in the hall or in the church behind a locked gate and door.

Hervey Kellog, the son of our village butcher, was brought into the small room on the south wall. He had taken a spear through the gut and was not expected to live. His father and mother were with him.

Stephen Hawknose, one of my foresters, had sustained a wound to the thigh. The great blood line which is carried in the leg had been severed and he had bled out his life force onto the road way as he lay. We carried him to our little mortuary in the corner by the privy and the store shed.

His adopted son Cenric Hirst went into the mortuary with Crispin and they closed the door.

There too did we carry John Chalkhill who had died bravely defending the children at the well.

With grave honour, we carried Walter Reeve to the church and placed him on a bier in front of the altar. The others would join him there shortly.

There were many with lesser wounds. The women went about patching and cleansing and Janet, for want of something to do to ease her pain, aided Johannes as best she could. Her eyes were huge in her face and she cried silently for her gentle, kind and noble father.

It was late in the night when I climbed the solar stairs, sat in my chair and wept for that good and honest friend. They came to me at midnight to tell me that Edward too had died of his wound. Johannes had laboured to save him but he simply could not. I wept some more.

Hawise, who had not gone to bed, was sitting hunched up in front of the fire. When Hal delivered the news, she burst into tears for she had liked our amiable groom and he had looked after her pony Felix, since she was old enough to sit him. Felice, the childrens' nurse went to her but she would not be consoled.

She cried into my wolfhound bitch Mildred's wiry coat until she fell asleep. I left her before the fire and covered her with a blanket.

Her mother was supervising food from the kitchen for the assembly but few felt like eating.

Eventually the manor was quiet and we took it in turns to man the gatehouse roof, five of us in three hours stints just in case they returned.

But the dawn arrived and there was no return.

*****

We buried our dead in the churchyard the following day and folk returned to their homes to begin the process of clearing up and recovering from their losses. Everyone was jittery and cautious.

Rob Hartshorn moved into Plum Houndsman's cott by the manor wall for the two were friends and it was going to be a long process to rebuild his house.

He had lost everything.

I sent to the coroner detailing what had happened, telling him that we had several murders for him to pronounce upon.

We gave thanks that the damage had not been more severe but wept for our losses and mourned our friends.

I took Johnathan Reeve aside once his father had been committed to the ground and asked him if he might become the next reeve.

"If the villagers would have me, sir."

"You know they will, Johnnie."

"My father wanted me to take over last year but I couldn't, not while... he was alive," he sniffed.

"I know that he had been grooming you and that you'd become his ears and eyes, and his legs too, lately."

Johnathan gave a sad chuckle, "Aye... I had been doing a deal of stuff for him."

"Then put it to the village. They must vote. Do you know if anyone else in Durley fancied themselves reeve?"

"John... John Chalkhill did say he might put himself up... but now...."

"Aye. John is gone." I slapped Johnathan on the back. "I would be pleased to have you Johnnie."

"And I pleased to be the representative of the villagers, sir."

And so it was done.

All through that awful afternoon, evening and night, Thomas Potter lay on his pallet, in silence breathing shallowly and occasionally moaning in his sleep.

As the next day came to a close, he opened his eyes and groaned. Lydia, who was close by, saw him and came down onto her knees beside him. She told me later what happened.

"Thomas. We are glad you are with us once more."

She helped him to a sip of water.

"What happened, madam?"

"You came into the manor yesterday afternoon and collapsed in Lord Belvoir's office. You have a nasty wound on your head."

199

Thomas put up his hand to his bandaged head.

"Yes, I remember now." He screwed up his eyes. "And a few bruises elsewhere."

"Where you fell...?"

"No, where I was stoned."

Lydia rose up, uncertain. "Stoned?"

Thomas licked his dry lips, she said, and turned his head away as if he did not want her to see the tears welling up in his eyes.

She came to find me.

*****

Johannes looked the man over and pronounced him out of any danger. He stood at last and with folded arms, listened to our conversation.

"The Lady Lydia tells me you got the wound to your head by being stoned, Tom? How did *that* happen?"

"Friends... Pah!" Tom tried to sit up but grew dizzy and lay back down again. "What kind of friends take up stones from the ground and rain them down on you?"

"The crokerers stoned you?"

"Aye. God damn every one of them, except Alban. Alban got me away from them."

"I take it they would not listen to your explanation."

Thomas Potter laughed. With great anger in his voice he said "I have no explanation. They lied about me... and then...." He turned his head away.

"Thomas, listen to me." I pulled up a stool and sat leaning forward and over him. Johannes stood close by.

"This is no lie. If you like, I will swear on the Belvoir bible."

Thomas slowly moved his eyes to mine and screwed them up.

"I too have seen you. I saw you in the church, striking the priest, Crispin, with one of the silver candlesticks and make off across the fields with it."

"I did not!"

"Crispin will also swear to it, Tom."

"When was this?"

"An hour or so after noon the day before yesterday."

"No, no! I was at Cock a Troop Lane trying to convince them that it was not I who attacked and killed Anthony."

I looked up at Johannes.

"How do you think I got this wound....and others...look...look...?"

He thrust away the blanket covering him and pulled up his shirt. His ribs were red and blue with bruises, scratches and scrapes.

"I have a salve for those, Tom," said Johannes.

"You may have gained those wounds at another place."

"Where, God damn it?"

"When you attacked the glassmen in the forest, who fought back with whatever weapons they could muster."

Tom's face was white and his deep brown eyes showed huge in his face.

"I did WHAT?"

"The glassblowers were attacked in the same way as the charcoal burners and the potters."

"Why should I? Why would I be with these marauders?"

"That we cannot fathom."

"The village too has been attacked, Tom," said Johannes. "Though that act cannot be laid at your door for you were here, unconscious and oblivious to the mayhem, all afternoon."

Carefully Tom sat up. He rubbed his eyes.

"No...no...! That's terrible... I knew nothing... it was nothing to do with me."

I leaned into him once more. "Tom... there are many things in this puzzle which simply do not make sense. Johannes and I have given it much thought...."

"And you have come to the conclusion, my lord, that I am a felon and not to be trusted."

"No. Although we cannot disbelieve the evidence of our own eyes, we also

201

cannot believe that you are guilty of these heinous crimes."

"My lord... you are not making sense," said Potter with a worried look.

"The man I saw looked like you, Tom. Just like you."

"Admittedly, the Lord Belvoir was not as close to you as he is now, to look you in the eye," said Johannes.

"However, I was but a few feet away and my eyes did not deceive me."

"There is only one explanation for this, Tom," said Johannes, hunkering down before the young man. "You were speaking to the Lord Belvoir some time ago about your birthplace..."

"Aye, Salisbury."

"That you went to see your mother in that town, last March."

"Aye and she died in the April."

"You also said...," Johannes looked at me, "that you had a sister and a brother."

"My sister is married to a...." He tailed off. His mouth dropped open.

"Oh, Jesu, aid me," he said weakly.

Johannes smiled. "Then we were right in our thinking, the Lord Belvoir and I." He levered his tall body up again. "You have a brother."

"I...I...." stammered Thomas. He took a deep breath and started to cough. Johannes leapt to the table and fetched him a beaker of water.

"Drink."

Thomas grasped the beaker with two shaking hands and drained it.

He looked at it in his hands.

"One of mine, m'lord." He chuckled desultorily, "A good honest trade... potting."

"Your brother is not a potter, Tom?"

"No, sir."

"He did not come to Durley with you and your father, you said, but stayed with your mother in Salisbury."

"Yes, sir."

"What does he do, Thomas?" asked Johannes.

Tom sighed and put the beaker on the floor. He swung his legs over the edge of his pallet and leaned back against the wall and grimaced as his bruises made contact with the stone.

"William went to Winchester, sir, when I left at the age of seventeen to come here. He went to train as a soldier at the castle there."

"I thought as much."

"He was always the restless one. Eager for the pennies which the life as a castle soldier could give him. He was always one for danger and trouble, always the one in the centre of the fighting, should there be any."

"Whereas you..?"

"Was always...," he laughed quickly, "the one who pulled him out of the mêlée before he got his head broken." He put up a hand to his wound.

Johannes sat down on the bench close by.

"I need to know something from you, Tom," he said.

"Aye, sir."

"I know that it is possible that two children can be born of the same mother at the same time... one a little older than the other of course... by heartbeats."

"Aye sir...we have had such children here in the village."

"The Brookers, before their untimely death, were twins were they not?" I said.

"Aye Edith and Edmund. And there's the Peddler twins sir... Janet's boy and girl," said Tom.

"That's right, Marin and Martel."

Johannes leaned in close. "These children are however, unalike."

Tom looked down at his clay coloured hands and at the scar on his palm. "Whereas my brother and I are identical, sir."

"Yes," said Johannes. "I have heard of it but never seen it. I do not know how it can be, I do not know how it happens but...."

"It is true, sir. Two children may be so alike that no man may tell them apart."

"Apart from their mother and father that is."

Thomas laughed "Even then... it was not easy, sir."

"No. If your parents had trouble how are we to tell you apart?"

"We are as alike as the flowers on the orchard trees."

"The same height, build, the same hair, the same eyes." I said.

"Aye."

"Tell me true, Tom. Could this be your brother, your identical brother?"

Tom grimaced. "Aye sir... it could be William."

"But...?"

"Why, sir. Why would he do these things?"

I leaned back.

"I don't know."

"He isn't an ogre, sir."

"Perhaps the company he keeps has made him so, Tom?"

Tom looked down at his scarred palm again. "I have not seen him for years. Our paths have simply not crossed."

"The woman Cille, I think he knew her. I think he seduced her in Hereford and told her that his name was Thomas and that he lived in Durley."

"This is why she was so convinced, that she was in the right place. He'd promised marriage to her, in your name," said Johannes. "The poor woman. She followed him to where he told her he came from. I suppose he had no idea she'd do that."

"She knew you had entered the church that evening. In the poor light, that first day, she saw you enter and recognised the man whom she thought was her lover. That is why she was at the lychgate calling you names. Poor deluded woman," I said.

"But it wasn't me, sir."

"No, Tom. It wasn't."

Tom put his face in his hands.

"I think he came into the courtyard, pretending to be you that next night. Wyot saw him and was taken in no doubt, by his ready smile. The same smile you give folk, Tom. Your brother ran up the stairs but did not enter the hall. When Wyot was gone, he ran down, and went into the small room to find Cille. He did not want her to see you in case she managed to detect a difference between the two of you. He knew that the crime would be laid at your door. I do not know how he knew she was here but gossip travels. It may have been known by then in the town."

"He purposefully framed me?" whispered Tom.

"Aye I think he did. I'm sorry to say."

"Oh God. This is just a bad nightmare. I shall awake in a moment."

I reached out and squeezed his shoulder gently. He grimaced.

"Tom, I have read that such twins have a certain bond forged in the womb. Those I have known are very close. They can anticipate each other's words, can without words understand what the other is thinking. Is this true?" asked Johannes.

"Aye sir. Before we parted we were very close. There was a great affection there."

"It's a terrible shame this affection had to turn so sour, Tom."

I lifted myself to my feet.

"We shall let it be known that you are innocent and that we lay these crimes at the feet of your brother. Your brother who is your perfect image. Your brother who, though he be made of the same clay as you, has a soul as black as the devil's cotte, Tom."

"Some folk think, Aumary, as I've said, that such natural births are the work of the devil" said Johannes. "We must tread carefully."

"We know what it was like here in Durley when Janet was delivered of two babies. It was difficult to get folk to appreciate that Janet had not committed adultery and had had two men, separate fathers to her children. It took a while for the village to come to terms with it.

"We must, as I say, tread carefully."

"Yes, Johannes," I said, "But so must Tom's brother William. For we now know he is here."

"Yes, but we can be taken in by him."

"Ah no my friend... no longer. Never again." I smirked.

Johannes folded his arms again and cocked his head to one side.

"There is one major difference between Tom and his brother which we must make sure we look for."

"And that is?"

"Oh no...not the fact that he wears colours...ah yes...Tom. He has learned that you wear nothing but brown nowadays and has changed his appearance accordingly."

"No!"

"He is cunning, of that there is no doubt. However, we cannot be fooled by him again."

"How so, sir?"

I reached for Thomas' hand.

"You bear a scar he does not, Tom." I said smiling, turning over his palm.

We all looked down at the puckered scar on Thomas' right palm, red still but now healing well.

Tom grinned up at me.

*****

I retired to my office and wrote down, as was customary, everything I had learned.

I leaned back in my chair and tapped my pen end on my lips.

Now I had a shrewd idea of where my 'outlaws' were hiding. I knew that Tom's brother was one of them. How I was going to flush them out of their hiding place as I might a covey of partridge from the downland grasses, I didn't know.

Suddenly an idea came into my head.

I jumped up and went back into the hall.

"Tom, have you any idea what your brother and his murdering gang are looking for when they dig behind the buildings at Cock a Troop Lane and the charcoal burners? They had no chance at the glassblowers nor here at Durley for they were outnumbered."

Tom lifted his bruised head.

"No sir... no idea at all."

"They dig pits about three feet apart, not too deep. They are looking for something. Hal suggested that it's treasure of some sort."

"Aye, Will was always talking about treasure and money. He was much more of a seeker after coin than I have ever been. I am content with my craft and my earnings, my friends and my life here. He was always discontented with his lot, always looking for more."

"Hence his flight to Winchester and the castle there."

Tom nodded. "But treasure? Here? How would he know anything about this place? He doesn't know the area...."

"But do we know how long he has been impersonating you Tom? What might he have learned about Savernake and Marlborough by just pretending to be you?"

Tom scratched his head. "He only visited once, about five or six years ago. He sought out Da at the cottage. Da was not best pleased with him, he told me. He'd become haughty and proud. He'd forgotten he was a potter's son."

"He didn't meet with you?"

"No. Da told me he came to the little cottage in the wood and started to throw his weight around. Boasting and telling tales about what he'd done and what he was going to do. Da gave him short shrift, sir. It upset him, something shocking it did. Not long after Da was dead. By then, of course, I'd taken the workshop here."

"Thank you, Tom. I have an idea which might... just might, be something with which we can lure the gang to the forest. I'll need your help. But let me think on it for a while."

"You know sir, that you have my help. You don't need to ask."

"Good man."

*****

I went down to the courtyard and sought out Hal in his little room which was tacked onto the end of a series of buildings on the south wall. Johannes was sharing an ale flagon with him.

"Hal...Johannes, I have an idea and a theory, if you are both willing to listen."

"About what, sir?" said Hal sitting up from a reclining position on his bed.

"About our 'wolfsheads' and how we might catch them. All of them."

I had the attention of both men now.

"How, Aumary?" asked Johannes.

"What did you say that you thought they were looking for, Hal?"

Hal furrowed his brow, "Well, stands to reason du'n't it... buried treasure. Why dig if it i'n't treasure?"

"What if we give them some treasure?"

"What?"

"What if we put it about that there's treasure to be had somewhere? What if we bury, say, some of the Belvoir regalia, perhaps a few bits and pieces of gold and some coin...just enough to pique their interest...?

"We might catch them red 'anded," said Hal.

"We might...."

"Ah, but Aumary, we'll need some professional soldiers to round up this lot," said Johannes. "It's one thing for villagers to defend their manor, family and home from a gang of marauders, quite another to take on such a bunch of armed men in the open. Ruthless and expert as they are."

"I am in charge of the castle garrison again. I have those soldiers. I can use them."

Hal and Johannes exchanged glances.

"You reckon you can do it before 'ol de Devil comes back with the King?" asked Hal.

"I can have a really good try," I said.

"Now this is what I think...."

It was dark before I had finished expounding my theory and putting before them my idea for catching our villains.

I left Johannes and Hal thrashing out the problems they thought inherent in my plot and went to supper in the hall, my mind working hard on how I would make it known that there was treasure to be found in the forest. I needed to draft my old friend Andrew Merriman into the story once more.

That night I explained to Lydia what had happened and how Tom was totally innocent of the crimes laid at his door.

"I told you there would be something," said Lydia, "I said it couldn't be true."

"We didn't know that he had a brother who was his twin, his complete likeness. He never spoke of him did he?"

"Not to me...not to any of his friends. It would have been known by all else."

Lydia reached out for me,

"Aumary, Johannes thinks this is perfectly possible? It's not some trick?"

I laughed. "What happened to your absolute assertion that Tom is innocent?"

"Ah well... it just seems... so... impossible."

"That a man may be a copy of another? Johannes has known about such a phenomenon for years but has never seen it in the flesh. It is, we are told, not something which happens often." I sat down on the stool before the fire. "We are told, are we not that, Romulus and Remus, the founders of Rome, were twins. We know that sheep may have twins...."

"But they are not like Tom and his brother, not absolutely the same."

"Until we see the two of them together, how are we to know we cannot tell them apart, that they are absolute copies?"

"You say their parents sometimes had a problem."

"They played jokes on them, now and again, Tom said. I think he is quite sad about that now."

"He must be sad that someone to whom he was so close has become so evil, for evil he is, Aumary," said Lydia.

Suddenly she gasped and put her hand to her burgeoning belly. "Oh Aumary... you don't think...don't think there might be *two*?"

209

I laughed. "No, Lydia...I don't."

*****

"Andrew. God keep you. How is the throat?"

Andrew Merriman turned in the action of scanning the castle wall walk for someone, with his hand over his eyes to screen out the sunlight.

It was a beautiful winter's day and the day before the feast of Saint Andrew, his saint, November 29th.

Merriman threw me a look which said, 'You know full well.'

He waved his arms and was answered by a wave from a man on the wall walk.

"So...." He gestured that I step into the guard room.

"No, let us go into my office. I have something to ask you."

"I am *so* sorry Aumary, about...."

"Aye...we lost six folk in all. Some died of their wounds later."

"And poor Walter."

"He died bravely and quickly and if I am able to put my plan into action, I'll see him avenged. I'll see his murderer hang, Andrew."

"And I'll help you in any way I can."

I unlocked the door to my office, entered and made sure the shutters were all across the windows. I lit a candle.

"We must speak quietly. This must remain secret. I mean to set a trap."

Andrew felt for a seat and lowered himself to a stool before the table.

"A trap for the murderers?"

"A lure and a trap."

"How can I help you?"

"I need some seasoned and loyal soldiers from the castle garrison...."

"Men like Castleman and Hardcastle. Pearson?"

"Aye and Bunce and young Jem perhaps. He's young but quick witted."

"Men you can trust, who know you?"

"I need perhaps, fifteen. Can you find them for me? I cannot be seen going about recruiting them. It would ruin my plan. It must be done quietly."

"Oh no! Not again. Must I go without food once more in order that you appear not to be involved?"

"Ah no, my friend. If I catch these villains, you may feast at Durley all you want. I promise."

"Consider it done."

I fished in my purse.

"Here."

Andrew extended his arm and flattened his palm.

"What's this?"

I leaned forward and pushed his hand towards the light. "It's a piece of Saxon gold."

Andrew drew it up to his eyes.

"Oh, it's magnificent."

"Now and again we turn up a small piece from the field at the back of the threshing barn at home. We think this is where the man we buried in our churchyard, our Saxon Prince as we call him, had his manor."

"I remember when you found his body by the river. And I remember the beautiful things you told me he was buried with."

"Aye, his treasure."

"Which the King now has."

"Yes, he has. When we find some bits we keep them for a while until we have enough to send to him, for all treasure trove belongs to John."

"This looks like the end of a belt."

"And this is the buckle."

I put into his hand a large piece of gold.

The buckle was a D shape and its surface was chased with patterns. The middle of the curve of the D was made as the likeness of a dog's head and its tongue was the prong.

"Oh, that is a lovely thing."

"Guard it well."

"I shall." Andrew looked up quickly. "I...I am to have it?"

"For a while. You found it, you understand, somewhere in the forest. "

"I did?"

"You found it at the back of the cottage which Tom's father had in the glade behind the charcoal burners' works."

"I did."

"He had a small workshop there for his tasks. At the back of the cott. That's where you found it."

"Yes, indeed it was," said Andrew smiling and nodding.

"I want you to tell a few folk. Not many you understand. Today. Show them this."

"And later today you want those fifteen castle men out in the forest?"

"In twos and threes. I'll not have them noticed leaving en masse."

"I think we can manage that. We have several horses out at the fields around the grange at Manton, don't we? They can be taken from there and ridden into Savernake."

"Aye we do. The rest can go from here on some pretext. So, who is to know?"

And so I told him.

His face turned pasty.

"No."

"Aye."

"This I must see."

"Come if you wish. Be prepared for a fight."

"You are certain, Aumary? De Neville will have my head if you are wrong."

"He'll have mine too, Andrew."

*****

I rode home and collected together some of the men of my village.

212

They stood in the courtyard, quiet and watchful.

Hal stood on the lower steps of the manor stair and bellowed.

"Listen to the Lord Belvoir. He has a request of you all."

I nodded to him. I was standing on the third step of the manor stair looking down at them.

"If my plan goes aright, we *shall* have justice and revenge for the death of our friends."

There was a general muttering and nodding of heads.

"I am asking for volunteers to come into the forest with me. This will not be an easy task. I will coerce no man."

Men shifted their feet.

"My Lord Belvoir," said Richard Marshall. "Whatever you ask of us, we shall do."

"There may be fighting, though I have arranged that there be fifteen soldiers from the garrison at the castle to stand alongside us. Durley village may not have to raise a weapon. The sight of the professional soldiers may engage our wolfsheads and inflame their blood..."

"We'll fight too sir, if we have to," said Tostig. "We'll avenge our Durley dead."

I smiled. "I will have no man with me who does not wish to risk life and limb alongside me."

There was absolute silence.

I looked round the courtyard. Out of the corner of my eye I saw Lydia, standing in the doorway, staring out over the sea of heads. She caught my eye and smiled.

"Some of us may be injured or God forbid, killed. Therefore I will take only volunteers."

No man moved.

"We may not need to fight. I hope to subdue these wolfsheads and bring them to justice. That is my fervent hope, but if not...."

The group moved forward as one man.

Johnathan Reeve was suddenly their spokesman.

"I have been voted reeve of this village, sir. I speak for us all. We are *all* agreed. Lead us and we shall follow you. No matter how long we wait, we shall see these beasts spitted on swords, crushed under clubs or felled by our quarterstaffs."

"I hope we shall see them dangle at the end of a rope, Johnnie."

He nodded. "If that is as God wills it, sir."

I looked over them all.

My grooms. Some of my foresters. My new reeve. My tied workers. My youngest wheelwright and my farrier. And at the back of the crowd, Thomas Potter, tenant of my manor with his bandaged head.

I looked up over the gatehouse and scanned the trees visible over the guest rooms on the southern wall.

"The sun is now over the trees to the south. It is not quite midday. We go to the charcoal burners' glade at Le Broyle. Thomas Potter will lead the way. Those who have beasts will ride. Some may carry others on their stirrups or ride pillion. Horses are freely available from the stables for those who can ride them. We wait...all night if we must. And the next day, though I suspect that we will not wait until the first day of December, the feast of St. Lucius, for our villains have other plans for that day."

People began to organise themselves into their tithings.

"Take food and water for we do not know how long we wait. But wait we shall. Each mounted man must carry an axe or a scythe and a spade for we shall dig and dig deeper and more thoroughly than our enemies have done."

Men looked surprised, did not question me but nodded and melted away to prepare themselves and to gather their weapons. Henry had once again opened the manor armoury.

"And we shall have our revenge."

Chapter Twelve

We moved out in threes and fours, strung out along the road to Hungerford and went by the back ways through the forest where we could. Just before Stype, a tiny abandoned hamlet in the middle of the trees we came across Andrew and his men.

From there it was a short distance to the charcoal burners' glade.

Here my men rested and we began to file into the smaller glade behind the ruins of the charcoal men's cottages destroyed by the raiders.

Here stood the cott which once belonged to Tom's father. It was a desolate place; the thatch was ruinous, the daub walls were holed but I could see that at one time this could have been a decent dwelling for a man alone or a man and his young son. A small spring arose not a few feet from the cottage, so the place was well served with water.

I measured a hundred paces from the place and, taking several men with spades, circled the glade, stopping now and again. I asked them to dig.

"Dig down five feet where you can," I said and although they looked at me strangely, no man asked why.

"Hide the soil as well as you can. We shall backfill later," I said.

Taking another group with me I asked them to cut and pick up twigs and branches, scythe dead grasses, ferns and bracken from the area though no man should do too much in one place for this work must remain secret and invisible.

This, as you imagine, took some time. All the while, our soldiers guarded us and circled the glade.

Finally Hal, Andrew and I went to the back of the cottage and dug a pit. Firstly the Belvoir sword, part of the regalia of the Warden of the Forest, with its beautifully chased scabbard and silver worked hilt, was laid reverently in the earth, wrapped in a deer hide.

We laid another Saxon buckle and belt end, covered in cloth, into the pit and

215

over it scattered coins. Then we carefully filled in the pit and tamped down the soil as best we could. We hoped that our thieves would not notice in their haste and their eagerness to recover treasure, that the soil had been disturbed recently. Over this we laid an old and rather decomposed barrel which we'd found at the side of the cott. We hoped this would complete the deception and fool our malefactors into thinking it had lain here some time. The barrel's bottom was quite rotten and hundreds of woodlice clung to it. This would give our trickery some realism.

I then went about the groups and asked men to cover the pits they had made with the branches, bracken, cut grasses, ferns and twigs.

Our villains would not escape, for if they *did* try to run, they would, we hoped, fall into the pits. It could not be helped that a mounted man might stumble and injure his horse in one of these holes. I fervently hoped not, but I couldn't have any escapees. Every man was to be apprehended.

Then we sat, concealed on the forest floor, and ate and drank our fill.

Hal, Andrew and I sat in the cottage with Tom. If we spoke at all, it was in whispers. All had had strict instructions to speak quietly and not allow noise to penetrate too far into the forest. I knew that our raiders would approach from the west and so our horses were hobbled at the eastern side of the charcoal burners' glade, well out of the way of the ears and eyes of our enemies.

Then we waited.

We waited and it grew dark. I did not think that our raiders would make a foray into the trees at night and so we wrapped ourselves in our cloaks and slept fitfully until dawn.

*****

Sometime after Terce, the morning prayer, the men I'd left at the main road came running into the glade.

Our band of raiders had left the main road and were travelling the charcoal burners' lane. They were however, said the man, dawdling and taking their ease.

216

They were in no hurry to reach their destination. It was easy for the watchmen running on foot to keep ahead of them and be here with us in reasonable time.

I deployed the men around the glade. They loosened their swords and knives and hefted their clubs, though I begged them that they were to be used only in self-defence.

I knew this was going to be a difficult thing to monitor, for the Durley men had lost friends and family, had been injured themselves or had had others close to them injured. They would want revenge. The revenge I sought was of the kind which kept within the law and ended on the gallows and I was by no means sure I could achieve my goal that day. I sent up a prayer to Heaven that no further man of Durley or castle be injured or maimed by this gang.

Finally I circled the glade imploring my men to wait for my signal to move and that they must remain silent and still. They all nodded their understanding.

Then I ducked into the small house and covered myself with old thatch so that a cursory glance into the dark interior might not reveal my presence.

Absolute silence was necessary and in that silence we heard the approaching group's laughter. We heard the thud of their hooves on the forest floor, their horse tack jingling. Not far from the glade, these men dismounted and came by the path to the cottage, leaving their mounts a little further off.

Again voices called to each other, giving each other instruction no doubt, but we could not hear clearly what was being said.

We waited.

The group came on; laughing, talking; one man was even whistling a tune. I recognised it as one I'd heard whistled at the castle many times. One man coughed with a terrible rattle.

I could not see of course, hidden as I was, but Andrew, hiding in a yew, one of the few trees which kept their leaves this season, a few feet to the perimeter of the glade, saw all and told me afterwards. Over the shoulder of two men, were laid leaf shaped spades, he said.

A discussion followed and the two men walked to the back of the house.

I heard the barrel being moved. I heard behind me kicking in the timbers at

217

the back of the house as they made more room for their labours. Leaning against the back wall of the house perched a small workplace with a pent roof. Much of it had fallen in, for it was merely made of planks of wood laid on the earth. The marauders laughed at their destructive work.

Then I heard the spade strike the ground. And another. They were digging close but not close enough. Ah well...let them dig. They would expend their energies before they found the 'hoard'.

The other men were milling about in the centre of the glade but at the sound of digging, the activity became too much for them.

Six, I'm told, left the front of the house and wended their way to the back. I thought their curiosity had got the better of them. Only two then stood in the glade.

Still my men remained hidden in silence.

I heard one of their horses neigh. I hoped that Hal and Cedric had managed to cut the saddle straps of the waiting beasts. This was a trick I'd learned from my young groom Nod who had saved the day, back in January, by such an action.

If our felons managed to make it to their horses, they would have to ride without saddles to make their escape.

The two men, said Andrew later, who were left in the glade started to become a little agitated.

They cried out to their fellows, to hasten, get a move on, dig faster, I supposed. We did not understand their words.

Then we heard a cry from the back of the cottage. They had struck gold.

All their voices were raised at once.

The two men left in the glade, unable to resist, ran to the back of the house. Frantic digging ensued.

Laughter, delighted screeching and then silence as, no doubt, the men lifted the hoard from its hiding place.

Then there was much more screeching and laughing. I heard what sounded like scrabbling with hands as other men tried to dig the ground to see if there was more.

Over all this, one deep voice, the man in control of it all, kept his calm.

Now all the men were at the back of the cott. Hal came zigzagging across the glade and ducked into the house place.

"All done" he whispered.

"How many?"

Hal lifted his hands and put up all eight fingers and two thumbs and then one more.

"Eleven?"

He nodded.

"Tom's brother?"

He nodded again. "I think so. Humble is amongst the horses."

Whilst the noise at the back of the house continued, I rustled my way out of the thatch and at a crouch made for what was left of the door.

Listening carefully, it seemed that an argument was going on.

Two men, voices raised were shouting at each other.

The deep voiced man bellowed for silence and silence was what he achieved. Quietly he explained what he wanted.

I put my fingers to my lips and blew a piercing whistle, hoping that Bayard would not think I wanted him, slip his tied reins and come thundering from his eastern hiding place into the glade. He didn't.

My men and the castle soldiers reared up from their concealment and made for the glade.

Some stood in a semi circle at the front, others closed in the sides. Our soldiers made an inner ring and advanced on the gang.

There was a deal of scurrying behind the house as the gang realised that they'd been spotted.

There was a collective metallic scraping of swords drawn from scabbards.

"I am the Lord Aumary Belvoir, constable of this county. Put up your weapons, or you will not leave this glade alive." I shouted. I pulled up my maille coif onto my head.

I strode to the back of the cottage. I had not expected immediate violence.

219

I expected them to feign surprise. To ask what I was doing there; to pretend innocence; to talk their way out of the situation.

Eleven men, all armoured in maille, some facing me, others with their backs to their comrades crouched ready to spring.

"I repeat, surrender. You are surrounded...."

I had not finished what I was going to say when one man rushed me; I took his blade on my own and pushed it aside.

As if by a signal, the other men engaged the castle soldiers and hand to hand fighting ensued.

A gap opened up as one castle man went down with a vicious blow to the knee. He would not walk well again on his own two legs and three of the gang ran past and out to the glade.

I saw Rob Hartshorn engage one of them with his sturdy quarterstaff and land a searing blow to the man's head but, helmed as he was, it merely dented it and he staggered and ran on. Two further raiders had had the time to don their helmets to fight. Others drew up the mailed coifs of their hauberks.

Bunce fired an arrow to stop one garrison soldier being skewered and it caught one of the gang fair and square in the chest and he fell. Our first casualty.

I bellowed as I followed the men giving and taking blows as we went, "Capture... capture them...."

Two or three Durley men attacked one of the felons and jumped on him to pin him to the ground.

This one's helmet was knocked off. I saw who it was, before a well aimed kick to the head disabled him and he was out cold.

My Durley men closed in.

One or two more arrows were loosed but none found their mark.

Two of the gang ran past the figures of Johnathan and his brother Athel, giving blows and missing but managing to evade the quarterstaffs kicked up in their direction.

They plunged into the undergrowth and made for their horses. The brothers followed.

"Johnnie," I shouted. "ALIVE!"

"Aye, sir," came back the answer from the trees.

Then I was engaged fighting a huge man who wielded a sword as if it were a mere twig.

He growled at me and advanced planting his feet heavily on the earth.

I tried a blow to his middle but it rang on the mail under his surcoat.

Then I had to turn and deal with another man. I wounded him on the arm and he reeled away howling, to come back a moment later and be felled by a blow to the back of his neck, by a powerful thump from Hal's sword pommel.

I heard a horse riding away followed by a neigh, a shout and a scream of anger.

I laughed. At least one man had fallen foul of one of our pits. Now a Durley man would follow and pin him to the ground.

Gradually we managed to contain them all. Even with our superior numbers, it was most difficult to capture the men without injury for they fought like the devils they were purported to be.

They backed together and fought in the glade.

My forehead running with sweat, I threw off my maille coif and ran my arm across my brow.

"Archers!" I yelled and seven of my men who were good with the bow came up.

"Surround them, nock and draw your bows."

My men of Durley fanned out and pointed their arrows at the men.

Although each of the felons was armoured in maille, at this distance, their covering was no protection from an arrow.

Only those who had lost their helms were open to scrutiny. Four still wore their head protection.

One went down on a knee pouring blood. He was a spent force. He bowed his head.

I heard a horse scream as it fell into yet another pit. One more raider had tried to escape and fell foul of our trap, this time his horse with him.

221

I felt sorry for the beast.

"Cedric, Richard… go and see what you can do for the horse."

"Aye sir." They loped off.

"Surrender. Surrender or I will have my men spit you like roasted boar!"

Still it took a few heartbeats before the men in the centre of the glade admitted defeat and ceased to struggle.

The castle soldiers backed off and rested behind my Durley archers.

"Unhelm! Now!"

There was a reluctance even so, but eventually those who still wore them dipped their heads and took off their helms or pulled back their mail coifs. Some still wore the bindings around their faces underneath.

I knew them not. I had seen them though and I knew what they were.

I heard a cough from the trees to my right.

With a shout of, "Bind them and guard them, Hal," and a yell of, "Andrew, to me!" I plunged into the brush after the man I had engaged at the beginning of the fight.

Despite his size he was agile and quick.

He wove through the trees and attempted to get to his horse.

He would have made it had Thomas Potter not stepped out from the ferns and bracken and dealt him a blow to the lower leg with a club.

The man fell heavily and rolled into one of our pits, yelling.

Thomas ran after him.

Suddenly, he disappeared. "Oomph!"

"Thomas you idiot…!" I cried, "You have forgotten where we dug the pits!"

There was some coughing and spluttering as Tom righted himself and fought for breath. Once recovered, he laughed. "Aye sir…I had." He brushed aside the bracken and fern which had fallen on him.

I reached down to pull him out.

His scarred palm reared up to me and I grabbed his arm and he walked up the side of the pit and out.

"Did I get the bastard?"

"You did."

"I broke his ankle I think."

"Aye, I think you might have done."

Andrew was leaning over the man who had remained in the pit. The villain stood now on one foot supporting himself on the earthen side. Andrew ducked and pulled off the felon's helm, none too nicely.

"Well, well," said Andrew as the ugly, grimacing and bearded face came to view.

"It's nice of you to drop in, Master Clijster, I said.

*****

What a job we had to disable our prisoners, bind them and set them on the road to Marlborough.

One dead man was slung across his horse. The badly injured man with the knee wound clung to his horse, leaned on its mane and moaned. Hal had to right him a couple of times.

Two other injured men were allowed to ride for it would only have slowed our progress to have made them walk.

We sent all the injured, including those from the castle back to Durley with Doctor Johannes.

All the way Master Clijster declared that they had done nothing wrong and that the deaths of the potters, charcoal men and glassmen, not to mention the villagers at Durley had nothing to do with his routiers.

In the end I had Hal bind up his mouth with a piece of cloth.

He complained that he had a blockage of the nose and could not breathe. He struggled, gasping and coughing and so I allowed him freedom again. At last he was quiet, sniffing and coughing into his chin.

I had my men take the head bindings from those who were trying to remain anonymous.

Yes. All these men were amongst those left behind at the castle when de Neville had ridden out to Malmesbury to meet the King and when he had left to go to Faringdon. All of them the King's Flemish mercenaries.

I counted them.

There were eight alive.

Thomas' brother was not there.

We made the castle in the later afternoon and I had the mercenaries thrown into the gaol at the base of the keep. Luckily, Andrew had prepared Master Gayle for our arrival and although he was nervous about imprisoning them, he shackled and manacled them all the same. We spread them out in the gaol for these were dangerous men and we dared not allow them to plot and plan together.

Doctor James bound the ankle of the mercenary master and pronounced it badly bruised but not broken. It would mend of its own accord he said.

The other injured man would probably lose his leg. Those with lesser wounds we left.

Before I committed Master Clijster to the gaol, I had him brought into my office.

"You deny that your group of devils is responsible for the deaths of many local men, women and children?"

"I do, sir."

I sat down and steepled my hands. "I grant you, I did not see you amongst the men who attacked my village. I would have known you by virtue of your size."

"I was not there, I tell you."

"I do have descriptions of other men—the glassblowers for example tell me that they saw your men—they can describe them quite well. I'm sure if I got some of the surviving potters up from Cock A Troop Lane, they too would swear that they knew them."

"No, My Lord Belvoir."

"I *saw* your men. The one with the bandaged hand. The spear man who tried to spit a four year old girl with a lance, the man with a scarred nose, oh yes, he was the one who struck down one of my foresters. I saw too, the man who attempted

224

to fire the thatch of Mistress Giffard. And the man who murdered my reeve. I can swear I saw these men. They were with you in that glade."

"It was nothing to do with me."

"Where is William? I think you might know him as William of Salisbury?"

Clijster shrugged "I know no William of Salisbury."

"He goes by another name?"

Cliijster shrugged again. He leaned forward and rested his hand on my table. "When my Lord de Neville…."

"When the King hears of this, whatever the Lord de Neville says will be as a puff of air, Fleming!"

Clijster laughed and his loud bass voice boomed up to the rafters.

"Oh… you are a young and foolish man. You think the King will give… that!" He clicked his fingers.

"We shall see. The King charged me with finding the group of murdering devils who were terrorising the forest. I have found them. You may be his men, he may rely on you but he will not allow your crimes to go unpunished."

"Then you do not know your King," said Clijster in a menacing tone.

I sat and stared at him.

"Oh take him out of my sight, boys!" I said.

I pulled parchment and a pen to me but found that I could not concentrate. I worried my lower lip with my teeth.

Would John, as Clijster seemed to think, forgive his mercenaries their murderous behaviour? He had been known to discipline his routiers and fine them heavily but none of them, I had heard, had committed so grave a crime as the multiple murder of his innocent subjects. Not until now. He had never hanged them.

As I have said, later on in John's reign he used his routiers increasingly and gave them more power. This caused much discontent, hardship and difficulty and of course inevitably ended with a meeting of barons on a waterlogged island in the middle of a river and with the making of the Great Charter.

At that time I did not know that. Then, on the last day in November 1207,

Susanna M. Newstead

John was not yet the creature he had become in 1216.

Hal came back into the room.

"Tom's brother William i'n't with 'em," he said seriously.

"No, and I want him, Hal."

"Tom went 'ome to Durley with the others."

"Aye, in a way that's good. I don't know what would have happened if he had come face to face with his brother in that glade."

"No." Hal grimaced "A' course... it's something I wanna see...."

"What?"

"The two of 'em stand side by side. I don't suppose I'll ever get the chance to see such a thing in my life. I i'n't never seen it before."

I snorted. "There were ten men at the potters, Hal. William was one of them. He killed Anthony Wright. He was with the routiers when they raided Durley. He killed Walter. I want ten men to hang for those crimes. I want William."

"Clijster?"

I shook my head " He wasn't there, at Durley, Hal. You know that."

"But who's to say he wasn't everywhere else."

I stood. "Come on… let's go and search their things at their lodging. We have a list of some of the chattels stolen from the potters. If we find them amongst their possessions, it's evidence."

The potters had very little, the charcoal burners even less. There was nothing which we could absolutely say was looted from either camp.

"We must ask Master Bartholomew to come up and check. He will know."

"Nah... I don't think it's worth it. There's nothing distinctive enough. The buggers'd say it was theirs and who's to disprove it? T'in't worth it m'lord."

"No, Hal. I suppose you're right."

I threw down a small knife which I'd found in one man's pack.

"Wait!"

I picked it up again and scrutinised it carefully. I closed my eyes. "Yes.... yes...." I pictured that day up on the side of the hill above Stitchcombe. Anthony Wright, Tom's lover, looking up at me. In his belt was this knife, I was sure.

"Hal...this is Anthony Wright's knife. If the man who has it now did not steal it from his dead body then how did he get it?"

"Aye, I think you're right."

It was a slightly larger than normal eating knife with a bone handle. On the hilt was carved the likeness of a hanap, a cup with two handles. In the cup's body was a pattern which seemed to me to be an 'A' and a 'T' entwined."

"We must ask Tom. Tom will know for certain if I'm right and if this is Anthony's"

"And if it is?"

"We have... at least one of them, Hal. Where one goes, the others follow."

*****

Stuffing the knife into my belt, I went in search of Andrew.

"When I get back to Durley, I'll write an account of today's events, Andrew," I said. "I'll make sure to add how helpful you have been."

He made a mock bow. "That is most thoughtful of you, m'lord."

"I left John Brenthall behind to supervise the filling in of the pits we made. I can't have deer or forester's horses blundering into them."

"That too is thoughtful. One horse had to be put out of its misery, Aumary. It broke a leg."

"Aye, I heard and I am most upset about it. If there was any way I might have prevented it... but I simply could not let the felons get away."

"At least it was one of the routiers' beasts and not a castle horse. We shall not have to make a report about its demise to the stable master here."

"No, each mercenary man owns his own horse, tack and weapons."

"Will they be confiscated do you think?"

"I can't say, Andrew. I can't even say that the King will be pleased that I've done exactly what he asked me to do. Master Cliijster seems to think John will not let them come to trial."

227

Andrew's eyebrows rose into his hair.

"Does he? Well, I know that de Neville will not be pleased."

"No, he won't and how much might he prevail upon the King? I have no notion."

I sat down and wearily rested my elbows on my knees.

"Why Andrew? What makes a man turn to such deeds? They are well paid, these mercenaries, well thought of by their monarch and those who use them. Why do they have the need to turn on the populace, killing and maiming?"

"They are vicious men. Violence is just under their skin. It doesn't take much to make them gleefully take up arms and strike."

"But they seem to enjoy killing. The look on that man's face as he took his spear from its saddle and threw it... to kill a four year old girl! I'll never forget it. The smile on his face was such a smile as we might wear when *we* look on someone we love," I added.

Andrew shook his head.

"I saw that smile on their faces when I showed them the gold I'd 'found' in the forest," he said.

"What was their reaction?"

"Great grins and knowing nudges," he replied.

"There were four of them lounging about in the guard room, not doing anything much except drinking and talking in that abominable language of theirs, laughing and joking."

He pointed.

"I sat there and fiddled with the bits of gold you gave me. You know, holding it up to the light and generally letting them see I had something of value. One of them, the one who spoke most English, came up and asked me what it was I had."

"You showed him?"

"I made a small effort to conceal it at first but then yes...I showed them. I told them that they were honourable men...King's men and so I trusted them."

"Pah!"

Andrew laughed. "And eventually I told them that I had found the pieces at the back of the cott in the glade to the rear of the charcoal burners' huts in Savernake. I swear that the man said to his mates something to the effect that they'd been close but not close enough."

"You understand their tongue?"

"Just a few words. The others then crowded round."

"They didn't threaten you?"

Andrew made a moue, "They weren't what you call friendly but, I am master of the garrison and can call on soldiers should I need help and they no doubt knew I would. They couldn't afford to be too unpleasant to me."

"Hah!"

"Here in the castle they must be seen to be under control. I told them that I'd probably not had everything that was hidden there and they were welcome to go and look. One man tried to keep hold of the buckle and belt end but I stood up to him and it was handed back. It was coin they were interested in mostly and I told them that there was probably more coin hidden there."

"Well, done."

"I made sure I was in company the rest of the day and was off into the forest with my men as soon as I could."

"I am sorry about John Pleasant. They tell me his knee will not support him. He'll go on a crutch for the rest of his life."

Andrew looked down at his hands. "Aye. I'll try to make sure he is well looked after—get him the King's stipend if I can."

"Johannes is looking to him at Durley. I'll get him home and get the doctor to do what he can. I'll tell Johannes I will pay any fee, though I doubt he'll take it."

"I will do what I can."

"So now we search for Thomas' brother. What I don't understand is, he is not a Fleming. Not a routier. How did he become entangled with them?"

"I've never seen him about the castle."

"No, he couldn't afford to be, could he, with Thomas so well known after the fire trial?"

"But he *is* a soldier you tell me?"

"That's right, but Thomas doesn't know where he has been, with whom he has served."

"He's a Wiltshire man, perhaps he's an Earl Salisbury fellow?"

"John's half-brother?"

"Aye, William Longspee."

"William was Sheriff here until 1203, was he not?"

"When we got Geoffrey de Neville."

"You came in...?"

"I came in June 1203. As you know we have a small garrison here and a guard for the royal treasury. In times of peace that's all we need. It's supplemented by others as is needful."

"And when the King's in residence."

"That too but he rarely stays long."

"Tom says his brother went off to Winchester in 1199."

"The Earl of Southamptonshire maybe?"

"But John has only just appointed Saer de Quincy to that county so...."

"Aye. He has powerful relations and as you know he was in Normandy where he surrendered a castle to the French."

"Do we think this is where he's been, this William of Salisbury?"

Andrew shrugged. "It makes my head ache just thinking of it all. All the to-ing and fro-ing. I'm a Wiltshire lad, the second son of a minor knight of Calne. I don't aspire to rise any further than I have."

I slapped him on the shoulder.

"Ah Andrew. God grant you your wish." I shook my black curls, "Some of us have no choice in the matter!"

Andrew put his feet up on the table and leaned back on the stool, resting his back on the wall.

"I like my life here in Marlborough. I like my little castle. I like you in charge of it."

I chuckled. "You are a good friend, a valuable soldier and a stalwart supporter. May God keep you always under his hand."

I heard him laughing as I went to collect Bayard from the stable and ride home.

*****

Hal and I rode for home before it grew too dark.

The first thing I did was ask after our wounded.

Tostig had taken a knife scratch to the arm and wore a bandage. He grinned at me as I inquired after his health.

"Fine as a bird on a branch, sir."

"And the others?"

"Rob is more upset about the loss of his quarterstaff than about the wound to his thigh. Cleaved it straight in half...."

"His thigh...?"

"His staff."

"Ah."

I chuckled as I made my way to the hall where the wounded had been laid. Johannes and Janet Peddler were busy and Lydia was supervising the doling out of soup and bread. I thought she looked very weary and I told her so.

"I will go and lie down in a moment, Aumary. There has been much to do."

I touched her shoulder gently, "Let others do the work Lydia. Go and rest."

"I am the lady of this place and it is my responsibility to see our people tended, comfortable and fed."

I smiled. "I am here now. I'll take over."

She smiled back and pushed a wave of her black hair back into her veil.

"You too are weary," she said.

I smiled and caught sight of Thomas sitting on his pallet talking to Annot Pierson who was rebinding the hand wound of one of the garrison soldiers.

Tom rose when he saw me walking towards him and Annot turned round quickly and curtsied. I saw that our little orphan Algar, was lying on Thomas'

231

bed fast asleep.

"Thomas, might I have a word with you?"

"Aye, sir."

I drew him away to a quiet corner.

I took the knife taken from the routier, from my belt and turned the hilt to him.

"Have you ever seen this before?"

His eyes fixed hungrily on the knife and they glistened with tears.

"Aye...aye I have, sir."

"Tell me."

He took it and turned it over in his hands.

"It is...was Anthony's. I gave it to him. Where did you get it, m'lord?"

"It was in the possession of one of the devils we took to the castle. It was in his pack. I searched for items which may have been looted and there it was."

"It was Anthony's. The cutler from the fair in the town last year made it and I carved the cup on the handle."

"And the 'A' for Anthony and 'T' for Thomas."

Thomas passed his hand over his nose and sniffed.

"Aye, m'lord. Daft really as Anthony could not read and did not know until I told him that it was the first letter of each of our names."

I nodded. "I need it Tom. It's evidence but when all this is over, you may keep it. If the King does not see fit to sell it."

Tom chuckled low and quietly. "Aye...methinks he would sell his mother if she were still alive, if he thought it would bring him coin." Immediately he was contrite. "Oh, my lord, I... I didn't mean to be...."

"No, Tom," I chuckled. "You are probably right. He makes money where he can. All monarchs are in need of money and John is no exception."

"You are his friend, sir... I should not have said...."

"Yes, Tom. I am his friend but that does not make me blind to his failings."

"And these devils he employs, sir. They want nothing but riches it seems."

"Many of them are greedy, violent men with little honour."

"They were lured by the promise of gold at the back of my father's little place."

"I think they came across the charcoal men's huts, Tom and decided to try their luck there first."

Tom's face grew grave and puzzled at the same time. "But sir... there was nothing at my father's house until you put it there."

I leaned on the wall.

"Tom, at each place they have visited, they have been digging. They dug behind a workshop of some kind at each site. No doubt they would have tried it at the glass worker's place but they knew they were outnumbered and foiled and so they fled. Someone has told them that there is treasure to be had at the back of a workshop in the forest."

"You think there is something of value buried at the back of Da's cott? No sir, it can't be. If there was he would have told me."

"I don't know."

"What might my father have that was of such value, sir? He was a simple man of very modest means. If my brother knew, he would have led the routiers straight to Da's cottage."

"I do not think he was with them on every foray into the forest. It's my belief he came and went. I don't know what connection he has to the mercenaries. They deny knowing him but he was the tenth man, of that there is no doubt. Master Clijster, the mercenary master was not with them on every occasion either. For example he was not part of the group who attacked us here at Durley. His size would have given him away to us."

I scratched my head. "Master Bartholomew told me that one man was as huge as a house. I thought it the simple exaggeration of a working man in awe of a mounted fighting man."

"Ah, I see, sir."

"These routiers have been to and fro in the forest looking for workshops - buildings in which men manufacture things. They found some workplaces. They did not find treasure."

"Until today, sir," he grinned.

233

"Aye, until today."

"So...." Tom scratched his scarred and bruised head. "So, who told them that treasure was to be found at this so-called workplace?"

I shrugged "I am sorry to say it, I think it might have been your brother...."

"No sir, he...."

"But he was purposefully vague. 'A workshop behind a dwelling place.' "

"Why would he say it?"

"Many hands are needed to dig efficiently and distract the occupants. He didn't want to do it by himself. He probably asked for help in return for a share of the treasure. But he didn't want them to know exactly where in case they dug without him."

"But how did he learn of it? I have never heard of any treasure in this locality, sir."

"Neither have I and I was born here. I suppose, someone had told him and although he...."

"Not me sir. I haven't seen him, not for years...."

"No, not you."

"Then who sir?"

Suddenly Tom's face creased in agony.

"Oh no! No sir. Oh no...," he said, as realisation dawned.

Chapter Thirteen

John and his team of foresters returned a while later after backfilling the pits they'd dug.

He carried a cloth bag with him.

"Here, sir. The Belvoir Regalia and the other items you buried."

"Thank you, John. It was a good day's work."

"Can I just say sir, that when we were working, filling in the pits, we felt as if we were being watched."

"Watched…? Our escaped raider, John?"

"I sent a few men out but we could find nothing. We had no glimpse of anyone. It was just a feeling on the backs of our necks."

"Aye... I know that uncomfortable feeling."

"Humble was missing of course."

"Ah, yes. He made his escape on the stolen horse. Without a saddle."

John ducked out of the office door. "And then there's this, sir."

"Hmm?"

He gestured to a loosely wrapped bundle, which was stained and covered in soil and debris, sitting on the screens passage floor.

"I don't want to bring it into your office - it's a mite dirty. But you should see it, sir."

I left my table and came out into the passage.

"Light, John... open the door." I reached for one of the candles lit in the evening and held it over the bundle.

The afternoon was fading but there was still some light to see by.

John stooped and opened out the folds.

"It was buried a little way in, at the digging at the back of Tom's father's cottage. Peter was about to make sure nothing had been left in the hole when he spotted this piece of old cloth poking up. He wondered if you had buried more than was recovered by the routiers and so pulled it."

"How far down was it?"

"The edge of the rags, only a foot but the rest a little more. Been disturbed I'd say by animals and the digging of the foreign mercenaries."

I bent my head. I was looking at a collection of bones.

I hunkered down and looked closely, frowning.

"A jumble of bones?"

"Not deer."

"No John, not deer."

I stood. "Put them in the stable and I'll look at them in better light tomorrow. No! Wait."

I poked my head into the hall. "Johannes, might you come here a moment."

The doctor had finished his work and was taking ale with a few of the lads.

He put down his pot and sauntered over to me.

"What is it, Sir Aumary?"

I gestured to our pathetic little bundle.

"What do you make of this? Recovered from the back of Tom's father's cottage."

Johannes took the candle from my hand and also hunkered down.

"Buried... some time ago. All flesh is gone but the bones are still quite intact."

"But jumbled."

"Ah well, they are easy to reconstruct."

I chuckled. "For *you* perhaps," I said, remembering the time we had found the Saxon prince at the back of the manor and Johannes had managed to put his bones back together again in the right order.

The doctor clattered around in the pile of bones and came up with the skull.

"Not a human then?"

"No." He held the grinning and somewhat toothless cranium to the light.

"It's a large dog, Sir Aumary," he said.

*****

I went to bed that night furious with myself that I had not managed to secure Tom's brother William, the murderer of Cille of Hereford, Walter Reeve and Anthony Wright.

Nor had I any idea how I might bring him to justice.

I tossed and turned in my bed and heard Lydia sighing as I woke her several times. In the end I rose, wrapped myself in a blanket, banked up the fire and sat staring at the flames. At an hour near dawn, I fell asleep and snored, my chin on my chest.

I awoke with a start.

"Dada, you're snoring," said Hawise, standing in front of me holding out a beaker of warmed ale.

I took it and thanked her.

"If you do not hurry, you will be late for church."

"Ah yes... it's Sunday isn't it?"

"Will you wear your new shirt? The one I made for you."

I smiled. "I will. Ask your mother to get it for me."

"I'll get it!" she shouted and ran to the chest where my clothes were stored.

I washed, brushed my teeth with salt and a willow wand, and dressed in new clean clothes, I went to church.

Standing there in the cold, I thought back to how all this had begun. Tom, coming in the door of the church late and Cille of Hereford screeching at the lychgate. My river project had been forgotten in all the fuss. I must take it up again.

I was tired. My mind yet again would not stay on the mass. I kept thinking of poor Walter and his terrible death; of Cille lying in our churchyard, unknown and unmourned and of all those others who died at the hands of the mercenaries.

I prayed fervently that I might bring them to justice and eventually catch William of Salisbury.

I stood at the church door as my manor people filed past me and watched as a messenger on a sprightly horse trotted down the lane and into the manor courtyard.

It had begun. I had been summoned to the castle.

*****

De Neville stood behind the table, his arms folded over his chest. John paced back and forth by the window.

He stopped and, smiling at me quickly, with no warmth in the smile, he took a deep breath.

"My Lord Belvoir, tell us again and this time in detail, why you have these men, our loyal soldiers, locked up in our castle gaol."

"Your grace, not to beat about the bush, these *are* the men who have been terrorising the forest. They are guilty of the deaths of dozens of hard working charcoal makers, potters, glassmakers and soldiers...."

"They are guilty of nothing more than the greedy searching for gold after being led to...."

"Hush, Hugh!" shouted John and sat down.

"I have sworn statements telling of men resembling the Flemings attacking the potters and the glassmen; their horses, accoutrements and how they seemed."

"Absolute recognition?"

"Of one or two of them."

"One... or... two...?"

"An item stolen from one of the dead potters, this knife." I laid it on the table, "was found amongst the possessions of one of the soldiers named Gerhardt Weylandt. Their particular language has been recognised as being spoken by them when at their killing in the forest by Sir Andrew Merriman and others. I too can testify that I heard them speaking as they attacked my man at arms, Doctor Johannes and myself when we returned home one day in the fog."

John's nostrils flared.

"In the fog?"

"Yes, my lord King. I recognised, as have others, their beasts in the castle stables."

I plunged on despite John's angry face.

"They raided my village and I recognised them and the stolen horse belonging to my deerman being used by one of them. They killed some of my village folk. I have made inquiries my lord; these men have been missing from the castle at every instance these crimes were being perpetrated."

"My Lord de Neville was not with them at this time."

I saw Hugh de Neville stand up straighter. "My liege, I protest!"

John skewed in his chair. "Only Hugh, that you were not here at Marlborough and had not control of them at that time," said John. "You left them here and rode out."

"I left some of them because I felt that a few should stay here to be a presence in the castle... a steadying force since the countryside was in turmoil...."

"At their very hands, my Lord Belvoir tells me," chuckled John.

"Sire, the glassmen, who are intelligent and observant men, tell me that their attackers targeted the soldiers left for their protection and called them by name, thereby disarming them. They knew them. No doubt, were billeted with them here at the castle of a night. Friends and acquaintances do not call you by name and then make for you and spit you on their swords."

"They attacked you as you called for their cooperation in the forest?"

"They did, sire. I have no doubt they will tell you that they were taken by surprise. I made them aware of who I was and asked them to surrender. They would not."

"I have no doubt they knew who you were, Belvoir," said de Neville, "but you had no right...."

"Be quiet, Hugh. I'm thinking," said John testily.

He drummed his fingers on the board.

"They killed some of your men?"

"They attempted to bargain for my reeve's life sire and then killed him, in front of my very eyes and those of the people of my village. They fired our property and attempted to abduct our women and children. They attacked us in the forest and injured some castle guards and some of my foresters whom I had taken with me to help in apprehending them."

"Self-defence," muttered de Neville.

"Self-defence, sir... against a four year old girl who would have been spitted through by a lance had Hal of Potterne not recovered her?" I said through clenched teeth. "This was purely revenge. I was becoming a nuisance. They wanted to frighten us."

I saw John wince.

"One of them is responsible for the murder of Cille of Hereford, a guest at my property. He struck my priest Crispin Darrell and stole a silver candlestick from our church."

"Have you recovered it?"

"No sire, nor have I the felon who committed this particular crime locked up with the others. It's merely a matter of time."

I did not want to elaborate that this man was the absolute image of Tom Potter and an Englishman.

I passed my hand over my forehead.

"Sit, Belvoir," rapped out John as if I were a dog. "You look weary unto death."

"I am my lord, I have not slept for three nights."

As requested I pulled up a stool.

"You knew, you said, that they were searching for some treasure about which they had been told, treasure which lay in the forest?"

"Yes, my liege. No doubt it's a fable."

"You have never heard of this treasure?"

"No, sire."

"Hmmm."

I could see my King weighing up the possibility of it existing and of sending out search parties to look for it himself .

"It is a mere fiction put about by idle storytellers no doubt, as much as the stories of ghosts in the forest are also the product of over-imaginative, drunken or febrile minds."

"Hmmm."

"In order to trap them and make sure I had the right men, I buried some coin and other things"—I leaned sideways and out of my purse fetched the gold belt end and the buckle which I had found at Durley and laid it on the table top—"in a pit behind the house and waited for them to come and retrieve it."

John examined the pieces I'd given him.

"Ah... more treasure from Durley?"

"Yes, my lord. We turn it up now and again as you know."

I saw de Neville lean over and screw up his eyes to catch a glimpse of it. It went quickly into the royal purse.

"Why?"

"The men who had perpetrated these crimes were looking for something, as I've said. Something they'd been told lay in the forest at a certain place...."

"You say... behind a workplace."

"A forge, a kiln, a pottery.... They tried them all."

"So finally, you gave them what they looked for."

"They took the bait, my lord."

I saw de Neville retreat a foot or so towards the wall.

John heard him move and looked over his shoulder.

"What say you now, my Lord de Neville? Shall we have your Fleming in here and ask him a few questions?"

Ah, so the man was now de Neville's and not his monarch's faithful soldier.

"By all means, sire. I'm sure he can explain."

There was a silence as no one moved. John did not give his permission. Again he drummed his fingers on the table.

"We doubt he will confess."

"No, my lord King," I answered.

"I doubt we can get him to swear on the Bible," said John, an absent look on his handsome face. "They are a Godless lot. They'd lie as soon as spit."

He scratched his beard. "God I need a bath."

He looked up. "*You* will swear Belvoir, on the Bible, that all this is as you say?"

"I will, Your Grace," I said, bowing my head.

John stood. I raised myself wearily.

"Petit!" shouted John.

Footsteps came running and the door opened a crack. "Yes messire."

"Prepare me a bath."

*****

Petit told me later that John sat soaking in his bath and that he had the felon Clijster brought before him in irons.

The conversation was amicable and then turned to the accusations I'd made.

Petit, standing in the dark of the royal chamber, was asked to find a scribe to write down what the Fleming said.

Cliijster naturally denied it all. Everything except the trip into the forest after gold.

This he said, he'd been told by a man of the Savernake, someone who would know about these things. It was natural. Any man would try to recover such treasure. No mention of Andrew and his lure. No mention of resisting the constable of the county and his men.

John listened patiently, lifted himself from his bath. The steam was still rising

Two soldiers guarded him as he wrapped himself in his dressing gown and was seated.

"Ahhhh, but," said John languidly, "had you found treasure, it would naturally have belonged to me. Of course you would have given it up to me wouldn't you?"

The Fleming's puzzled expression made John laugh to the ceiling, Petit told me.

Quick as a stoat for a rabbit John grabbed the huge mercenary and thrust his head into the hot water.

The soldiers took over and John stood back and laughed.

Cliijster was dragged up coughing and spluttering, beard dripping to the floor.

"Now we shall have the truth."

The mercenary was dunked again. A little longer this time.

Petit chuckled as he related it to me. "Oh my Lord Aumary, it was all I could do not to laugh out loud. This great huge man bound by the feet and hands, spluttering and dripping and my Lord John hopping about semi-naked shouting, "Torture is illegal in this country, did you know, Fleming? But then you are not an Englishman. We can do what we like with you."

Yes, I know Paul. It was one of the things that was levelled against John before the Great Charter was sealed. That he tortured folk. I'm sure he was capable of it but whether he did or not... I don't know. I am sure that there were times when it was necessary. I felt no revulsion when Petit told me John had tormented the Fleming. But dunking him in hot water was a mild thing to do... upon consideration of what the mercenaries had done to others.

Petit shook his head.

"Five dunkings it took and more hot water, before the beast confessed."

"Confessed, Petit? To everything?"

"Almost. But it was enough for John."

"What did he say?"

"That he knew his men had been out in the countryside burning, raping and killing but was powerless to hold them back. He said that William of Salisbury had told them that treasure was concealed somewhere and they went in search of it. This was the man you failed to arrest wasn't it, sir?"

"Aye, Petit, it was. De Neville?"

"Red faced rather."

"Hmmm. What will happen?"

"It has happened, my Lord."

"Oh?"

"The lesser Flemings were hanged. Clijster was fined and sent packing with a brand to his cheek."

"He's gone?"

"He was accompanied from the castle, sir. No horse and nothing but the clothes in which he stood. Soldiers took him to the London Road and set him on his way. If he goes through the forest... well... I wouldn't like to give odds on his survival. Folk know him, he's unmistakable. I doubt he'll get to London."

I rubbed my aching forehead. "I doubt he'll get out of the county. I hope I don't find his body in my forest, Petit."

He smiled. "Ah no, sir. I doubt you'll find it. Find it anywhere."

*****

So my villagers and forest folk were revenged.

But not entirely.

I still had to find William of Salisbury.

It was the rouncey, Humble, we found first, or rather she found us.

Things had returned to normal and everyone was out about their work or such work as they could do in December. It was mild and grey that month, with no frost and so we were able to go about without hindrance, unlike that terrible winter of 1204 and 1205.

Whatever maintenance could be done was carried out by my foresters. Animals which had not been slaughtered, salted and pickled were cared for. Dung from the barns had been carefully stockpiled to be mixed with marl and spread upon our fields, though the villagers never had enough to fertilise more than the closest strips.

I stood by the back of the church and looked up at the field as my folk toiled in their plots. It would soon be Christmastide and we could look forward to a time of merriment and rest for twelve days.

Thomas came striding up the road.

"Ah, Tom. Have you been to Cock A Troop Lane?"

"No, m'lord. I doubt I shall ever go there again." He fingered the white and red scar which disfigured his handsome face.

"That's a shame."

He smiled and wrapped his brown cloak around his body. "Some things, sir, you cannot forget."

"Nor forgive Tom? Even though it was a mistake?"

"I...." But he didn't have time to answer me, for along the road behind him came a trotting horse. A little thinner than when we'd last seen her, scratched and scruffy in appearance.

"That's Humble," I said and shouted for Nod who looked to our rounceys and lesser beasts.

Nod was at that moment sweeping the church as a penance. He had been set this task by Crispin who had caught him blaspheming and swearing. He had confessed the sin to the priest, Nod told me and reluctantly, on Crispin's part, the task had been given as a punishment.

Nod came running out of the south door and round the west end.

"Yessir."

"Humble, Nod. Can you catch her?"

Nod's eyes widened. "Where the Hel... hempen halter has she been?" he yelled.

"I don't know but she's in a bad way. Take her down to the stable, lad and see what you and Master Richard can do."

The horse snorted and threw her head about, her tangled mane spraying about her like a shower of water.

Nod and Tom managed to grasp hold of her and they walked back to the courtyard together.

I stood for a while staring into the trees at the Ramsbury road end of the village.

I had a bad feeling welling up inside me.

I stayed there a while just staring and then walked back to the hall.

It was Sunday. The courtyard was deserted. Richard and Nod, no doubt, were seeing to Humble. Some other grooms were sleeping off their dinner. Hubert our farrier was out at one of our farms, where some of his family lived. Cedric had gone to Marlborough and Bill was out on the downs exercising an injured horse.

Our wheelwrights were visiting friends for dinner in the centre of the village. Wyot was asleep in his cell by the gate. There were no guests in the south rooms. John, Peter and Agnes were at home; Henry and Annot at his mother's in her house in the village. Alfred Woodsmith was visiting his mother. Hal was...I did not know where but guessed he was with the Widow Giffard and her newly brewed ale.

Lydia and Hawise were in the solar. Crispin was at home.

I heard Matthew Cook singing in the kitchen and then the door slammed.

It was very quiet.

Then I heard a scuffle from somewhere to my right. I paid no heed and kept walking towards the manor steps.

It came again. I turned and looked.

No doors were open.

I listened.

There it was again. A scuffle and a clinking. The sound of someone moving, and none too gently, something which had a metallic ringing sound.

I thought, 'Perhaps Hubert has returned, and is in his forge moving about.'

I came to his door and tried it. He locked it rarely, only when he went out of the village and today it was locked.

"Hubert!" I cried. "James."

James was Hubert's apprentice, the son of a villager.

There was no answer nor sound.

I moved along the row and approached Tom's pottery.

I listened again.

There came the noise. This time it was a rustling and snapping as if someone were shaking out a blanket or a cloth of some kind.

I reached out for the door handle.

"Wait, sir...," said a voice to my left hand side. "I'll open it... I locked it when

I went out."

I turned. There was Tom. He'd come out of the privy, I guessed.

The noise had ceased.

I put my finger to my lips and bade him be quiet. Tom looked at me as a frown creased his brow.

"What's the matter, sir?" he whispered.

"Intruder."

He waved the key at me.

"I locked it, sir...."

I shook my head and slowly lifted the latch.

It was as I'd thought, open. The lock had been forced.

I pushed Tom behind me and carefully released my knife.

With the flat of my hand I opened the door.

The room was empty.

*****

We moved to the middle and scanned the room. No one.

"Mice, sir," said Tom laughingly.

"No mice make that amount of noise, Tom," I said, "unless they have large nails in their boots."

Tom swung off his cloak and made to go to the brazier he had in his workshop. It could be quite snug in here. He had a small pallet and a trestle, a stool on which to rest, racks of stored pottery. The kiln was out in the field at the back of the wall, a humped clay construction with a small wooden building alongside it.

Tom turned to the peg on the wall where he kept his spare clothes, to hang his cloak.

"Oh...!"

"What?"

"My clothes. I have a tunic and another cloak. It's identical to this one."

"Brown?"

"Aye, brown."

Tom looked worried as he threw up the lid of a chest sitting by the side wall.

"Gone."

"What else is gone?"

"Spare chausses and shirt. All gone."

I laughed "Are you sure you haven't given them to Joan the laundress and it's slipped your memory?"

"No sir. 'Tis not the season for washing. Besides, I don't have that many clothes that I don't know what's missing."

"Anything else missing?"

"I'll have to look, sir. I can't see anything obvious."

"All right. I'll see you at supper. Let me know what you find then. We must get back to our project for the river."

I turned my back and walked towards the hall steps. A moment later, there was a whooshing sound and a yell and something fell from what sounded like the rafters of Tom's work room and there was a scuffle below.

Tom came running out of the pottery and made for the salley port.

"Where're you going?" I yelled.

"Felon... over my roof and away over the wall," he cried.

I followed him for a short while, until I chanced to look back into the workshop.

A humped brown figure was just picking itself up groggily from the floor.

"Tom?"

"Aye, sir?"

"Tom what's happened?"

"My brother, sir... he was hiding in the rafters and jumped me."

Tom staggered into the light.

His clothes were now covered in dust, both from the floor and from the earthenware pottery he made, a rusty grey colour.

"What?" I looked from Tom to the position of the salley port door behind the kitchen.

He clung to the doorpost of his pottery.

"He's wearing my stolen clothes, sir," he said.

*****

I ran out of the salley port telling Tom to go out of the main gate and wake Wyot to set up the hue and cry.

I could see no one running in either direction. Neither towards the river nor the orchard.

Yes... there was the threshing barn.

A man might hide there.

I freed my knife once more and made for the barn at a trot.

It was a large building. I opened the door a crack and light flooded onto the threshing floor. The threshing had been almost finished a few days ago and the whole place was dusty and untidy with bags and rubbish. Folk would finish the jobs when the weather got worse and they must work indoors. The threshed grain would go to the miller a few hundred yards down river.

It was silent. Tom came running in behind me.

"Anything sir?"

"No. He's away."

Tom had been running hard to get round the manor walls to reach me.

"Did you tell Wyot to sound the alarm and get the hue and cry going?"

"Aye, sir."

It was then I heard Wyot blowing his horn to summon the hue and cry.

I pushed open the furthest door and stared out over the meadows.

"Nothing."

I closed the doors and stood biting my lip for a moment.

"Meet me at the front. I'll go via the orchard, you the riverside."

"Aye, sir." Tom turned tail and ran.

When I reached the main gate, Wyot was out gathering a few folk together and blew his horn again.

"Which way did he go, sir?"

I scratched my head.

"Out of the salley port, Wyot but then... he disappeared. Best to fan out through the village and search. Everyone to look for...."

I stopped. What could I tell them? Look for Thomas Potter, who at that moment came trotting around the edge of the wall by the dovecote.

"Thomas! Go into the manor hall and stay there. I only want to be looking for one man in brown clothing!"

He jogged up. "But sir...I...."

"No, go Thomas. It's safer and easier."

"Aye sir."

He backed through the gate looking affronted.

More people were coming onto the green space before the manor gates.

"We are looking for a man who looks like Thomas Potter," I shouted. "Be careful. He is armed and is a very dangerous man."

Although some whisper had leaked out about how Thomas' brother was a felon responsible for the death of Walter, few yet knew 'looked like' meant that he was the actual image of his brother. They were going to be quite surprised, I thought, when they came upon him.

Hal came running up, buckling on his belt. John and Peter followed him from the church lane.

"What's up, sir?"

"William of Salisbury is in the village."

"God's teeth!" said Hal.

"He attacked Tom and made off through the salley port though he seems to have gone to ground now."

"Tom all right?"

"Aye, he is."

It was then I heard a shout behind me.

I turned quickly to see what looked like a brown tunic disappearing round the edge of the kitchen building.

Hal pushed past me and ran under the shadow of the gatehouse.

We all squeezed through the gate. Wyot was left scratching his head.

We lost both brothers for a moment.

"Everyone who is out there," I yelled and pointed to the folk by the main gate. "Out the back."

The salley port gate clanged with force, didn't engage the latch but opened again.

A man in brown approached.

"Tom?"

The man turned. "Yes sir. He's out of the salley port again."

"Go to the hall as I said."

He nodded and ran off up the manor steps.

I took the key from the lock and held it in my hand.

"Hal, John, Tostig. Out the salley port. I'll lead the party...."

We all dipped our heads under the lintel of the small door in the six foot thick wall.

Then, there came an hysterical scream.

"The hall! That's Lydia."

Hal did a rapid volte face and came running back through the salley port opening.

"This is gettin' ridiculous!" he spat as he passed me. I threw the key to John and saw him secure the small gate.

As we neared the steps I found, discarded by the undercroft door wrapped in a black cloak, a sword and a large knife, both in their scabbards. William had divested himself of his weapons. Why?

I pointed to them and said, "Tostig, take charge."

Hal and I took the steps two at a time.

We slid through the screens passage and entered the hall. The door was, as usual open.

251

At the top end by the dais, stood Lydia, her face pale, her hand to her bosom. Hawise stood on the bottom step of the solar stairs, her mouth open. Felice, nurse to our children, stood on the top step, muttering.

In the middle of the hall, four paces apart stood two men in brown. Both with their backs to me. They turned as one as we entered and one of them then looked back to Lydia and nodded respectfully.

"Sorry to frighten you my lady. It's only me, Tom."

Hawise shut her mouth with a snap and turned to Felice. "Oh do be quiet Felice. It's just Tom Potter... twice," she said and her nurse, not usually spoken to in this way by her charge, was instantly quiet.

The other man in brown looked thunderous.

"No, I'm Tom, mistress. Don't take any notice of him. I'm Tom."

Lydia felt for a chair and sat. Hawise helped her and stood protectively by her side.

"Well... I'll be bugg... buried in Burbage," said Hal as he slowly walked up the hall. He kept his distance from the two men but his eyes on them both. He also kept his hand on his sword hilt.

Tostig came into the room behind us. John and Peter were not far behind.

Peter let out a small whoop of surprise as he saw the brothers.

"Jesus!" he said, "There are two Toms."

I walked close to the two brothers scrutinising them both, trying to remember what exactly the Tom I'd seen earlier was wearing. It was impossible. No one took much notice of a plain brown tunic, brown chausses to the legs, a brown belt. There was nothing to distinguish one from the other.

Both of them bowed, then glowered at each other.

They wore no knife, no distinguishing purse. Their clothes, both, were dusty and stained. Their hair was disordered from running. Two identical pairs of brown eyes watched me as I walked round them peering at them deeply.

Hal came up.

"Well, I never thought to see the day."

"No, Hal. It's remarkable isn't it?"

252

John came up, his eyes blinking rapidly.

"This can't be true. It's some trick of the devil as Agnes said."

"It is true. Perfectly true," I said. "One of them is our Tom Potter and the other, his identical brother William of Salisbury."

"Which one is which, sir?" asked Peter, coming out from behind his father.

"Ah... that we must find out."

I walked to the dais.

"Close the door John."

John walked backwards, never taking his eyes from the phenomenon before him. Before he pushed and latched the hall door, Tostig slipped in silently with a pair of manacles in his hand.

"Stay there."

"Yessir."

I sat down on my chair. Elevated as I was, I had a good view of the two brothers.

"Come closer."

"Sir...," said one of them....

"No, you will not speak. You will do as I ask."

The man's face fell and he glared at his brother.

They took two paces nearer.

Hal jumped....

"No, they have no weapons Hal. I think I'm safe."

Hal stood quite close to them both and folded his arms.

"Thomas Potter...."

"Yessir?" said two voices.

"Thomas Potter has, a few weeks ago, undergone a trial by fire and will have a scar to his hand. Put out your right palms."

The men looked at each other and then quite confidently put out their hands.

"Hal?"

Hal stepped forward to stand before them.

I heard a short, sharp intake of breath.

253

"God's cods!"

He turned to me, his face wide and incredulous.

"They bloody both 'ave!"

I swallowed and sighed.

"Then Tom's brother too has been subjected to a trial by fire. I have no doubt he's a murderer and a felon."

Lydia, who had been silent all this time, shifted on her seat to look at me. "But Thomas was proven innocent, Aumary."

"Aye. He was."

"And as I said before, what sort of man would allow himself to be subjected to this ordeal before God...." She trailed off as she saw my face.

"No, my love, if a man is as Godless as we are led to believe Tom's brother William is, he will have no misgivings about subjecting himself to such a trial."

"But Aumary...," she began and then fell silent as she digested the enormity of it.

Tostig stepped forward. "Sir, our Tom has a wound to his head."

I put out my hand to Hal.

"Fore'eads...," he said sternly to both brothers.

With a sigh the first and right hand brother lifted the locks of chestnut brown hair which fell over his face.

There was a pink scar starting at the middle of the hairline and disappearing into the hair at the ears on the right hand side.

The second brother threw up his head and confidently lifted his hair.

Hal grunted. "Two scars..."

"Does anyone remember how the scar on Thomas appeared?"

All shook their heads.

"Janet would know. She stitched him," said Lydia.

"John, fetch Janet."

"Aye, sir."

He opened the door with a scrabble and was gone.

Tostig took his place.

I jumped down from the dais.

"So, this is a pretty parcel."

I walked around the two brothers.

"Show me your hands. Palms up."

Both men looked at each other again and held out their hands.

"Sir, I cannot...."

"Quiet!"

I lowered my eyes. Both palms were dirty and both had a slight reddish tinge. I leaned to look down carefully.

It seemed to me that one man was a little redder than the other. Though I knew that Tom had done little potting lately because of his sore hand, his hands would not be as ingrained as they had been. The felon had been scrabbling around on Tom's floor and he was wily enough to try to make himself look like his brother; that was assured.

"There is one easy way to settle this."

I stood before them, my feet planted wide apart, my hand on my sword hilt.

"One of you is a potter, the other a soldier."

Both men underwent some sort of facial change as they anticipated what I was to say.

"A contest perhaps...?"

They looked at each other.

I swear that they both thought their own separate thoughts. A contest...? One might challenge the other to a duel. One might fight with sword and buckler. The other, create with potter's clay.

I smiled. "No, I have a better idea."

I folded my arms.

I walked away again and leaned on the table with two hands.

"The Tom Potter I know, will know the answer to this one question."

One of the brothers lifted his face and I swear I saw worry there.

"And the question is. What is it that I, Sir Aumary Belvoir, wish to build here at Durley to prevent the flooding of the village?"

The brother to my right hand looked at the other. His lip curled.

I saw the left hand brother's face crease in a broad smile.

"You wish, sir...," he said bowing, "to build a sluice gate such as they have at the castle moat and the town mill. You asked me to draw it and Hubert the farrier and Alf Woodsmith to fabricate it."

I folded my arms. "Well done Thomas". I nodded to the other man. "Bind him Hal." Hal stepped forward, as did Tostig.

With an almighty roar the face of the second brother and right hand man, whom we now knew was William, changed. His lips drew back over his teeth.

"I'll see you in Hell brother!" he shouted and launched himself at Tom.

Tom fell and scrambled away backwards.

Hal grasped the felon by the neck and pulled hard.

Tostig managed to snap the manacles on him as Thomas struggled upright and brushed himself down.

William of Salisbury bucked and fought.

Tostig punched him for good measure in his midriff. "That's for Walter," he said.

The man doubled over and staggered forward. Hal pulled him back by his chestnut hair.

Eventually he regained his breath.

"Peter, can you fetch the gyves... I think we shall need those too."

Peter followed his father John out of the hall.

I was just seating myself again when John Brenthall came in with Janet.

"Just to be sure, absolutely sure. Janet, will you look at the scar on Thomas' head and tell me if this is the wound you stitched some weeks ago?"

Thomas turned his head and looked at her sweetly.

"Aye, sir. This is the wound here." She caught sight of the other man, the perfect image of Tom and a small "Oh," escaped her lips.

"You are certain that this is not the man Thomas, whose head you mended so beautifully?"

With a certain amount of trepidation, Janet approached the man William.

Hal pulled back his head and yanked his hair again.

"No, sir. This wound is further to the temple. Tom's, as you can see, is a jagged line down his forehead on the left hand side. Made by a sharp stone."

William lunged at Janet and she stepped back quickly. Tom placed himself protectively in front of her.

"Will, give up. Confess your sins…it's no use…."

William snarled and then spat at his brother.

"Go to Hell, little brother!"

"Little?" I said.

"I am the younger by three minutes, sir," said Tom.

"Ah…."

"I will always be the little one."

I smiled at him.

"So, William…," I gestured for Hal and Tostig to bring him up to me as I sat down by Lydia and reached for her hand.

Hawise came to stand between us.

"Tell your story… I will listen."

Now that there was no possibility of dissembling, the face that stared up at me was not that of Tom Potter. It was harder by far; cruel, sneering and over confident.

He said nothing.

"You know that you will hang?"

His only reply was to lick his lips.

"If you answer my questions I will make sure they break your neck. I can have you dropped. You will not throttle to death."

Tom looked sadly at him. "Will… tell the Lord what he wants to know. What good can it do you?"

Tom was favoured with a sidelong look which told him to go to Hell again.

"Where did you go when you left Salisbury, Will?" asked Tom.

"I went off with Earl Salisbury's men."

"The Earl William?" I asked.

"I learned soldiering there. Then we went off to France."

257

"Yes, I was there when William was there." I said. "Not in any military capacity but... I was there."

"We ended up in Sussex... the cinque ports."

"Yes, I remember when John posted him there." I leaned forward.

"How did you become attached to the Flemish routiers?"

"I killed a fellow soldier in a brawl. Had to flee. What else could I do? I hired out my sword... no questions asked."

"Why did you come home, Will?" asked Tom

"I wanted to see Da."

"But Da had been dead many years then."

"No one thought to tell me."

"We might have told you if we knew where you were," said Tom.

"Your father, am I right, Will, had previously told you that there was a treasure buried behind a workshop in the woods somewhere?"

I saw Tom flinch.

"He told me that there was a treasure beyond compare. Who wouldn't want to come back and find it?" said Will.

"Ah. That is why you really returned."

"I'd had enough of living the life of a wandering soldier. I was getting older... I wanted to...."

"You wanted what you could never have. You were always the same!" said Tom.

"Whereas you... you apology for a man... oh yes... don't think I don't know what...."

"That will do!" I shouted.

Will sniffed, looked away and wiped his manacled hands over his mouth.

Tom looked up at me under his eyebrows.

"Back you came with the routiers attached to the Lord de Neville's men."

"Aye. They were billeted in the castle. I had to find my own base. I wasn't a *Fleming*!" he spat. "I was only a poxy Englishman."

"Where? Where did you live."

"Inkpen. In an abandoned shepherd's hut."

"And naturally because you were simply a foot soldier, you had no horse."

"'Twas all I could do to get me a sword and maille."

"I expect you stole that too."

Will glared at me.

"So here you are. Not able to ride out all the time with the routiers, until you find yourself a horse which you did in the form of my Deerman's rouncey, Humble."

"Just going begging wasn't it?"

"And then when you were horsed you could have some fun. Where did you get the saddle and tack?"

"Stole it."

He smiled that feral smile again.

"And then that day, it dawned on you didn't it... that the place your father had been talking about was much closer to home."

"Gerhardt saw the garrison man with some gold and yes... it just clicked."

"And so you took my bait."

Will growled low in his throat. "He lied."

"Andrew?"

"My father!"

All at once Tom threw up his head and laughed. We all looked at him in concern, such laughter in Tom was so uncharacteristic.

"Oh you idiot! You absolute idiot!" He doubled up laughing.

*****

We weren't expecting the huge amount of venom with which William was filled. Again he launched himself at Tom and fell on him trying to get the chain of the manacles to his throat to throttle him. Tom toppled backwards and fell on the flagstones.

259

Tostig threw the cloak, belt, sword and knife that he'd been holding onto the table and lurched forward. The knife skidded out of the scabbard and lay on the polished oak.

John, Tostig and Hal pulled William off. He bucked and fought and again Tostig had to give him a punch to the belly to subdue him.

William went down on his knees gasping.

Lydia reached for Hawise who was fascinated by all this and pulled her to her side.

Tom got up to his knees, shook his mane of hair and rose to his feet, brushing the dust from his brown clothes again.

"Never call me a fool!" said William breathlessly. "Never!"

Tom fought for breath. "Well, you are. Taken in and blinded by your greed."

"Wha...?"

Tom leaned over his brother. "Father told you all those years ago and, yes, he told me too. Only I had the wit to understand him, Will... so I say again... you were blinded by your greed. You idiot."

"Bastard!"

"What was it our father prized above all things in life, Will... think... what was it?"

William, gasping, looked up at his brother, his face twisted in hatred.

"What. Was. It?"

Will's face suddenly creased in puzzlement.

" 'A possession more valuable than gold,' he'd say. 'More desirable and loyal than the love of a good woman. More worthy than the worthiest King.' "

"The bastard! If he were alive now, I'd cut out his living heart...!" shouted William, spittle spraying from his lips. "Stupid old man." He shook his head, fighting the hands which held him; his hair splayed out around him.

"A treasure beyond compare, Will," Tom roared.

"Pity you didn't have to marry that whore, Cille," spat Will. "That would have been torment to you wouldn't it? You with your love of m...."

Tom's face hardened. "You killed her? Killed that poor girl? Killed her in my name? Made her believe it was I who loved her? You abandoned her and her unborn baby? You tried to blame me? You evil...."

He breathed through clenched teeth.

"And you killed Anthony. Killed him. Murdered him. For that may you rot in Hell, William of Salisbury."

Before any of us knew what was happening, Tom reached for the knife which had been lying on the floor, fallen from the table where Tostig, in his haste to help subdue William had thrown it. Tom grabbed it.

"Tom, put down the knife," I said quickly and quietly but he was not listening.

"The thing which my father prized above all things...that treasure which was beyond compare, more noble than the noblest King, an affection more worthy than the most wonderful woman, was that of his dog, Will... HIS DOG!" he shouted.

William of Salisbury growled low in his throat and lunged at Tom.

"Bastard!"

And Tom, gritting his teeth stepped forward and thrust the knife up into the black heart of his twin brother.

There was a sharp intake of breath. William looked thoroughly surprised, gurgled once and fell onto his knees, glanced quizzically at the red stain growing on his chest and then toppling onto his face on the flagstones, lay still.

I stepped forward in shock, a moment too late.

"Oh Tom...."

Tom Potter moved back one pace, a strange look on his face. He dropped the knife to the floor.

Everyone was paralysed into inaction.

Then Tom looked up at me, swayed, fell to his knees and started to weep, his hands over his face.

"Oh Tom," I said again, my throat constricting, "Tom, Tom, what have you done?"

GLOSSARY

Amerced - Punish with a fine.

Assoil - Pardon.

Bailey - Or ward, a courtyard of a castle or fortification, enclosed by a curtain wall.

Bothy - Small simple building often of daub and wattle, roofed with thatch and with a beaten earth floor.

Bliaut - Voluminous overgarment worn by both sexes, (but mostly women) and pleated to the waist or under the bust.

Braies - Underclothes, like shorts, worn by men.

Buckler - Small round shield.

Burh - An Anglo Saxon fortification - particularly of the 9th century.

Burntwine - Brandy.

Capuchon - A hood which goes over the head and shoulders.

Cist - Chest, coffer.

Chapel of Ease - A church building other than the parish church, built within the bounds of a parish for the attendance of those who cannot reach the parish church conveniently. Usually of the 14th century. I have brought the date of the chapel forward.

Chattels - Goods.

Cordwainer - Shoemaker.

Coif - A mailed head piece like a hood.

Coroner - Also called the crowner. The man appointed by the crown to deal with unexpected deaths. The Coroner was the man who drew up the jury of twelve men to decide the cause of death and if need be, impose fines.

Cotte - A long sleeved shift or tunic. A coat.

Cutler - Man who makes knives and other small metal items.

Dais - A raised platform at one end of a manorial hall.

Deer Fence - An artificial barrier to keep deer in a particular area of the forest.

Farm - A form of taxation.

Frankpledge or Tithing - An Anglo-Saxon legal system in which units or tithings composed of ten households were formed, in each of which members were held responsible for one another's conduct. It was still in use in the 13th century.

Hauberk - a coat of mail

Hounds of Hell - A supernatural pack of dogs in legend.

Keep - Stone or wooden tower on top of a small manmade hill.Large towers in a castle that were fortified residences, used as a refuge of last resort should the rest of the fortress fall to an adversary.

Lychgate - A covered structure at the gate of a church where coffins were often rested.

Lyrwite - a fine which unmarried mothers must pay.

Mark - Not an actual coin but an amount to the value of thirteen shillings and fourpence

Mercenaries - Or routiers, professional soldiers hired to serve in a foreign army.

Nock - Put an arrow to a bow but not let it go or loose it.

Oath Taker - Someone who will swear an oath for another's good behaviour.

Portcullis - A strong, heavy grating that can be lowered down grooves on each side of a gateway to block it.

Posset - Milk curdled with wine or ale and served hot.

Rouncey - A smaller horse used as a workhorse often ridden by servants. Rounceys were not fast but they were possessed of great stamina.

Sanctuary - A sacred place, such as a church, in which fugitives were immune to arrest recognised by English law. They had forty days to make up their mind to either plead guilty and go into the hands of the law, or leave the country forever.

Scrip - A purse hanging from the belt or a larger bag.

Screens passage - The corridor between the hall and the service rooms of a mediaeval manor.

Sext - The sixth hour of the day, roughly midday.

Solar - A private room reserved for the lord and his family, often positioned to catch the sun for much of the day.

Tag and Go - A children's game - meaning an uncertain outcome.

Vallum - Latin for wall.

Vespers - Evening prayers.

Villein - Peasant, churl.

Warren - An enclosed place where rabbits are farmed.

Wicket - Small personnel door in a larger gate.

Wolfsheads - Another name for outlaws.

AUTHOR'S NOTE

King John began to use routiers, paid mercenaries from Belgium (then called Flanders) in his army, quite early in his reign. It wasn't an unknown practice. Other monarchs had used them as they were greatly feared and had a reputation for being organised, merciless fighters and very loyal to those who paid them.

Bands were let loose in England and terrified whole swathes of countryside. There was nothing one could do but run and hide. Most were not brought to justice.

Wolfsheads were the scourge of the forest. These outlaws were men who had been pushed outside the law for one reason or another. They were so called because they could be killed on sight, as could a wolf and their heads taken to the authorities, a reward being claimed for their demise.

Cock a troop Lane is still in existence. Its origin seems to be Crokerer-troupe or potters' settlement, indicating the presence of a pottery industry in the Saxon or early Mediaeval period. There is a small wooden bridge over the river nowadays which meets Thicketts Lane.

The (now) footpath does indeed go from the London Road, the A4, (off Chopping Knife Lane) down the hill to the river to Mildenhall (pronounced Mine-all by the locals). Stitchcombe is a sweet little hamlet on the River Kennet in an idyllic setting even today.

It was not uncommon for a lord to let out places in the village to tenants who could work at artisan crafts. Potters, bakers and wheelwrights might have been amongst these men. Land was also granted to them in return for rents, collected by a bailiff or steward.

Twins were not unknown in Mediaeval Britain though they were rare and identical twins very rare. It was thought that twins were the product of a woman sleeping with two men. Of course they had no knowledge of genetics or DNA in the 13th century. Identical twins might have been viewed with a great deal of horror as the work of the devil. What they thought about the mother's morals is not documented.

Many people could go their whole lives and never see an identical twin or even know about it. It was only as people began to travel further and more often, that these occurrences came into popular knowledge, as Shakespeare will attest.

Women who were unmarried and had children were chastised and fined a lyrwite by the church and wherever possible it was desirable to find the man who made her pregnant and make him marry her.

It was not a fanciful thing for women to follow a man who had promised her marriage and left her in the lurch.

At this time in history, it wasn't customary for folk to have two names. This practice came in fully, when we had universal taxation in the form of the poll tax of 1377. It was then helpful to know every man by two names.

I have given people names which we might recognise now, for ease of reading. They fall roughly into four groups. Those which are nicknames. Those which describe the things someone does for a living. Some names are patronymic i.e. named for the father, Haroldson, Peterson etc. though in the 13th century it was more likely you were Thomas son of Harold. You could also be called after the place you were born or lived in. There were not too many common names then. Thomas, William, John. Some were Norman, some Saxon and as time went on and intermarriages became the norm, one might have a Saxon and a Norman name in the same family. I have also given folk two names to distinguish one from another. In one village you might have three Thomases and six Johns, as you have in this tale in Savernake.

Though I Live Not Where I Love

Now to Aumary. He is a minor lord, not terribly wealthy and more a businessman than pure aristocracy. As warden of the forest he has quite a practical job and needs to know about the forest and its trades. He is a knight - yes, but first and foremost, a forester. I have made him a sympathetic character as so many folk of his class in novels are portrayed as proud, haughty and nasty. I fail to see how many of them could be so. They were dependent upon their peasants for their livelihood. If the peasant didn't prosper, neither did they at this level of society. Grander folk perhaps could be less amenable. Aumary takes every man as he finds him and isn't averse to rolling up his sleeves and getting on with it.

What happened to Tom? It was likely he would not be charged with a crime but a record would have to be made and attested by witnesses that he was 'defending himself' and that he was a man of good character. A sin like this might be purged by going on a pilgrimage to a holy place. Perhaps this is what Tom does. In any event, he crops up in later novels and so escapes any major punishment.

When I was writing this book, I lost my beloved four year old dog to a freak accident under the wheels of a car. This might have been a different tale and had a different ending if Samos hadn't died in the middle of writing it. This book is for him and in his memory. Samos, a wire haired fox terrier, as precious to me as was Tom Potter's father's canine companion, to him.

Sleep deeply my little lad.

Samos WFT Newstead, August 10th 2013 - January 14th 2017

Susanna M. Newstead © March 2021

ABOUT THE AUTHOR

Susanna, like Aumary Belvoir has known the Forest of Savernake all her life. After a period at the University of Wales studying Speech Therapy, she returned to Wiltshire and then moved to Hampshire to work, not so very far from her forest. Susanna developed an interest in English history, particularly that of the 12th and 13th centuries, early in life and began to write about it in her twenties. She now lives in Northamptonshire with her husband and a small wire haired fox terrier called Tabor.

Though I Live Not Where I Love

ALSO BY SUSANNA M. NEWSTEAD

The Savernake Medieval Murder Mysteries
Belvoir's Promise

She Moved Through the Fair

Down by the Salley Gardens

I Will Give my Love an Apple

Black is the Colour of my True Love's Hair

Long Lankyn

One Misty Moisty Morning

The Unquiet Grave

The Lark in the Morning

A Parcel of Rogues

Bushes & Briars

Kennet Valley Tales Medieval Romances
Forceleap Farm

Hunting the Wren

Illustrated Children's Books
Tabor the Terrierble: The Gardner's Dog

Tabor the Terrierble: The Dark Knight

Please visit the website for further information

https://susannamnewstead.co.uk/

Printed in Great Britain
by Amazon